10,00

From Caranga she learned of pirates' ways;

Her valor was all her own . . .

Tiana's search for her half-brother Bealost takes her on a harrowing journey, bringing her to a land ravaged by vampire nuns who worship

a giant bat fed on human flesh . . .

then on to a realm where people fly . . .

to a village deceptively bewitched . . .

and finally, to the secret place where the enchanted Bealost is hidden.

Demon in the Mirror
is the first book of the trilogy
War of the Wizards.

D1572181

THE DEMON IN THE MIRROR

ANDREW J. OFFUTT AND RICHARD K. LYON

A KANGAROO BOOK

PUBLISHED BY POCKET BOOKS NEW YORK

Distributed in Canada by PaperJacks Ltd., Licensee
of the trademarks of Simon & Schuster, a division of
Gulf & Western Corporation

This POCKET BOOK edition includes every word contained in
the original, higher-priced edition. It is printed from brand-new
plates made from completely reset, clear, easy-to-read type.
POCKET BOOK editions are published by
POCKET BOOKS.
a division of Simon & Schuster, Inc.,
A GULF+WESTERN COMPANY
Trademarks registered in the United States
and other countries.
In Canada distributed by PaperJacks Ltd.,
330 Steelcase Road, Markham, Ontario.

Copyright © 1978 by Andrew J. Offutt and Richard K. Lyon

All rights reserved, including the right to reproduce this
book or portions thereof in any form whatsoever.
For information address Pocket Books, 1230 Avenue of the
Americas, New York, N.Y. 10020.

ISBN: 0-671-81720-5

First Pocket Books printing January, 1978

Trademarks registered in the United States and other countries

Printed in Canada

"To Ina and Jodie
without whom,
precious little

Contents

1

Snakes in the Door

The larger ship, a Narokan merchantman, flew no flag and bore the marks of fire and sword. The other vessel's flag still fluttered in the gentle breeze: the black banner bore the outline of a fox's head in the scarlet of new-spilt blood. A pirate craft she was, *Vixen*, out of Ilan. Locked together now like lovers, the two ships rode the moon-bright water almost in silence. Attack and battle were long over. The vanquished slept in the sea; the victors, pirates and newly freed galley slaves, slumbered nigh as deeply from much ale and strong wine.

The night was silent, save for the gentle liquid sounds of a calm sea. Having posted no watch, the victors had left themselves defenseless. Yet danger of attack was minimal, and the pirate captain's judgment was that it were best to let the men drink until they knew not the color of their own skins; the corsair crew was white and the galley slaves black.

The piratical ranks held but one black, the first mate Caranga. It was his conceit that he slept with one eye open, thus ever keeping watch. The sprawled man's heaving chest was broad and powerfully muscled as that of a hibernating bear—and presently produced a snoring quite as loud. For all his strength, Caranga was not a tall man, and his hair showed gray at the edges.

Not all the victors slept so comfortably.

Near the starboard rail lay three blacks whose first taste of freedom had been bitter indeed. They moaned from time to time, their skins tinged with green; nor was there aught remaining in their stomachs to hurl into the sea. Having found a keg of ale, the delighted trio had either not heard or ignored the order that all such finds were to be fetched to Caranga. Narokans were fond of posthumous vengeance, and their ships generally carried a poisoned keg or two to abbreviate the triumph of successful pirates and mutineers. When no such keg was brought Caranga, he went seeking, and the new freedmen were happy to have him quaff their ale.

A single touch of his tongue to the brew was sufficient. Caranga spat vigorously.

That the trio had drunk the poisoned ale was too bad—for them. But the act itself was a matter of less import than its being a direct violation of Caranga's order. Punishment for that offense was the returning of all that they had consumed. The miscreants might have preferred death by poison: both pirates and their fellow blacks joined in the sport of alternately forcing water and feathers down their gullets.

Aside from the moaning, listless trio of former slaves whose education had been thus furthered, the victors were in good condition. Their dead had greatly outnumbered the seriously wounded—and they had taken no prisoners. Who, after all, wanted to buy a Narokan?

Linked like friends leaving a tavern, the two craft slid over the moon-bright water. Snores were the only sounds that rose from them, and ale-induced sleep gave to few movements. They might have been ghost vessels under the wan circle of the moon.

Not quite all aboard were asleep. Two had transferred to the merchant ship, where both were on quests, though of different natures. Belowdecks of the Narokan craft, a single candle ghosted about. *Vixen's* captain explored the prize.

Captain Tiana had fought hard and worked harder afterward, at surgery. Yet she was not a tippler and her curiosity would give her no rest. Alone with her candle, she searched the gloomy passages of a depopulated ship.

"There must be something of extraordinary value aboard this accursed hulk, Rarn—else why was it so well guarded?" But a glance told her that Rarn had departed swiftly, on his own mission.

She moved on, reflecting, wondering. Had it not been for the slave mutiny, she mused—and of course her own superb leadership—the battle for a merchant ship unexpectedly filled with marines would have ended very differently. Yet, while the cargo appeared to be readily marketable at a good price, it comprised nothing of unusual value. So, with her candle and while her men slept, Tiana searched.

Until she came upon the mirror. Full length it was, and one glance at her reflection told her this glass was of the highest quality. Tiana stopped.

No doubt lingered in her mind that she was no less than beautiful, and this opportunity to inspect and admire herself was irresistible; there were no mirrors on *Vixen*, in grudging deference to the Sinchorese who thought them bad luck. Assuring herself that a nearby keg held naught but nails, she waddled it forward and rested her candle on it. With a toss of her deeply red hair she stood before the glass and gazed into her own green eyes, below brows arched with a confidence Caranga called o'erweening, and occasionally supercilious. She frowned at her long black cloak with its gold braid at the shoulders. During the victory celebration she had worn the concealing mantle and kept herself apart, so that her men might think of her not as woman or companion but as their captain.

The night was not chill and vanity warmed her; she removed the cloak.

Tiana was dressed as she'd been during the battle—indeed, for the battle. A wide black belt girt short breeches and a loose-sleeved shirt that was signally tight in the torso. Shirt and breeches were of shimmery green silk; the leather boots were glove-soft. Bloodstains marred her garb now, but she smiled. The clothing had been calculated; Tiana well knew her looks, and she well knew men. She'd been much on display, and, if those fool Narokans had chosen to gape at her body when they should have been plying their swords, why then that was their problem. The rapier and dagger at her belt had punished their error and ended all their problems.

Busy inspecting herself with uncritical eye, Captain Tiana of *Vixen* paid no mind to the two strangely bright spots in the mirror's upper-right corner.

She turned in profile to the excellent mirror: she stretched forth a leg of uncommon sheen and shapeliness; she jiggled with fully satisfactory results. "Look like you're trying to smuggle a pair of tahlequah melons," Caranga had observed with asperity, nor had he exaggerated overmuch. Again she smiled at her reflection. *And what*, she mused, *might you bring on the slave mart, my beauty?* She could fair hear the clammer's voice: *What am I bid for this fire-haired darling with a body so perfectly formed and her still young as well?*

"Hmp!" Tiana pursed her lips. That would depend to some extent on the market. In Sinchore the nobles favored women like dolls, tiny fragile creatures, while in Aradot the aristocratic taste ran to tall, large-boned girls and strapping women. True, over most of the world demand was for women such as herself, of medium stature and frame, well endowed with curvature, not muscular but with firm strong limbs.

Of course, anyone buying Tiana of Reme would soon discover that she was considerably stronger than she appeared. She mused, smiling, giving her hair another shake and a few touches. Not so bad a thought; were piracy to become unprofitable for this reason or that, she could arrange to have herself sold. Once inside the home of a wealthy purchaser, she'd loot it and vanish. If any sought to deter her—so much the worse for them. Being Tiana was of great advantage in a world peopled with fools who considered combat a matter of brute strength rather than skill and speed, and women something for the using.

More than one man had sneered at the long needle of a blade she had unsheathed to daunt him. Each had learned that one last lesson.

She flouted and flaunted before the mirror, and its two areas of brightness gazed down upon her, unblinking. Without thinking about it, she assumed them to be reflections of her candle; there was naught behind her to cast such reflections. Nor did she note, in these few moments she had stood before the mirror, that the light-flecks had grown a bit brighter.

Stepping back a pace, Tiana whipped out her rapier and fought a mock duel with her reflection. Booted feet danced on the rough planking with swift easy grace as she parried and lunged. The rapier was a weapon well suited to her; its length compensated for the shortness of her arms and its lightness enabled her to make the very most of her agility and swiftness.

A small sound behind her brought her whirling, rapier ready. Instantly its point lowered; she recognized the sound of well-padded little feet, followed by a brief angry tussle slashed by a tiny shriek. A moment later *Vixen's* cat appeared, carrying a still-twitching rat.

"Good for you, Ram," Tiana told the triumphant cat. "You're about your business—as I should be."

She was picking up her candle when she thought to examine the mirror. The perfect image it provided made it rare and valuable—but its wooden frame was an anomaly. It was not even well made. Elevating the candle and peering close, Tiana saw that the wood was old, very old—while the mirror's silvering was in faultless condition. The glass did not approach the mirror's true age.

"Rarn . . . consider. Why would anyone place a highly valuable glass in a poor frame that does so little to protect it from breaking?"

She did not ponder long. Seeing no immediate profit in the solution to this mystery, Tiana moved on. The mirror was left in shadow. She was gone when the cat stared at the glass—and with a hiss, arched its back. With the candle's light removed, Rarn saw the evidence of his nose: the two spots of brightness on the glass were . . . eyes.

Though largely in darkness, the owner of those eyes was visible to the cat: a tall man who stood not before the glass, but *within* it.

The eyes did not focus on the alarmed animal or indeed on anything else. They stared at infinity. Their owner's hands moved in a gesture that puzzled the cat. Rarn was a keen observer of humankind in all matters pertinent to the obtaining of food. The gesture he saw was one made by fishermen to signify that the bait had been taken. Rarn perferred fish; rats were for sport, and strokes from his human. Yet no fish appeared for him to steal.

While the cat watched with eyes no less green and no less curious than his master's, the man faded from the mirror. His image was replaced, but not by a normal reflection. Rarn hissed and backed a pace, gazing into the image of a second mirror. It too held an image. . .

No reflection of himself or a ship's hold Rarn saw but of an empty tavern.

Then that mirror faded, with its image . . .

It was replaced by a normal reflection. Rarn grasped the rat jealously, made sure its neck was broken, and growled his warning. The other cat, too, held a rat—and was fading, blurring. The blurring increased; Rarn blinked. A network of cracks raced through the silvering. The glass was warping even as he watched. In a few heartbeats both glass and silvering were as old and time-ravaged as the wooden frame.

Stalking forward, Rarn sniffed. His tail moved restlessly. The cat's knowledge of mirrors was limited to the fact that they held strange, handsome tomcats one could not fight. This mirror was strange. It had exuded the odor of Bad, rather like a stalking great beast.

Now Rarn smelled only glass and wood. Rarn consulted his stomach and decided he was hungry enough to eat two rats. Too, it would be easier to catch the second on an empty stomach. The cat acted on that notion with alacrity.

Two knobs adorned the door at the end of the narrow passageway. The inner one was round and plain; the other was formed in the shape of a serpentine head. Tiana bent to examine them. The round knob was unmarked, while the other showed small scratches, as though it had been opened only by a mail-gloved hand. A faint green discolored the knob at the left of the snake's mouth. It seemed to stare at her while Tiana considered.

Just like Narokans to guard a door with poisoned needles! Yet . . . . if there is venom in the snakehead knob, is the plain one harmless?

Careful not to touch either as she pressed her ear to the door, she heard a faint slithering sound within. *Within what?*

Tiana vanished from the corridor to reappear in seconds, carrying a length of rope. With care, she knotted one end to the plain knob set almost in the door's center. She stepped back a few feet, set the candle on the floor and held her rapier ready for a swift thrust. She tugged hard at the rope.

The door did not open. A compartment did, within the door. As Tiana stared, three ugly cobras dropped thumping to the ship's planking.

Tiana snapped out a curse. She had half expected a single snake and had known little apprehension; the greater reach of her rapier would result in its swift demise. But three!— The captain of *Vixen* faded back, hoping one hooded reptile would rush ahead of the others. Instead, they advanced on their liberator in perfect side-by-side formation. Tiana's nape prickled. Hooded heads wove invisible designs a foot or so above the floor while the creatures stared with unblinking eyes green as her own but hardly comparable. Malign they were, and . . .

A chill slithered along her spine. There was intelligence in those eyes! It was no illusion, and neither was their continuing formation—a perfect defense against rapier thrust.

Great Cud—I've loosed sorcery on myself!

She backed another pace. She could easily slay one, but before she could recover for another thrust, no matter how swiftly, she'd be twice bitten. Had she a weapon designed for edgework, she could have lopped off those three broad heads at a single stroke—but she was bode by an uneasy conviction that against a broadsword or saber the snakes would have chosen a different formation . . .

Tiana took swift stock. She had rapier and dagger, flint and tinder, and naught else of use. Her soft leather boots would no more stop a cobra's fangs than would her silk clothing. *Curse me for not wearing mail to battle!* Retreat was possible but disadvantageous: in the main hold, the cobras could attack from three sides at once.

The concept of racing back to her own ship for help never entered Tiana's mind.

Her left hand shot to her belt, and the dagger leapt forth to fly at the center cobra. The dagger's aim seemed true, but the snake's head was like the smoke above a candle; the knife passed (through?) without effect. With her heartbeat increasing its tempo, Tiana stepped back, and back and, with a running start leaped over the leftward cobra. Its head flashed up and fangs narrowly missed her bare leg—while, in air, Tiana slashed down at the rightward snake.

Thumping lightly to the deck, Tiana instantly whirled and thrust. Her point skewered the center snake. The right serpent lay motionless, its head bloody. As swiftly as she'd stabbed, Tiana freed her sword from her second victim.

"Two down! Now, you demon from the—"

Tiana broke off. Rather than turn and recoil or strike, the third reptile slithered rapidly *from* her—and knocked over the candle. The flame was snuffed and the instant blackness was total. Tiana's heart pounded and her armpits prickled. Fighting down panic, she moved silently through the darkness. The advantage was clearly the snake's; Tiana knew she could move as soundlessly, but a misplaced thrust would betray her position, while the cobra could strike and miss without a sound. Her skin tingled. Would she feel only a blow at one leg, or the needly piercing of the fangs? And then how long would she have? Would it strike again—and again? If she succeeded then in slaying it, would there be time for the horror of trying to saw off her leg—or would she faint in pain and slide into the coma that would precede death by venom?

She stood motionless, straining her ears for the slightest sound. The pounding of her heart seemed a drum shouting her location to the enemy.

A faint slithering sounded to her left and on the instant her rapier streaked down. It impaled something soft, then the floor. She felt her victim wriggle; felt it go still. Relief weakened her. She wanted to shout her victory—

A terrible suspicion entered her mind and paralyzed her lips. Freeing her sword of the floor and raising it, she examined the snake's corpse with trembling fingers. Her rapier had entered the creature just behind the head—but there was a wet cut *on* the head.

It was the rightward cobra. The slash she had given it as she leaped over it had laid open its head, but merely knocked it temporarily senseless. And now all this noise had surely betrayed her position to the real enemy, the unscathed snake that had formed the left element of the formation.

It must be near—very near! Panic rose and she fought it. With a jerk and snap of her arm, she sent the dead snake thumping noisily to the floor. *Strike at that!* she urged mentally, while she stepped silently back to the door. Had that been a rush of air, past her leg? Gooseflesh leaped up and made her shiver.

If I miss, it won't. I must strike quickly—and true! The snake's keen sense of smell would soon penetrate the darkness to find her. Her mind boiled with self-reproach: *fool to think the careless slash of a rapier's edge might kill, vain fool to wear perfume!*

Yet there came no thought of regret at not having run for help. Her brain was busy elsewise, intensely busy.

A plan crystallized. If she tapped her foot, the snake would certainly come. If she then aimed her rapier's thrust parallel to the floor and a few inches above it, she need only guess the cobra's direction, not its exact location. Despite the snake's obvious uncanny intelligence, it must still be a creature of habit. It would approach along the left side of the corridor. Tiana chewed her lip. Her instincts cried out against betraying herself with sound in the protective darkness. Yet though her logic might well be faulty, better to try even a bad plan than wait in growing terror for certain death.

Her foot tapped, and the sound was as of a hammer's falling in the silent darkness.

She waited, poised for her planned thrust. Sweat was like cold grease on her face and hands. She felt its trickle down her back. Her hand quivered, wanting to leap forth. A quiet voice in the back of her mind whispered *Not yet, not yet,* while eternity seemed to pass. *I'm standing here, dying of old age,* she thought, as if arguing with her own inner voice of counsel. Her heart thumped hard and fast and the veins in her temple stood out from the strain while sweat tickled its way down into the crease between her tensed buttocks—and the voice said *Now!*

Tiana thrust—and felt her rapier's point encounter flesh. She skewered, panting, shoving the point away from herself with all her strength. In the darkness, it was eerily as if the rapier itself was amove—something was impaled and writhing on her slender sword. There was a sudden wrench and she felt a sharp blow at the hilt, just beyond her knuckles. The blow was accompanied by a click-snapping sound. Then the weight on her rapier went dead.

Tiana panted, sweat-drenched, trying to suck deep, slow breaths. Her legs quivered with the after-tingles of relief. All was quiet. Were all three snakes truly dead?

Suppose there's a fourth! Her imagination soared, flourished, filling the darkness with an army of huge-fanged cobras. She fought the fantasy; she dismissed it.

"No!"

Nonetheless her flesh crawled when she stepped away from the door. From the pouch at her belt she produced a piece of flint. She found the candle, lit it, held it high.

All three reptiles lay dead where she'd slain them. The last she had impaled well behind the head, and she realized the snapping sound had been the breaking of a fang when the creature struck her swordhilt, less than an inch from her hand. Tiana drew a deep breath, expelled it slowly—and stared at the door. Again she spoke aloud; questions and tension remained, and her voice was a comfort still.

"Now, *why*? A ship guarded like a harem—and a door guarded by *those*. And . . . what else?" *Not to mention*, she mused, *what's behind this accursed door!*

With the door's secret compartment open, she could see the inner workings of the other knob. As she'd suspected, a needle would be released by the turning of the snakehead knob—a needle well envenomed, naturally. Her dagger broke the mechanism. Nevertheless she exercised care as, with rapier ready, she opened the door of death.

Tiana blinked. A hanging oil lantern illuminated the cabin beyond the door. The room was empty save for a small casket or chest and an unusually beautiful girl.

She was nude but for the silver band about her waist, which was fastened behind to a silver chain, long and delicately slender. The chain was, in turn, secured to the floor—by bolts of silver. *A rich tether indeed*, Tiana mused, studying the girl's face; it was a cameo of perfectly formed features, but showed no apparent emotion. With a lifted eyebrow, Tiana regarded a feminine form that was a dream of lust come true. Luscious limbs were as exquisitely formed as Tiana's own, and the man-

tantalizing, full, sculpted breasts were both firmer and of more size than her own.

Hmp. The whore's top-heavy.

"Free me—oh, please, free me!"

Tiana returned a cool gaze. "Why? You didn't fight for your own freedom! There's strength in those lovely limbs of yours, I can see that. You . . ."

Tiana trailed off. Why hadn't the girl twisted and worked and broken that so-slender chain, to break free? Why was she here in the first place, fettered so—and so guarded? True, she'd fetch a fine price on any market. But she could hardly be the treasure the Narokans had guarded so well. There was something wrong, Tiana realized. Her eyes shifted nervously to the little casket.

Was that the prize? Then . . . the girl? . . . The cloud of suspicion in Tiana's mind began to take form as she noted the captive was holding her hands oddly—the fingers could not be seen. Concealing her fingers? *Why?*

The serpents had not been natural ones, but products of some dark sorcery. . . .

"Show me your hands."

At Tiana's words, the girl leaped up and sprang at her as if launched from a catapult.

Her intended victim was hardly a mere woman, hardly inexperienced, and already suspicious. Tiana stood her ground; her rapier darted forth to meet the fierce charge. Pierced through the brain, the girl fell. Her perfect brow was marred now by a wound like a blindly staring red eye.

It was the hands that drew Tiana's stare. The captive had not been hiding her fingers; she had none. Each hand sprouted razor-sharp claws that were the ghastlier for tipping the perfect arms of such a lovely creature. Aye, creature. . . . Even worse than the claws was that revealed by the mouth that now gaped in death. The girl—the creature—possessed fangs, not like a tiger or a bear, but long, slender needles, slightly back-curved. They were obscenely hideous, marring that lovely face.

And hollow, I'd make wager. The fangs of a cobra!

Revelation brought relief; relief brought laughter. The "girl" was neither the prize nor a girl; she was a *lamia*, a monster set to guard the real treasure.

"By the Sacred Cud—what sort of treasure needs a hundred marines, two death traps, and a monster to guard it?"

One worth fleeing, one part of Tiana's mind told her, but her more piratical side responded that it was one worth the taking, particularly after so much work and death-dealing. As she started toward the chest, she gave the lamia another glance of helpless fascination. Her eyes widened; was it imagination, or was the death-wound *smaller?*

It was. Tiana froze, staring in awe as the red eye closed, then vanished to leave clear, unmarked skin. The beautiful monster's real eyes flamed anew with life, and a heartbeat later, it was leaping at Tiana.

Still dazed at this unholy resurrection, she only just evaded the rushing claws—and lost her rapier to one set. Even while it clattered on the cabin's floor, Tiana was dodging, pouncing sidewise, twisting back. She grasped the silver chain, so close up to the thing's back that it could not get at her. The monster bucked and lunged while Tiana clung with desperate tenacity to the chain. Daring to trust to a one-handed grip, she snatched out her dagger. She reached around to drive it deep into the inner surface of one breast, the left. Surely that reached the heart—but though the abominable creature screamed and staggered, it continued to struggle. When claws barely missed tearing open her arm, Tiana withdrew the dagger. Immediately the wound shrank, closed, vanished.

Hanging onto the thing's leash and swerving her body this way and that to avoid back-clawing talons, Tiana stabbed again and again in quest of a vital spot in a monster that seemed to have none. Each new wound closed with nauseating swiftness. Twisting about a head whose human beauty was rendered a ghastly mockery by the fangs, the lamia spat on Tiana's arm.

She groaned. The venom burned like a red-hot iron.

Defensively, Tiana jerked up her dagger as the monster spat again. Venom splashed the blade and Tiana moaned at the tiny droplet that touched her finger. She plunged the dagger into the monster's neck. Instantly the creature went rigid. Its face writhed, and its stiffness lurched into the increasingly violent activity of convulsions. Tiana released the dagger; her hand, gripping the chain, was drawn down as her inhuman foe slumped to the floor. It thrashed, twitched, made a hideous belching sound, and was still.

Hurriedly spitting on her venom-splashed arm, Tiana rubbed it against the leg of her short breeks—hard. Twice more she did that, until the burning abated. She stood panting and disheveled, staring down at that which had nigh slain her. *I really should carve off that head—but I like the dagger just where it is. There's always the one I took from the Narokan captain's cabin. Let mine stay in her neck—its neck—with the venom that slew the monster.*

Tiana looked about, considering. Obviously the creature should have been able to break the chain. Silver, like its own venom then, must be its nemesis. The chain, Tiana the pirate reminded herself, was valuable for its metal. *Well, I'll promise it to the harbormaster in Reme. Let him take it off! Meanwhile, just in case* . . .

Retrieving her sword, Tiana toed the chest to a point well beyond the reach of the silver chain. The casket was not so large as a helmet for that great head of Gunda's. Surely it was too small to house a fabulous treasure, let alone both that and another death trap.

Nevertheless, she exercised great care in examining the plain chest of red-brown hardwood. It seemed no more than a valuable, locked jewel-casket sufficient to hold, say, a large ale stein and little else. *Or a hundred Atean pearls, perhaps, if there are so many in the world; the ransom of a halfscore ships!* That was an exciting thought and, once she had the chest braced against one wall, she was able to pick its lock with the needly tip of her rapier. Standing, she used that same tool to lift the lid.

"Dung! RAT dung!"

The chest contained three books of considerable age, a roll of parchment and a disgusting mummified hand. And naught else. Nor was "rat dung" sufficient for the occasion. A deaf ear three leagues distant could surely have heard Captain Tiana of *Vixen* cursing all the gods, the several Fates and all the idiot humans— men—who oversaw and conducted the affairs of the world. All this work! All this—nervousness, she told herself, not fear—and all her sweat. And to show for it: *junk*, junk that would not fill Gunda's helmet!

She, cursed by the gods, bright and dark, even invoking that formless nemesis, Drood of the Thousand Arms, and she swore by the Cow whose rumination created the world and by the Turtle on whose back the world rested and was sustained and— she caught herself. Even in her rage of disappointment Tiana would not swear the dread third oath, which was the Means That Shall Destroy the World. That final oath was seldom sworn, for its consequences were never pleasant.

Given voice, Tiana's rage subsided. Her commercial sense reasserted itself.

This junk was better guarded than any king ever was. Surely someone will pay well for its return—a one-handed bibliophile, mayhap! And . . . he'll pay the better when I know why these things are so valuable—and who else might buy them. . . .

When Tiana squatted beside the chest, she noted the patch of her breeks that had been eaten away. "And may Drood grasp the creature who raised up that lamia and its venom, too! The finest silk I—ahhhhh!" With a jerk of her head, she fell to examining that which the casket contained.

The hand was just that, but made extraordinary by the fact that a plain iron ring had been left on each finger—or slipped onto them. Ah! And the rings were *nailed* to the bottom of the hardwood chest!

With a jerk of her head, Tiana smilingly admonished the hand not to run away. She checked each book in turn. Each was written in a language she could neither read nor recognize, and if that rusty-brown ink was what she suspected . . . With a start and a most unpleasant twinge, she decided that it in all likelihood was indeed blood—the pages were human skin!

The parchment was not. Breaking the seal without a qualm, she unrolled it. It was short, and so was its message, written in Narokan:

To Lamarred, my Brother Sorcerer, a greeting:
    We both despise Pyre and must cooperate to
complete our plans. Accordingly, I agree
to your terms, and send that which you requested.

                                                    Ekron

Tiana's body betrayed her with an unworthy little shudder. The books *were* valuable, then . . . to any who wanted the vile secrets of black magic.

As she aversely returned the letter and books to the chest of evil, Tiana's heart nearly stopped. Very slowly, the fingers of the mummified hand were . . . moving.

Tiana slammed the lid.

2

Bargaining with the Devil

On a dark street in Reme, chief port and capital of Ilan, there is
an establishment called the Inn of the Smiling Skull. None
remembers why it is so named. The wine on King Hower's table
is not half so rare of vintage or delicate of bouquet as the wine
served there. The fat chef buys the finest prime beef and serves it
cooked to perfection that all may partake of the descendants of
the Cow. The other meats and fish, pastries and manifold
delicacies are all of such quality that no honest traveler of the
world's back has claimed to have tasted better. Despite this
veritable pinacothek of excellence, prices are higher in the
poorest pigsty masquerading as inn. It is known that boys,
clammers, are paid to apprise newcomers to Reme of the
felicities of the Smiling Skull. Nevertheless the inn's patrons
remain few, for too many men and women therein have from
time to time met their demise. Some have said 'twas coinci-
dence; since the dead bore no mark of violence, no tinge of
poison, no hint of foul play, these numerous passings must have
been natural. Even those who have argued thus, however, dine
not at the Smiling Skull.

This night the inn's patrons were three, and them together. A
curtain of mauve king's-cord draped one wall; seated at a table
there were Tiana, Caranga, and Gunda, second mate of *Vixen* .

With them, recently brought ashore from the ship on which it had been well guarded, was a large cloth bag. Within the bag was a smallish chest or casket, wound about with a delicate silver chain. Nor had Tiana opened it since slamming the lid while aboard the Narokan merchantman; nor had any touched it ere this night when she had carried it ashore. Nor in fact did her gaze long leave it.

The trio, well got up as gentlefolk, awaited a most important appointment with a certain Lamarred.

Caranga would have it not otherwise: he tasted Tiana's wine, first the glass and then the bottle. With the tip of his tongue he touched her fork and each side of the knife. As he checked the roast beef, huge Gunda spoke.

"Why look ye for poison? The king's spies have proved there be none here."

Caranga growled, "And how did they accomplish that?"

Between great mouthfuls of his own succulent beef, Gunda made reply: "King Hower was angered because of all those who died here, and so he sent two of his best spies. Neither ate nor drank aught. Both died. This proves it be not in poison that the trouble lies."

The black man but snorted—and continued to check the meat. Gunda shook his hairless head. "Now I know why you made end to retirement and returned to the sea," he said, amid mastication hardly silent. "Ye've no happiness but when you're afret over the cap'n."

On the point of making heated reply, Caranga paused. The second mate's words were true. When a dozen years ago the black pirate had given shelter to a homeless white orphan, he had expected to keep the child a short time till a suitable home could be found. To his amazement, she took to him and the piratical life like a fox to the chicken coop. In combat Tiana's speed and agility bested the strongest of enemies, and that before she attained twoscore years. In leadership and strategy she soon surpassed her foster father. At length forced to admit that he was aging, Caranga retired his command in Tiana's favor—nor could any criticize his choice (or so dare). Within a short time, though, the peace of retirement had palled. Too, he could not bear the thought of his beautiful daughter's facing daily danger without him. Claiming that her curiosity would kill her and that only he was blessed with the good sense to turn his back on this and that, now and again, he rejoined the crew—as mate.

Now he snapped, "Well, someone must fret over her. Look at

the wench, here without her rapier and with her bosoms on display like a doxy clamming her wares.'' Seeing those green eyes narrow and her lips draw tight, Caranga covered one of her long-fingered hands with his and hurried on in tone more fatherly. ''Tiana, Tiana. Peddling this so-called treasure has us bargaining with Drood himself! The secrets of thaumaturgy and necromancy are evil. Books written in blood on human skin— gained by murder, for mere paper cannot hold such ireful knowledge. Such things are not objects of ordinary commerce. They change hands only by dark means; fraud and theft, murder—and conspiracy to perform monstrous acts.''

''I've not heard such a speech from you in twelve years, Caranga. And are not fraud and theft and murder and fell conspiracy part of ordinary commerce?'' Tiana responded, in high innocence.

Caranga jerked back his hand and gusted a sigh. ''Perhaps. But you're involving your darling self in a war of wizards, girl. You'll be sucked into a whirlpool of their sorcerous intrigues. Come, let's be off before it's too late.''

''It is already too late.'' The voice was passing quiet, almost a whisper.

The trio whirled to stare at the speaker; the curtain at the wall had parted to reveal a small alcove, and a man. Robed he was, and tall, thin as though he dined but occasionally and then not well. Yet his color was good, and strangely pale, almond-shaped eyes were bright with vigor.

Eyes like a . . . cobra, Tiana thought, but she said, ''Well, Lamarred, we meet at last. As we are all doubtless hurried, what offer am I made for these rare old books of ours?''

'' *Your* books?''

''Certainly ours,'' Tiana nodded. ''By right of salvage. We found a Narokan merchant ship adrift, locked to a pirate craft. The corsairs had slain all the Narokans, but had drunk of the wrong cask. All were dead.''

''And for believing that bit of imagination, the harbormaster receives a fourth part of the spoils,'' the wizard said, without smiling.

''Fifth,'' Tiana corrected.

''No matter, Captain Tiana. We have no need for haggling. When you examine your find, you'll discover the books gone and a large bag of pearls in their place. They are Atean pearls, be assured; each is worth several pieces of gold.''

''Impossible!'' Gunda snapped, but Tiana soon proved him wrong.

Having slashed off the sack—still bound with her knot—and

clankingly unwound the silver chain, she opened the chest. She hefted the knobby bag she found within.

"You've robbed us!" she accused, squeezing the bag that seemed miserably small for all her trouble.

"Hardly; the books were not your property and the pearls are valuable. And as Caranga said, such things do not change hands by ordinary commerce." Lamarred spoke ever in a murmur, seeming to caress each word that emerged almost as a purr.

A purring cobra? Tiana thought, even as she noted that the mummified hand was still within the casket—slowly wiggling its fingers. It had given her no trouble; she treated it cavalierly.

"Be still, hand. Lamarred—and what will you offer for this very rare and most unusual hand, which as you see moves without attached body?"

"They are Atean pearls, right enough," Gunda said.

"Nothing," Lamarred said. "For the time being, Captain Tiana, you must retain the hand."

"Must?" Tiana echoed, with a slight taste of fear in her mouth. "Why?"

"Because Caranga was right to be nervous of involvement, but many years too late." And the mage spun his web of words. "Captain Tiana, you were *born* into this intrigue of sorcerers. You are the daughter of Sondaman, Duke of Reme, by a union . . . not recognized under Ilan law. When you were nine, the dukes of Arcone and of Palance conspired with the wizard Derramal to overthrow King Hower. Because of your father's loyalty to the king, the dukes had him slain and kidnapped his heir."

"Bealost," Tiana whispered.

"The same," Lamarred nodded. "Your infant half-brother. The conspiracy failed and the conspirators were executed. The dukedom of Reme being vacant, the king thoughtfully conferred it on his cousin, Holonbad Lacklands."

Mention of the dead brother she had loved deeply brought on thoughts that cut like knives into Tiana's brain. Her voice was harsh. "So I am a bastard." She shrugged. "My father and brother died years ago. All you speak of is over and done. Here sits my father."

But even as her hand closed on that of Caranga, ghosts of memory awakened and Lamarred's face became familiar, the face of a forgotten enemy.

"No, Tiana of Reme, your brother is not dead." The cobra eyes stared into hers. "Derramal realized the babe was a valuable pawn in the game of Empire. He hid Bealost—and took the secret to his death. And that brings us to the present problem. As

the lawful heir to the Duchy of Reme, Bealost is a threat to
Holonbad—who no longer stands so high in the king's favor.
Pyre, aye, *Pyre*, has discovered your brother's hiding place and
offered to sell his death to Holonbad in exchange for . . . certain
concessions, which I would find disadvantageous.''

Caranga spoke in a quiet growl. ''You want us to assassinate
Duke Holonbad?''

''No, for then Pyre would but sell Bealost's death to Holonbad's successor.''

Gunda made as if to speak, but his tongue locked. Logic
seemed to call for their slaying of Pyre, the dread most powerful
of wizards.

''No, Pyre is invulnerable,'' Lamarred said in answer to the
unspoken thought. ''I have already succeeded in slaying Pyre's
emissaries to the duke, as well as the duke's emissaries to Pyre.
The circumstances are such that each will blame the other. This
little delaying tactic will give us time to find Bealost and estab-
lish his claim to the Duchy of Reme.''

''And how,'' Caranga demanded, ''is this severed hand to
help us find Tiana's bro——half-brother?''

''A discerning question.'' Almost, the purring mage bowed.
''In some of what I said I have . . . oversimplified. When his
enemies overcame Derramal, they only partially neutralized the
spell which protected him. In consequence, though they dismembered his body, he did not as you see gain the peace of
death. The hand is alive, in a way, as is each severed portion of
his body. These are scattered over the world, for as the faithful
use the relics of saints in their prayers, so do wizards use the
remains of mighty sorcerers in their spells. With Derramal's
body, ummm, collected and reassembled, I can neutralize the
protective spell. He will then truly die, and by now he is ready
. . . but there will be a few moments, Tiana, in which he can tell
us where your brother is hidden.''

''A grim treasure hunt!'' Caranga growled. ''How much of
the body have you?''

''Only the right hand, which Ekron sent, but it will aid us to
gain the rest. Tiana—will you remove the tablecloth?''

Tiana had long said nothing, while her brain worked furiously. Lamarred's face was familiar, but impossible to remember.
Whoever he was, he was deadly. Without knowing how she
knew, she was sure that the slightest sign of recognition on her
part, any hint that she had guessed the riddle of his identity, and
the mage would slay her and her companions as a man might
callously swat three flies.

"Tiana," the sorcerer insisted. "The tablecloth."

Not yet trusting her voice, she hastened to comply. The cloth's removal revealed the tabletop indited with a large map of the known world, a map more complete and detailed than any Tiana had seen. Lamarred spoke, purring forth words like water flowing over butter, but the words were not such as human ears might hear. To Tiana the murmuring voice was an icy breath from the realm of death, a blurred echo of insanity.

From the chest came a creaking sound, a cracking, a tearing—and with a splintering of wood the hand stepped forth to walk on its fingers like a baneful spider.

Eyes stared from frozen faces while the repugnant thing tick-ticked across the map. It stopped; the index finger tapped at a small village named Woeand, fifty leagues north of Reme. Moving northward, the hand tapped on the mountain Erstand. In quick succession it indicated Calencia, capital of Nevinia; Escallas capital of Bashan; Lieden, capital of Collada. Pacing southward, the hand indicated a small island off the coast of the black countries, and then the abandoned city of Killiar, each with two taps.

These things done, the revolting relic collapsed, its unnatural life spent.

"Perfect," the sorcerer breathed, "perfect! This confirms my previous intelligence—and adds to it! Each of the areas located is the hiding place of a part of Derramal's body. Tiana, you must go alone on the northern route while you, Caranga, must take *Vixen* and her crew south to the island of the wizard Serancon and thence to Killiar."

"By the Back!" Caranga swore. "You expect us to chase all over the world on no more than your word?"

"I do," the mage said easily. "You must know that no wizard can break a promise and oath made on his Power. I swear and promise on my Power that Bealost, Tiana's half-brother, is not dead; and that if Derramal's body be brought here, it will tell the boy's hiding place and I will effect its disposal. If I break this promise, may my name which is part of my Power be changed and my Power lost."

"And Drood grasp you in each and every arm." Gunda added with virulence.

Lamarred did not so much as blink. "For solid evidence, here—Bealost's locket. Pyre's emissaries were carrying it to Duke Holonbad when I . . . deterred them."

Tiana snatched the locket almost before it clinked on the tabletop. Indeed, it bore the family coat of arms—aye, and on the back was the tiny inscription she herself had scratched one day when the jeweler wasn't watching his tools. It was in truth her brother's locket—but it was wrong side to. Both the armorial bearings and her inscription were reversed.

Tiana felt as if she stood on the brink of a chasm of madness. Suddenly she knew the true identity of Lamarred, and it was an impossibility, a blasphemy against natural order. Previously she had feared showing some betraying sign of recognition; now she feared to think lest her enemy read her thoughts.

After a moment her strength reasserted itself. Though Lamarred was clearly an enemy, he had struck her heart, where only Bealost and Caranga dwelt. *I must play this cobra-eyed wizard's game—and beat him!* Yet how to solve the enigma, the dark riddle of insanity that was Lamarred? *Many a knot is unraveled by the road*, she recalled. Aye; somewhere on her distasteful quest she would find the answer to the mystery. Controlling her voice, she spoke.

"It is my brother's locket. I have no choice. I will undertake your grisly quest."

"*Our* quest," Lamarred purred. "Good then, Tiana of Reme. You are strongly allied. What useful knowledge I have is written on the back of the map, which you will find can be slid from the tabletop. And now—farewell."

The wizard turned and seemed to vanish even before the curtains fell before the alcove where he'd stood. Caranga cursed, but it was Gunda who leapt up to whip back the arras. Wordless exclamations broke from three pairs of lips.

The small alcove was gone. It did not exist. It was as if it had never existed.

In its place stood a tall mirror.

"Again," Tiana whispered, "a mirror . . . or *the* mirror. . . ."

Perhaps Gunda thought the glass concealed a secret door; perhaps he merely had need to express anger and frustration at Lamarred's abrupt departure. Whatever the reason, Tiana's second drew ax from belt and, with the full power of his brawny right arm, struck the mirror. It rang from the blow that would have splintered a city's gate . . . rang, and was neither shattered nor so much as scratched. Without a sound but an aspirant gasp, Gunda crumpled to the floor like a puppet whose strings had been cut.

His companions needed no examination to know that *Vixen's* huge second mate was dead.

Caranga stared, dumbfounded, a large black hand on Tiana's

bare pale back. He turned that expression of mingled astonishment and anguish on her.

With her lips close-pressed, she answered her foster father's unasked question: "We will go. When we finish our vile quests, we must learn the secret of the Inn of the Smiling Skull . . . and avenge our friend."

3

The Sisters of Death

Hot moist breath blew on Tiana's face and was followed by the slurping over her cheek of a large wet tongue.

Tiana's transition from sleep to full alertness was instantaneous. Even while her eyes focused, her dagger sprang into her hand. She gazed into great somber gray eyes, which stared back. A mule!

Relief did not completely replace apprehension; mules had masters. She rose, grasped her long, nastily slim rapier, and surveyed the forest clearing. There was neither sign nor sound of another human. Tethered as she'd left him, her horse calmly cropped grass. With a little frown, Tiana turned to examine the mule. It was dirty, unkempt and wore neither bridle nor harness. A small wound festered on its left fetlock, she saw; it should have been lanced and cleaned at least a day ago. Evidently the beast was masterless but not wild; it had come to her seeking human care.

Good. I can use him. But—why would anyone abandon such a sound and valuable beast? An answer suggested itself, pleasant or no: *perhaps no one did. His master was slain by robbers? Forest thieves?—and the clever animal fled the murderers.*

"Clever fellow. Here, stand easy now."

The mule did, placidly accepting her tending of its wound,

and she sat down to a breakfast of the cold roast rabbit that
remained of last night's supper. The meat was doubly delicious
for its seasoning of self-righteous satisfaction.

As she had prepared to depart Reme, Caranga had remembered that for all her expertise asea, his piratical stepdaughter
could hardly know aught of woodcraft or forest lore. She could
blunder all too easily into any of a host of deadly traps. Tiana had
listened with what she thought was considerable patience, while
Caranga explained that in the forest one was ever both hunter and
hunted. (And how, she mused, did that differ from the pirates'
life he and she had led all these years?) Pay attention to the
principles he explained, Caranga bade her, and she'd be able to
follow any trail through the forest while leaving none herself. He
expounded at length on various methods of stalking game and
men, on leaving false trails and deadfalls to evade or ambush
pursuers and on which wild beasts were most dangerous under
which circumstances. In the middle of why one should always
approach a water hole from downwind, both Tiana and her
stepfather had run out of the patience that was a virtue of neither.
Heated words were exchanged. Caranga swore that his foolish
daughter would never so much as see the hand she sought; she
would starve in the midst of plenty for inability to catch so much
as a rabbit.

All of which made the rabbit especially delicious. With or
without Caranga's tediously detailed knowledge, she'd caught a
fine fat rabbit on her first night in the woods. All she'd done was
stand quite still while the little animal took his time hopping
within rapier reach.

Now Tiana wondered idly if it mightn't have been a bit too
easy, if perhaps the abundant animals of this forest were unac-
customed to hunters—or unafraid of them. Could she have
wandered onto some nobleman's game preserve? Such lordly
dogs were frequently too lazy to hunt, yet hanged starving
peasants for "poaching." Small matter, she mused with lifted
brows. If she met a gamekeeper, she had plenty of gold and
silver for a man reasonable enough to accept a bribe. And if he
insisted on being honest to his lord, why then—her hand touched
her sword.

She finished her repast, saddled up, and was out of the forest
by noontide. The mule followed her like a devoted dog.

According to the map, the village she sought, Woeand, lay but
a few miles along this dirt road. Strange; the fields on either side
were overgrown with weeds, and cows feasted merrily on what
little corn and wheat struggled up without seeming attention.

The three farmhouses she'd thus far passed were ramshackled and weatherbeaten, their windows laced with cobwebs.

Why do these foolish people abandon their farms?

Reining in, she dismounted to examine the soil, even to test its arable depth with her dagger. By the Cud! Rich and moist it was, and dark, the topsoil extending down and down. With such land even an indifferent farmer should grow fat and rich! Their counterparts to the west scratched out a precarious living from a hostile earth; up north, farmers plowed land not half this fine in daily fear of the savage woodlings. That this fine land was idle and waste was . . . obscene.

Pondering, aware of mystery, she rode on, followed by the mule. Even the graveyard she passed was deserted. No, the dead had hardly departed their abodes en masse, but all maintenance had been neglected. Headstones were overturned or poked forth at odd angles from masses of weeds. There was no sign that the nuns were performing their ceremonies—and duties!—and there was not one new grave.

What ails people hereabouts? Bad enough they've stopped hunting and farming—have they ceased dying, too?

At least the next farm was inhabited, though its proprietor's efforts appeared far less than wholehearted. Less than half his fields were plowed, and no furrow among those was straight. A weedy invasion seemed close to victory. Narrow-eyed, Tiana reined her mount up to the farmhouse. Curiosity tethered the horse there; curiosity impelled her through the open door.

She inhaled deeply; the perfume was that of bread freshly baked and hot beef stew. Beside the stove, a large fruit pie was still warm. So, at a table set for five was the stew on the plates! Frowning, hand on pommel, she looked about, called out. *Did I frighten them off? Hardly!* In less than a minute, she'd made sure the little house was deserted.

A chill of apprehension, awareness of the foreboding unknown tautened her nerves.

What emergency sent a family of five out of their home in the middle of the midday meal? A neighbor's house afire?—there was not so much as the odor of smoke. Grimly and with nervousness riding her shoulders like a brooding vulture, Tiana mounted and rode on toward Woeand. She'd had the presence of mind to help herself to the pie; riding, pondering the mystery, she munched.

"At least the cooking's good hereabouts!" She'd spoken aloud, full-mouthed; her mount put back one ear and the mule hurried to catch up. Tiana tried to laugh. She failed.

The village of Woeand carried on the nigh-abandoned appearance. Its few buildings were maintained only by patchwork and make-do. Tiana saw with new shock that the people were a sickly lot, pale and drawn of face and sunken of lackluster eyes. Slump-shouldered, they walked in listless shuffles and seemed to fear her glance. It occurred to her that the region must surely be afflicted with some whelming plague that did not slay, but sapped vitality and spirit. The thought sent a nervous shudder running through her. At least she'd not be here long.

Even so, she felt the temptation to forget her mission and hold her breath until she was many miles distant.

She reined toward a listless youth. "Ho there—does this town have an inn?"

The boy stopped to stare up at a magnificent woman astride a chestnut horse. Her face, framed by sun-glinted red hair, was alive with beauty; deep-green eyes stared down at him and burned with authority. Though she was enveloped in a long black cloak with gold braid at the shoulders, such of her supple limbs as were visible or outlined showed superbly molded shapeliness and an unusual lithe strength. A woman, beautiful, bosomy, and armed as befitted a man of arms.

"May it please your ladyship," he drawled, "there is no inn, but the widow Mordabot takes in such travelers as pass our way." The boy pointed at a tired-looking house at the edge of the village.

"And where lies the convent of the Sisters of Death?"

"Theba's temple is there, your ladyship—about a quarter of a mile to the east." Again he pointed, lifting his arm as with considerable effort.

"Do you bring a sack of grain to the widow's, for my animals," she said, "and do you be quick." To observe his reaction, she deliberately overpaid; she tossed the boy a small coin of gold. It was worth more than the larger ones of silver that crowded her bag.

Though his eyes sparkled with instant greed, his hand was too slow. *Listless*, she mused. *No vitality.* She watched him retrieve the coin from the dust and shuffle off with what was probably his notion of haste. It cut Tiana's heart to see such waste of a lad who should be full of energy and mischief. *He didn't even ogle*, she mused, for Tiana of Reme knew her body, and she knew males.

The widow Mordabot proved just as tired-looking as her little weather-bested house. After tending her animals and buying a halter and lead line for the mule, Tiana examined the room the listless woman had rented her. Like all the town, it appeared past its prime. At least the place was clean; despite the harsh life that had been hers, Tiana loved her comforts. She looked fondly upon the bed with its feather-stuffed mattress and clean white sheets—and at the strong bolt on the room's single door. It was firmly secured.

Perhaps, she thought, with an attempt at lightness, *the graveyard has no new graves because all the dead don't know it—they're still walking about, like Mordabot and that boy!*

She knew she was whistling in the dark. To offset the feeling of unease, she busied herself for her night's work. Whirling off her black cloak, she carefully daggered off its gold braid and other ornamentation. Then she stripped and sprawled to luxuriate on the bed. She'd simply sleep till midnight and then rise to go and do what she'd come for: steal the left hand of long-dead Derramal from the convent of Theba. The nuns surely regarded it as the prized relic of some saint.

But—*guard* it? *Nuns?* Tiana smiled at the ceiling. *Not likely!*

Still smiling in confident anticipation, she lowered herself into sleep.

Slumber slid into formless nightmare, vague and shadowy and red-shot, full of a brooding, heightening menace she could not name. Fear, then intense anger rose in her breast and she fought, seemingly clawing her way through a maze of cobwebs. Waves of warmth and erotic desire swept over her, enveloped her. It was lovely . . .

Submit . . . submit . . . submit . . . so sweet, so lovely, submit . . .

Tiana did not hear the urging; she *felt* it, as desire spread a tingling glow through the heaving fullness of her breasts, down her muscular stomach and into her loins, throughout every part of her nakedness. *Submi-i-it. You will be delicious s s s . . . submit . . .*

Her limbs quivered in anticipation, expectation. So nice. . . . Her breath came in rasping gasps. Sweeter than honey was the demanded submission, sweeter than that its promise. It challenged even the fiercely independent spirit of she who had been captain of *Vixen,* preying on other ships—

Preying! Submission was *too* attractive, and Tiana resisted. Her efforts intensified; she seemed to be enveloped in moist pink silk. Anger flamed. With all her will, all her strength, she struck out at the sweet pink haze that enveloped her. It retreated; again she struck.

The haze dissolved like fog beneath the sun. Her mind struggled—and was clear.

Yet wakefulness was as disconcertingly unreal as dream-filled sleep. She was astonished to discover herself in the center of the room, still naked, covered with sweat—and clutching her dagger!

She lifted her fisted hand and stared. The dagger's blade was red-smeared and dripping.

By the bright moonlight streaming through the window, Tiana's wild eyes saw that her bed was not empty. On it, swathed in black lay a nun of Theba—a Sister of Death. Her eyes were wide open, but she was motionless. Her throat was slashed out. That scarlet splotch indicated that her heart was pierced as well. Tiana stared, looked again at her dagger, glanced about.

I . . . awoke from a nightmare, still dazed, and . . . slew a nun?

The door was open. The bolt was back, showing no sign of having been forced. It was as if the iron cylinder had come alive to slide itself back.

Tiana was shaken, but on the instant she firmed her mouth and stood straight. *Sorcery! I awoke from a nightmare and slew a sneak-thief who entered the room by . . . means arcane. That explains why I didn't waken as usual; totally, and at once. Explanations to the villagers might be troublesome—though surely she isn't a nun at all, but a thief disguised.*

"By all the mud on the Great Turtle's Back, too many mysteries haunt Woeand! Past time I fetched that accursed hand and departed this noxious place!"

Hmp, she thought, going still naked to the window, *second time today I've talked to myself. Tiana, Tiana—'tis unworthy!*

She peered out into the night. Every home in the village was dark. There was no sign that anyone else was awake at this late hour. Yet—a shuddersome clot of black figures moved slowly along the street. Robes dragged in the dust. While Tiana watched, pressed back in darkness with one damp hand to a bare breast that tremblingly bespoke her rapid heartbeat, members left the group by ones and twos to enter the darkened houses. After a few minutes inside, they came hastening back, flowing black robes flapping like the wings of bats, to rejoin the main body. She was surely looking down upon above thirty nuns—nor were they afflicted by the listlessness of this land!

Tiana strove to tell herself that the nuns were merely taking up a strange ritual collection. . . .

At midnight?

Her mouth was dry and her spine had gone chill and seemed acrawl with worms. It was not just that the Sisters of Death had

no difficulty entering the homes of sleeping folk through doors
that should be locked; there was an intangible aura of the *wrong*,
of a nameless loathsome evil hovering about those mysterious
figures in black. It seemed to emanate palpably from their very
robes.

Straightening from the window, Tiana ran her palms down
bare flanks. Hands and hips were dry; when confronted with
circumstances frightening or worse, she tended ever toward
calm and inflexibility of plan. She'd not be dissuaded. Thinking
apace, she whirled for her clothes. The fact that the nuns were
still up and about impelled her to hasten her planned theft, not
delay it. Dressing rapidly, she gathered up her possessions,
swung the unallayed black of the long cloak about herself, and
silently stole to the front door of the widow's house.

Tiana peered out into an empty, silent street.

Just as she started to step forth, a nun emerged from the house
next door. Raven robe fluttering susurrantly, she hurried down
the street after her companions. Suddenly she paused, glanced at
a house at the village's very edge, and entered.

Overpowered by curiosity, Tiana rushed after the Sister on
feet as silent as she could make them.

The door by which the nun had entered was only ajar, but
Tiana could see within. Around a table a family sat in the
darkness, seemingly asleep. The Sister, her back to the door,
was bent over a girl in her teens. Though no one moved, Tiana
heard an odd, sinister noise—a *sucking*. Easing out her rapier,
she kicked the door fully open.

"In Theba's name, what are you doing?"

The nun whirled, still a-crouch. The moon's glow highlighted
her face like that of an awful lich, and Tiana stared. Eyes that
were glowing pools of unnatural hunger glared at her from above
a mouth stained with the blood that dripped crimson from parted
lips—and ran down the throat of the seated girl.

Pure reaction sent Tiana lunging at the heart of that abominable apparition, her own face set in lines of horrified rage.

Partway to its target, her rapier seemed to enter soil; it slowed.
The eyes of the fiend glared, growing ever larger. Baleful power
seemed to issue from them in a palpable force that struck her
attacker. Clenching her teeth, straining, Tiana forced her blade
forward with an arm that was like lead packed in wet sand. She
was unable to wrest away her gaze; the ireful eyes of the vampire
now merged into a single great orbiculate light that filled her
vision, owned and *possessed her vision.*

Cold winds seemed to blow through her body, which prickled as though assailed by needles of ice. The eye, the eye . . .

The eye was a whirling vortex, sucking at her soul, seeking to wrest and drag it from her body. Tiana's teeth ground; her muscles quivered with effort; she strove to press on. . . .

Having reached the fiend's black-shrouded breast, the rapier point seemed frozen there, as the winds blowing through Tiana's body were freezing her, blood and bone. By the Cow whose rumination created the world—what *power* she strove against!

Tiana's long career as a pirate asea coupled with her certain knowledge of her own bastardy, had given her an ever-fierce thrust for independence and a will that was passing strong. Both drove her now. Her being flashed with scarlet anger. Every ounce of her strength channeled into the arm that strove to drive her sword into this monster in human form. Though she seemed set in a block of ice and there was a dull roaring within her head, her rapier's tip moved—and entered the vampire's breast. Black robe yielded and was pierced. The dreadful eye widened even more, but then crimson clouds appeared in its ghastly freezing glare.

Fear abruptly replaced the expression of unnatural hunger. The eye began to shrink as the vampire's power failed her. Quivering from crown to toes, Tiana forced her slender blade another inch into helplessly accepting flesh—vile flesh.

The eye filled with dread. It dimmed and shrank. Then it became two ordinary eyes, and Tiana completed her lunge as though a mighty ax had cleft through chains that bound her. The eyes stared—and glazed in death. Tiana nearly pitched forward as the human monster fell backward off her blade. With an unsteady hand on a poorly wrought chair back to support her on jellylike legs, Tiana of Reme stood shaking as much in horror of revelation as from the terrible strain of that unnatural duel. Her jaws ached from the long clenching of her teeth.

O Great Cow, small wonder these villagers were too weak to farm or hunt or make simple repairs! The convent of the Sisters of Death was a coven of vampires, whose ghoulish members nightly fed on the villagers' lifeblood!

Yet mystery remained, she knew as she stood, regaining strength and control of herself; not all was solved. Many of these people could not long survive this nightly taking of their vital juices. None could withstand it indefinitely. Then—why was the graveyard abandoned, rather than overflowing? *Where are the corpses*, Tiana demanded within her own mind, and with a sickly sinking sensation, she knew there remained a grisly secret yet to be discovered.

She felt an urgency in her to run, flee . . . but, again, that only firmed her to her purpose. She left the doomed village and walked eastward. Her sword, naked in her hand, was a comfort—small comfort! Yet it had slain, she told herself while she walked through darkness in which horror and the yet-unknown hung heavy as some noxious fog. The nun was a *living* vampire, a demon that could be slain, not one of the Undead.

The walk was at once too long and too brief; a stone building loomed before her. While it covered little more space than a house, its walls were high, running up into a rounded dome worked with the sacred symbols of deathless Theba. A chapel . . . she stared at it, the abode of Theba and the Sisters of Death, and the hiding place of the left hand of the dismembered mage, Derramal.

She had come far for that long-severed hand. She would have it, vampires or no.

No nun showed herself, nor came any sound from the chapel. A little distance away, a smallish shed was silent and dark, and that wooden door in the terrace must be a wine cellar. Circling warily, Tiana looked up. In windows thirty feet above, faint light flickered. Was the chapel empty, with a few ceremonial candles left to burn while the Sisters were absent on their ghoulish errand of sustenance? Or, Tiana wondered, were the nuns amid some silent, faint-lit ritual, following their inhuman repast from the veins of humans?

She circled the building until she was in shadow on the side opposite the moon. From her pouch of thieves' tools she withdrew her silken rope. But then, frowning, she stepped closer to the wall.

"Ah." The thick old ivy cloaking the wall held firm; it could be climbed in absolute silence, while even the padded grappling hook could make noise enough to betray her. She returned the rope to her pouch, took off her sword against its clanking and saw to her dagger.

With the consummate ease of the natural athlete in fine condition, Tiana glided up the wall, a shadow among shadows. She reached the window without experiencing other than the most minor of mishaps. Clinging to the ivy and with one foot braced on the sill, she peered within, and down.

The nuns had preceded her. They were there, in strange ceremony. In their black robes they were like large bats, kneeling before their high altar in absolute silence. The scene might almost have been one of normal worship of devoted adherents.

It was not. Behind the altar against the chapel's back wall stood a tall figure, its head and most of its body lost in the darkness. Apparently some sort of statue—not Theba—it seemed to preside like death itself over a tangled heap of white forms at the base of the altar.

They bring them here, she thought in new revelation. *Ah the monsters—those are the naked bodies of the villagers—or the farm folk whose home I found abandoned in mid-meal!*

She wondered. Did the Sisters collect blood by night and whole families by day? Why? What further obscenity did they perform on the innocent victims of their need and lust for human blood?

The head of the tall presiding figure was well above the level of Tiana's window. Most of that rearward north wall was covered by black drapes that swept out from the . . . figure. Tiana looked elsewhere. Just below her window she noted a thick wooden beam, one of several that spanned the chapel at regular intervals.

With a last look within, Tiana climbed down to consider her problem.

Somewhere within that temple of ugliness was a relic she sought. And so were thirty or forty of the nuns. She was but one; how to gain the hand—and preferably rid the world of the obscenity of this abominable company the while? True, she found them conveniently all in one place, with but one way out—but locked doors opened for them. Knowing they possessed deadly hypnotic powers, she had to assume they had other powers as well, though Caranga had taught her that the greatest abilities, natural or arcane, were little or naught without courage.

Tiana honestly believed herself fearless. If she was wrong, she had yet to come upon that which overpowered the courage that was like instinct within her.

She pondered, letting her mind range. That second nun she'd slain; her hypnotic power had failed when rapier point had first pricked her breast. At first blood, she had abandoned her horrid weapon—and since she had not fled, she had apparently frozen in panic as well as lost all courage. And the others? *If only I could lock them in the chapel!*

Are they demons? That lamia I slew aboard the Narokan ship that started all this questing and confronting the Otherworld;

*she was a demon, and was held by the slimmest chain—of silver!
By the Cud! Silver! Steel slays demons and were-things; silver
holds them.* She touched her money pouch. *If only I could find
the things I need . . . their shed!*

Taking her sword, she rushed to the little building just west of
the chapel. Inside, she drew the door behind her, sure there'd be
a candle or lamp just within. Within seconds she'd put her hand
on a candle; in less than a minute her flint and tinder raised its
flame. As she'd hoped, she was in a tool shed. Walls were lined
with shelves containing various supplies and tools, including
several large jars of oil. Their number indicated the nuns had not
burned the sacred lamps of Theba overmuch, of late! In one
corner squatted a small grinding wheel, a bucket of water beside
it. And there hung a hammer by its leathern handle-strap.

Tiana felt both elation and a touch of awe. Chance was
completely on her side this night—or the Goddess had appointed
her to work justice on the heretic nuns who were traitors to Theba
and humanity alike.

She set to work with the enthusiasm of a fanatic. From her
pouch she took out a dozen large silver coins of Bashan mintage;
good hard coins, and strong. It was the work of but a few
minutes, using the rotary whetstone, to put a sharp edge on each
Bashan eagle. With a couple of hide strips from hanging tools,
she rigged a little harness for a large jug of oil; now she could
carry it while leaving hands free. Smiling, humming, she doffed
her cloak and soaked it with water from the pail that was set to
cool and clean the grinding wheel. Her silken rope she soaked
too, and rubbed it in the silver dust from the grinding.

Jug bound at her side, Tiana snatched up hammer and bucket
and hurried to the chapel's door.

The unholy sisters gave voice now to what was superficially
an orthodox Theban chant—but which was strange, twisted,
seemingly in praise of evil rather than good. Tiana smiled anew:
Good! Chant on—loudly! The door fit its frame most accurate-
ly—wonderful!

Hoping the chant covered the noise, Tiana set to work: she
used her sharpened silver coins to nail shut the chapel door.

Once their chanting stopped abruptly, and she only just
checked the stroke of her hammer, gasping when she directed its
shortened impact onto her own hand. She waited, holding her
breath—and the nuns began a second, eerily repellent chant or
incantation. Tiana drove home the last of the silver coins-
become-nails.

By the time she had secured the door, Tiana's belief in her

being a divine instrument was running a bit thin. Fanaticism waned when it occurred to her that if her plan failed in any of its several parts, she'd simply have made the vampire nuns a present of a free meal: Tiana of Reme.

Well, this was battle, she told herself firmly, and no battle is without risk.

In the shadow beside the temple, she set down the pail, looked up at the window once more. Rope, dagger, and oil were what she needed for this task; the rapier would be of small value, and might well betray her with a clank. Again, she discarded it. Once again, jar of oil thumping her hip, she mounted the vines that hugged the wall.

She slid through the window and onto the beam just below. Aye, it was broad enough. After securing her rope in the window, she lowered its silver-coated end through darkness to the chapel floor. With a care for silence, she crawled along the beam toward the black drapes behind the high altar. She'd have a few moments' sanctuary there, behind the drapes. Twice she paused and held her breath, having by accident knocked off one of the pieces of plaster that littered the beam. The chanting continued; its noise covered the impacts of the plaster particles. Releasing her breath and drawing another, Tiana crept on.

She had crawled some ten feet when the incantation ended. Silence filled the chapel. She felt that she could put out her hand and *touch* silence; in its totality the slightest sound would resound like thunder. Aye, from below she heard the rustle of a death-dark robe.

Even more carefully, not daring to breathe, Tiana continued her tense advance along the narrow, plaster-sprinkled beam. Her mouth was dry. Her heart thudded hard. Her stomach felt as if she'd swallowed a great stone. *Wretched farmwife—what did she put in that pie I ate? Curse her for being the worst of cooks. May she—*

Tiana chased the thought and paused while she shuddered. The baker of the fruit pie was most certainly crumpled below, limbs entangled with those of her own family, stripped naked and drained of every drop of blood! *I shall weep later in repentance of my evil thought—the slightest sound and I shall join that pile of white bodies before their altar of obscenity!*

Despite the night's coolth and her soaking wet cloak, she was covered with sweat. Her breath came rapidly in short gasps and she feared her heartbeat must be audible for a league in every direction. She was within a few feet of the mass of drapery now—and she saw that she must rush. Below, a nun approached the altar, carrying a brazier in which she had kindled a fire. When that source of light reached the altar beneath Tiana, it would be as effective as sunrise in destroying the shadows that cloaked her.

Despite the danger of noise, she redoubled her speed and slipped behind the draperies—just as the shadows vanished before the flamelight from below.

Tiana was still for a time, swallowing again and again, carefully wiping her hands free of sweat and bits of plaster. Then she looked, and she was able to see the head of the great figure behind the altar, eerily illumined by the light from the brazier. Cud of the Cow—the Sisters of Death, consecrated to Theba, were in truth worshiping a repugnant image made in the likeness of a *giant sleeping bat*!

The black drapes were cut so as to resemble hugely spread wings. The realism of workmanship struck Tiana with a momentary horror that the thing was alive. But no—it must have been constructed here, for the bat was too tall and bloated to have passed through the door.

The horrid fear removed and the "wings" providing invisibility, Tiana deep-breathed while she worked at relaxing tensed muscles and quivering nerves.

Realization came on her that she mightn't be safe at all. She might have been seen and, rather than shouting alarm, the nun who saw might well have spread the whispered word among her loathsome companions that they prepare to *receive* the invader.

No matter, Tiana told herself. *It is time, anyhow; they'll be sure I'm here soon enough!*

Unstopping the jug of oil, she began to trickle its contents onto the drapes. Oil sloshed, and she barely curbed her reaction when *her hand touched flesh*—the bat was alive! It must have been *grown* to its prodigious size in this noisome chapel of abomination! But . . . how could the nuns feed a monster of such gigantic proportions?

Then she knew, and Tiana went sick and felt the weakness of horror.

This place demanded the cleansing of fire; it must be removed totally from the surface of the earth. An army of murdered souls screamed voicelessly for vengeance on the nuns who'd drunk their blood and the colossal bat that feasted on their flesh.

Swathing herself in her sodden cloak, Tiana drew its hood close about her head and made sure her mass of fiery hair was within. Then, with dagger and flint, she struck sparks to the oil. With a rushing sound as of wind, bright flames leapt up. Dagger in teeth, Tiana pounced onto the bat's wing and slid to the floor. The dagger was back in her fist on the instant she alit—but she had landed almost in the arms of the Mother Superior, who seemed to be awaiting her. She *had* been seen!

The fiend's hazel eyes seemed ordinary enough—until Tiana found herself completely incapable of movement. The Mother Superior possessed power far greater than that of the nun Tiana had slain earlier! Tiana was helpless.

Peripheral vision apprised her that the fire had thrown the other nuns into a howling panic. In a milling mass they rushed to the door. Bound with silver, it refused to open even for their demonic powers. Their fear redoubled; they milled in noisy terror.

Tiana could not smile at her success in trapping the unholy sisterhood; she was trapped with them. She stood powerless to move while the Mother Superior easily pushed aside her dagger and bent back her head. Tiana seethed in mute rage and strove with all her will to break the fell paralysis. Desperation enhanced her furious efforts, yet the only effects were that her frozen body went atremble, her heart raced and her veins, including those of her neck, stood forth. Demonic eyes flashed greedily at the sight. Baring hideous fangs, her captor slowly lowered its open mouth to the smooth skin of Tiana's throat.

She felt its approaching breath, and Tiana knew that she was dead. They would all roast together—they her victims and she theirs.

The monster bat must have been bound by spell or consummately deep sleep; only when its left wing was a leaping sheet of yellow fire did pain shatter its slumber. With a horrendous screech of pain and terror, it surged forward. Nuns scattered and some were crushed unnoticed by the agonized monster. The mad beating of its afflicted wing only fanned the flames, which spread to the chapel's furnishings and the creature's body. Higher sprang up roaring fire. A convulsion of the devil bat saved Tiana temporarily; she and her attacker were bowled over. The bat collapsed too, in the center of the chapel, a howling burning mass of flame that writhed in agony.

On the floor nearby, Tiana strove to free herself, but the vampire's power held. The intended victim remained unable to move. Once again the vampire lowered open, greedy mouth to the quivering flesh of Tiana's throat. Again she felt the creature's hot breath, close and closer to her pulsing jugular.

It was then that the Mother Superior seemed to become aware of the fire for the first time, so intent had she been on her victim.

She—or it—looked around in disbelieving horror. Terror clouded those dreadful eyes when it saw that the chapel had become an inferno of death. Its hands left Tiana; its hold left her as the horrified monster rocked up to its knees. Tiana stared up into the face of what seemed only a frightened woman—a terrified woman.

When it rose, Tiana followed. She gripped a fear-quivering shoulder and forced the creature about even while her other hand struck. Turning it to face her, Tiana drove her dagger into the vampire's heart.

Rushing past the falling chieftain of the Woeand monsters, Tiana pounced to the high altar. Aye, that glass box looked just right to house and display a hand—but it was shattered, and empty. The shattered glass lay outside. The box had been broken *from within*!

The hand of long-dead Derramal had sensed the fire, broken free, and fled.

Acrid smoke roiled in the chapel as the fire spread. Lowering her face to the clearer air just above the floor, Tiana saw something like a small animal a few feet away. She hastened to it; a smoke-blinded vampire nun blundered into her and was hurled athwart a blazing bench. Eyelessly sensing rising heat all about, the hand was running in desperate circles in a horrid spider-like gait. Tiana restrained the impulse to snatch it up; though she had sought it with such assiduousness, it was a fell thing, the hand of a dead sorcerer that obviously lived on, Undead.

Staring bright-eyed at the scuttling thing, Tiana lowered her cloak into its path. Instantly it buried itself in the cloak's folds. There it clung.

A nun with horrid eyes and bared fangs emerged from the smoke to lunge at her and Tiana kicked the vampire, almost carelessly, in the proximate center of the flowing black robe. With a cry the creature staggered back—and flame leaped up its robe from a crackling wooden bench that became a great torch. Groping through the smoke, Tiana found the west wall and followed it half-blindly to her rope. Either the nunnish vampires had not discovered it or had been baffled and repelled by its rubbing of silver dust.

"Hang on, hand," Tiana muttered. And though her arms felt like lead, she seized the slender silken cord and began climbing.

All about her fire crackled and roared; there were fewer cries from the dying vampire horde. The smoke was taking them, even while it choked Tiana as with demonic hands. Her eyes burned and streamed. Up she went. A new intensification of heat directly below her told her that the fire was coming for her rope. It seemed to stretch from hell to heaven as, gasping, blind, she forced her way up. Her wet cloak steamed and breathing became impossible.

And then clear night air struck her face and she dragged herself over a windowsill she could not even see. The silken rope smoked when she drew it up. Leaving it tethered, she flung it out the window. Tiana slid to the ground and allowed herself to fall.

Though her lungs ached and her eyes remained partially blinded by smoke-tears, she did not pause. First she recovered and sheathed her sword. Then she checked her prize. As she unfurled the cloak, the hand dropped free. It lay still, its unnatural death-life seemingly reserved for saving itself. Without hesitation she emptied coins onto the ground, stuffed the most valuable into her bosom, and crammed the lifeless, severed hand into her money pouch. She drew its rawhide string taut and double-knotted it. Then she plunged her hands into the water remaining in the pail.

I have you, hand. I . . . rescued you. Just in the Name of the Cud of the Great Cow, fear nothing—and remain still!

The air of night felt cold after the fiery interior of the temple, as Tiana ran many yards from it. There she collapsed, panting, to survey her bonfire.

Now she heard fewer cries from within the chapel, and those she did hear were all but obliterated by the roar and crackle of leaping flames. The place was evidently the work of superb masons; despite the intense fire that raged inside, walls and dome stood firm. Tiana was surprised that the stone building contained so much that was combustible.

Wait, she thought, *until the fire eats those beams—then we'll see if that place of horror doesn't fall in on itself!*

Judging by the screams, the bat-worshiping drinkers of blood were also burning rather well. Those vampire cries of anguish comprised the sweetest song Tiana had ever heard. A very pleasant night's work, she thought. With a perfectly sincere hypocrisy, she had already forgot her fright of this night—her several frights. Ever after, she would recall this as a glorious adventure and herself as a hero.

The people of Woeand would not know that they and their whole land owed gratitude to a mere thief, bent only on stealing a relic from the vampire nuns.

Hmm. The nuns had stopped burning the sacred lamps and in consequence there was a large supply of oil. No doubt they'd stopped drinking wine, too.

And I'll wager yon wooden door amid the bushes leads to a wine cellar!

It had been a thirsty night's work.

4

Paradoxes

Far beyond the northernmost borders of the civilized lands, a fertile valley sprawls amid cold and barren wastes like a serpent of green basking in warmth. Life is more than hard for the savages who inhabit the desolate land round about. Yet no matter how great their hunger, they never venture into the valley where both game and fruit flourish in abundance. The valley's center sprouts a lofty building at once gracious and austere. A castle rises within the protective ring of its moat, behind defensive walls narrowly sliced by archery ports. Yet it is no castle, for the edifice in the impossible valley has no conventional defenses.

A paradox, the valley; a paradox, the undefended "castle" that is never molested; a paradox, too, its name.

Its name is Ice.

Though surrounded by envious savages, he who dwells in Ice has no need for conventional defenses. Ice is the home of a man as greatly feared as he is little known. His name is Pyre. He is foremost among wizards of all the world.

The wizard sits this day before a table spread with arranged replicas of certain places in Escallas and Calencia, in Leiden and the mountain Erstand, and the chapel of the Sisters of Death. This last model, perfect in detail, is afire. After staring *deeply into the flames for a time, the sorcerer gestures. No eye could blink so swiftly as the three men appear before him. In the quiet, calm tone of command long held and totally assumed, Pyre speaks.*

"*Some idiot thief has stolen the left hand of Derramal. Should this thief succeed in stealing the rest of the corpse, incredible danger will be loosed upon all. All. The thief will be rewarded for his folly . . . by being eaten, body and soul, and we and all that live will pay a bitter price. Prepare. At dawn you will go forth and slay this idiot meddler.*"

Pyre gestured in dismissal, and the three men vanished. Next morning at dawn three large Arctic hawks rose from Ice and flapped swiftly southward.

5

The Elixirs of Serancon

With a great flagon of wine and his kingly personal goblet of gem-studded beaten silver, Tiana's foster father adjourned wearily to his cabin on *Vixen*. Caranga the pirate, formerly Caranga the cannibal and always Caranga the black, finest detector of poisons in the world, sat down at his chart table.

"Cud of the Cow and Susha's paps, what a day, what a day!"

First he filled the goblet, and emptied it in long gulps. He refilled it and pulled together the materials for the log he had promised that damned meticulous Tiana—Susha keep her well and safe from sorcery and pointed steel!

After a moment's thought, the mate of *Vixen* prepared to record his first part in this mad quest. (Lamarred indeed! Mummified body parts of a dead mage, indeed! Bealost indeed! Ah, he'd taught the dear girl too much of honor and responsibility, he had.) With a sigh and a sip from the great goblet, Caranga began laboriously to write:

The first part of our southward voyage went well, Tiana. A fair breeze in our sails and but a touch of unfriendly weather. I had time to pore and pore over the mage's map and its instructions and to worry over you, my sweet girl with no knowledge of woodcraft for she would not list to her

wise father. The map Lamarred gave us shows the isle of the
wizard Serancon a few leagues off the western coast of the
Dark Land. On its back he wrote that the isle is barren rock,
with Serancon's keep built on a hill shaped like a skull. He
noted too that Serancon was not deeply learned in the black
arts, but was the world's most skilled brewer of elixirs—
mostly, one assumed, poisons. From such a man, a poison-
maker living atop a skull, we were to gain the legs of
Derramal.

Ho! I'm sure you had no such difficult time with a few
gentle nuns!

When we arrived, we found not barren rock but a lush
green paradise, as lovely a place as these eyes have seen.
Made a man's blood rise and his brain turn to thoughts of
womanflesh, it did—and so did the naked girls who came
arunning down to the beach to smile and wave at us.
Naturally the crew wanted to go ashore at once! I was of
steel, though, and decided to sail first around the island.
Was this the proper place?

About halfway around there came . . . a strangeness.

The air shimmered like water somebody's thrown a stone
into. One second the island was lush and green. The next it
was black rock, devoid of vegetation. I had to pretend calm
to hold the sweet crew in check; they were shaken, muttering, ready to stampede. As you know, daughter, I myself
am without fear. To distract the men, I pointed to the stone
fortress that squatted high up on a rocky hill. The stones
were white as a marble but shot with red, so that the high
keep looked splashed with blood. It also looked invulnerable to frontal assault, with a lot of barred archery ports but
no windows and only one door—which we could see was
strongly made and reinforced. Too, the hillside was smooth
naked rock, without the slightest cover for attackers.
There'd be no taking Derramal's legs by force.

We sailed on around the island. Again that sorcerous
eeriness: the air shimmered . . . and the isle was again all
tropical beauty!

We anchored twenty yards offshore; I was cautious by
now, wondering what was illusion and what was not—and
why.

"No point in all of us going ashore into danger," I told
the crew. "I'll take six volunteers."

Since the girls were back on the beach, smiling and
waving, every man volunteered. The real problem was

making the others remain on *Vixen*. A threat and a few
promises accomplished that, and seven of us rowed ashore
in the smallboat. Sweet Susha's sweet paps! What a sight!
Not a one of those girls wore a sweet thing, not even a
flower in her hair. And believe me, considering what nature
had done for them, they needed no ornaments! Black as
night their skin, like the shining wings of raven every
maid's hair—but glossier.

As we landed, they squealed and ran into the jungle. At
that instant, your Caranga lost all control over the shore
party!

The girls led us a pretty chase, with me arguing that I
smelled a trap. Yet there was no sign of ambush. Indeed,
there was no sign that we weren't the only men on the
island. At last we broke into a small glade—and there they
were! As many smiling maids as I had leering crew on
Vixen. Only one of them wore aught—their queen.

She was tastefully dressed in a gold crown. Naught else.
And you know how I like my women, Tiana—with meat on
their bones! Oh, that queen was a prize. A head taller than I
she was, broad of shoulder and with superbly shaped limbs.
Skin like black velvet I could fair feel under my hands, with
great standing breasts large and firm as melons.

The sight of her set my blood aboil. My passion was at
such heat I could scarcely speak, much less think. For all
my years, your father still has a hard and powerful body,
daughter, and women look on me with pleasure. The queen
did, and smiled, and she came swaying forward. Ah, it was
utter delight the way those oval melons of breasts joggled
and danced so tantalizingly. I burned.

Her voice was deep, thick and sweet as honey: "Captain,
wouldst care to fetch the others of thy men, that I and my
girls may entertain thee all?"

"Aye!" I assured her. "Naught could please me more."

"Good," said she, "for we have been long without men.
Gladly shall we tender complete hospitality. Thou mayst
have us and all we possess for as long as thou wish, to do
with as thou wish."

A cheer rose about me. A cheer rose within me! I started
forward. With a temptress smile and a lifting of one fine
silky black hand, she made me pause.

"We first beg a small service," sweetly said that island
queen. "Though we be but weak women, we are at war
with Serancon. 'Tis he who stole our men and reduced them

to a state worse than death itself. We have made a vow to rest not till he is destroyed. Already we have reduced his power by stealing a magical leg from him. Slay him, and we are thine.''

"Gladly!" said I, bobbing my silly head—but I had some wit about me. "You will give us both . . . hospitality and the wizard's leg?"

"Aye, handsome captain, gladly. 'Tis an ugly thing, sorcerously preserved.''

The trek back to the beach was a blur in my mind, Tiana, for I admit I was deranged by passion. Only when the ship was under weigh could I think clearly again. I bent down to clean my boots—and shock came on me.

Though I had run through soft moist jungle, there was neither mud nor grass stain on my boots. Instead, they were scuffed and cut as though I had run over ground covered with rough stones. The boots of those who'd accompanied me told the same story, and Machelen had something caught on his right buskin. In the glade his foot had become entangled in a vine, he said, and he'd slashed away the vine with his cutlass. Yet what I found was no vine, but a length of rope unlike any I'd ever seen. It was white, light but strong, and uncommon *sticky*.

Much wonder and nervousness was in my mind when we landed at the base of the fortress's hill. I went ashore with most of the men and a large sack of gold. Once we'd climbed the hill, I saw the valley beyond. The soil was nearly as rocky and barren as the naked rock we stood on, yet it was producing a goodly crop of vegetables. Men tended them, watering, treating those plants as a mother tends her babe. I say men. . . .

Susha's loins, Tiana, those farmers were pitiful creatures, skin-covered skeletons. They spoke neither to us nor to one another, nor did they even show curiosity over us. Their eyes were . . . dead. We fell silent in f—in nervousness.

Other eyes did see us. From the archer's ports in the keep, numerous red eyes stared with a clear lust to kill. I hoisted high the sack of gold and made it clink. As I approached the fortress door, a port opened in it and a voice called out.

"Welcome, good captain. My humble home cannot accommodate so many men, but if you wish to enter alone, we can discuss your business.''

I opened the sack of gold and poured glittering coins on a stone for all to see, then quickly swept the coins into the sack. After I'd pointedly handed it to Machelen, I stepped through the keep's doorway, which was open a mere crack. It slammed shut behind me and the great bar dropped.

Before me stood a wizened old man, a bit beyond plumpness and gnarled like an old tree's limb. I could not tell his race, for years of experiments had stained his skin into a patchwork of many colors. Whether he was originally black or white—or indeed green or purple—I cannot say.

"You are most prudent, Captain," said he, "to leave your gold outside."

"It appears that you share my caution, Serancon." As I spoke, I was noting the men who guarded his keep.

All were hard, strong, black warriors of the coastal tribes. I saw no human emotions on their faces and their eyes were those of a wolf pack, filled with the slaying lust and no trace of compassion. Save for the wolfish eyes that followed my every move, the warriors of Serancon's keep were motionless as statues.

"You admire my guardsmen," the wizard hissed, and I saw that he looked upon me with the same smile a cobra gives a fat mouse. "They and the fieldworkers are among the proud triumphs of my art."

"I am told you are the most skilled brewer of poisons in the world."

"An unjust rumor! Men refuse to understand subtle distinctions—I do not deal in mere poisons. I neither make nor sell aught that can slay man or beast. Elixirs I create and sell, *medicines* that ease the way men fit into their society by destroying this or that tiny . . . weakness in them."

"Weakness?"

"Aye! For example," said the paunchy pruneface in his splotchy robe, with the excitement of pride on him, "the typical farm worker is lazy and inefficient and eats much of what he grows. *My* workers *work*, and never rest or eat. So long as one keeps them from salt, they are faultless laborers. The usual soldier is full of qualities that limit his usefulness: an instinct for self-preservation, initiative that interferes with obedience to commands and, too often, a conscience. One of my elixirs is a medicine that removes such unfortunate deterrents, filling him too with desire to obey—and a bloodlust. Many proprietors of pleasure-houses find that girl-stealers draft them recruits who are pretty enough, but emotionally unsuitable. They have silly ideals of chastity or of faithfulness to their lovers, or are simply too fastidious to receive many of the paying customers to their bodies. No matter! A mere drop of my elixir and these misfortunate qualities are washed from their brains, leaving only uncaring indiscriminate passion!

"Good Captain, tell me of your enemy, and why he is a problem. I will solve it in a way far more effective than crude killing. One of my clients feared to invade a neighboring country because its general was a great warrior. He wished to slay the general, not seeing that a new leader would be nearly as brave and strong and but take the other's place. I gave my client an elixir that made the general a coward."

"Fascinating, good and brilliant Serancon!" I told that monster. "I, however, am come only to purchase the right leg of Derramal. You have seen my gold. Suppose we trade on these terms: remain you within your keep, whilst I rejoin my men. Place a table in the doorway, and on it we shall make the exchange."

The wizard agreed. Soon I faced him across a table. My men were behind me, ready for treachery, and backing him were the fiends he had created. When I placed the gold on the table, he set down both the ugly leg and two goblets of purest gold.

"Such a transaction calls for a sharing of wine," he purred. "Choose the goblet you prefer and I myself shall pour." He showed me a stoppered decanter.

I indicated one of those admirable cups, and he poured wine into it, then into his goblet. When I pushed the sack to his side of the table, it blocked his view of the goblets for a moment, and gold clinked. Then were we raising our cups to each other in hail. We drank. Ah, excellent vintage!

Serancon smiled. "As you came up the hill," he said, for my ears only, "I recognized you as Caranga, a man noted for his skill at detecting poisons. Indeed, you fulfilled your reputation, for when you switched goblets I scarcely could detect it."

I gave him a sweet cobra's smile right back. "Ah, but had I *really* switched the goblets, you would never have known."

He stared, and fear came into his eyes like a stain on water.

Smiling and with an eye on his men the while, I said, "When you asked not my name, Serancon, I was sure you knew who I was. Thus you would logically expect a switch—and so you put the poison in your own cup, true? Ah, I see it is! Serancon, you have outsmarted yourself and got a dose of your own foul . . . *medicine*! And surely no man deserves it more." I waited for him to fall dead.

Instead . . . the light of intelligence flickered in his eyes like a candle in the wind—and then died! "That was very clever, master," said he. "Now how may I serve you?"

Oh but I was elated! A fine elixir indeed! Taking the leg of Derramal *and* my gold, I replied, "Your master requires that which removes the ability to lie."

"Readily," said he, "though I must warn that it is effective only for a few hours, master, nor can it be given with food or drink."

"Then how is it used?"

"By air," he said, handing me a vial. "As you see, it is a dry powder. Put a little in—ah, that kerchief about your neck, and raise it to your nose. It will make you sneeze, and thus spread it several feet. This method is impossible to detect, the only disadvantage being that you yourself can say only truth for a few hours afterward."

As we returned to *Vixen*, it occurred to me that Serancon's elixir was certainly effective for eliminating initiative—for lack of orders, his bloodlusting guards had done naught while I slew and robbed their master.

I held grave suspicions about the women on the other side of the island, but there was no question of not returning to them; a good captain as you know does not *beg* for mutiny! Nor would mere fears stop me, in view of the queen's promise of complete hospitality. The men shared my eagerness though not my doubts. Most of the asses wanted even to go unarmed ashore, so that I was forced to appeal to vanity. We must look our best, I told them, and that of course meant armed as befits brave strong men. . . .

The sun was turning the sky orange as we reached the glade once more. The smile the queen turned on me would have melted ice. She came to me, swaying her tantalizing body to my hungering eyes. That rich honeyed voice asked had I slain Serancon.

"Aye," said I smiling, "I tricked him into drinking one of his own *medicines*."

"How brave and clever thou art, O handsome warrior from the sea. Come, I shall entertain thee while thy men and my girls disport themselves. As thou seest, we have prepared soft beds of leaves and grass."

I saw! "Lovely. Oh—business before pleasure! The leg of Derramal?"

She led me around a great thick tree and I saw a crude stone altar bearing the ugly leg. I had brought a knapsack, that I might carry the legs and have both hands free. As soon as the leg was in the sweet sack, I put my neckerchief to my nose and sneezed, directly at her.

The transformation was instantaneous and horrible. The great "tree" was a rearing chunk of leprous stone. The altar remained. No more was this lush verdure, but barren rock strewn with stones, surrounded by a great network of white rope—an enormous spider's web. My men were not dallying with lovely maids in leafy bowers, but were being enwrapped in cocoons by spiders five feet tall. My beautiful queen was a monster, a great hairy spider no less than eight feet in height. Eh? Seven, then. It moved obscenely toward me. Enormous compound eyes flashed like thousand-faceted gems. Now that deep soft voice was a monstrous obscenity.

"What be the matter, my darling? Thou seemst disturbed . . ."

My answer was in my sword. Faster than I can write it, the blade smashed into that hideous head. Green ichor splashed burning on my arm. The queen's mandibles snapped inches in front of my face. Then, with a convulsion that hurled me several feet, she died with a great tremble of huge hairy legs.

I sprang up, for there was work for my steel. Those of my men who were free were fighting for their lives. At equal odds we might have prevailed, but too many were cocooned ere the battle started.

We took a bloody toll, by Susha's scarlet nipples, but one by one those abominations pulled us down. The monsters evaded close combat, where our swords gave us the advantage. Instead, they squirted sticky ropes of web stuff at us and, when a man was helplessly entangled, they pounced to paralyze him with their venom. The victims were wrapped alive, whether to be eaten later or to serve as food for hatching spiderish eggs, I know not. I shudder now, daughter; then I was too busy.

The sun had set in the sweet scarlet of blood and now growing darkness increased our plight. Ah, what a thirst-quenching of sharp blades was there! And what a falling and web-envelopment of men. . . .

Suddenly, a clot of scrawny black figures appeared, carrying torches. They sang a mournful low chant, but they fell on the spiders like Drood's own demons. With Serancon removed, the zombies in his fields had found salt! Now the wretches realized their true condition, and they'd come seeking and dealing death. The poor creatures asked the favor of death in a way not to be ignored—they seized spiders and tore off their loathsome legs!

To survive, the spiders must slay the Undead. This was not easily done. Their paralyzing venom was without effect, while torches burned their sticky web ropes. Zombies wrapped in webbing would set themselves afire and clutch a spider to their burning bodies so that both were consumed in a grisly funeral pyre. The stench was ghastly, staggering. I saw godsent opportunity for me and my men to escape.

We bore up all our fallen comrades we could, and fled. Twice had I to return to the scene of that awful battle of abominations to gather the rest of the crew. Never have I been amid such horror. Blood and ichor spattered like water in a storm and roiling smoke carried the stench of burning flesh and spider-stuff. Twice during those returns I was attacked by spiders; I slew them with pleasure. When a zombie attacked me, though, I dodged and held my steel. If I killed or hurt him, I thought, his fellows would see me as an effective source of death and fall upon me. He harried me for a few minutes, during which I but dodged. Then he went off seeking a foe who would fight back.

Finally, I and the crew were safe aboard *Vixen*. We pulled up anchor and sailed into the night, and not one of us but knew he was lucky to be alive. Call her but the goddess of savages or no, I hurled no less than two coins of gold into the sea, with thanks to Susha the Voluptuous. And tried to put from mind and loins memory of how that monster spider had *first* appeared. . . .

How that sweet war between the zombies and the spider

women ended, I know not. Whoever was the victor, I much doubt that Serancon's Isle will be a healthy place to visit. 'Tis well. The people who come to buy Serancon's elixirs—his "medicines"—will now receive precisely what they deserve.

As for me, my elixir of the grape has run out, and I am weary and ready to retire.

At least the spiders kept me so busy that my hours of enforced truthfulness were no inconvenience. . . .

6

Riding the Thunder

> To the north a towering mountain range marks the end of civilization and the beginning of Greenwood. Just south of the main range, the mountain Erstand rises to proud height. Ice-clad, its perpendicular slopes are unscalable; no man has ever ascended to its summit. Nevertheless, in a cairn on that summit rests the right arm of Derramal.
>
> —the map of Lamarred

From Woeand, Tiana rode north toward the mountains that divided the world and challenged the sky. As she approached Mount Erstand that rose like a mighty gate before the fortress of the main range, her mount entered dense forest. Within an hour she came afoul of the Woodlings, nor was it an occasion of pride for her.

There was no warning. One moment she was alone in the coolth and shade of the woods; in the next, six of the weirdly painted men were on her. She was shamed and galled; it was debasing so to be taken without inflicting so much as a scratch on her captors. In disgustingly short order, two of the silent men were carrying her along like a slaughtered deer; hair streaming down to sweep the forest floor, she hung head-and-bottom down from a pole to which her wrists and ankles were thonged.

Caranga was right about the value of my knowing woodcraft, Tiana thought. *How ignominious!*

Though it strained her neck, she watched her captors closely. Survival, she knew, depended on her finding a means to outwit them.

Little was known of the Woodlings—for the simple reason that any who met a Woodling raider must slay or be slain. Nothing was known of their homeland north of the mountains save that—at least when viewed from afar—it was lush and green. None had seen it up close, and returned to report.

Few, indeed, dared travel this near the Woodlings' lair.

Parties of raiders from Greenwood, conversely, ranged far to harass their neighbors. Strangely, Woodlings did not steal. They but slew. That was a further problem for Tiana, for most men could be outwitted by an appeal to their greed. Indeed, she mused as she was borne along, she might not be able to converse with these feather-wearers at all; thus far she'd heard not a single word from any of her captors.

Perhaps they're mute. Who knows? —But more likely it's part of their woodcraft to make only the totally necessary sounds.

Their captive swinging like a sack of meat, the strange men glided in eerie silence through the darkly shaded forest. Even up close they were nigh invisible; the men of Greenwood painted their obscenely naked bodies brown and green to match the forest.

Tiana wondered what they planned to do with her. She gritted her teeth. *They'll use me, of course. Who could resist?* An annoyance, that. It was one of the problems of being a woman. She put it out of her mind; of considerably more menace was the fact that these men's teeth were filed. Cannibals, surely. *Well, we'll see. They underestimate me, else they'd have slain me at once. The village must be far. All I need do is wait for an opportune moment—and think very positively about there being one!*

Her possessions, including both Derramal's hands, nestled securely in the pack on her mule. He was cheerfully following, not so clever after all. The Woodling chief had appropriated her weapons. She eyed his nakedly churning backside, and the scabbards swing-ing at his side. If she could regain her rapier, she was confident of slaying these silent green-and-brown men in a fair fight—fair meaning she'd not be taken by surprise; they would. Once weapons were out and death heavied the air, there were no rules; none at any rate that Tiana of Reme adhered or admitted to.

The disturbing aspect of the "plan" was that the savages were definitely heading for Mount Erstand. Surely their village lay not there . . . in which case they must have some particularly unpleasant intent for her, here in the woods.

Surely they'll free me of this pole first . . .

Though she caught no sound or sign that they were other than alone in the woods, her captors halted abruptly. They stood silent and still. Stepping noiselessly to Tiana, the chieftain placed his finger to his lips and her own dagger to her throat. To his men he made several rapid hand signs. Tiana was lowered to the ground. By the time she was able to turn her blood-thickened head, all five men were gone. She had no idea of the direction they'd taken; no broken leaf or bent branch or whisper of grass betrayed the passage of these men of the woods. It was as if they had sorcerously vanished.

The chieftain remained. Her own dagger remained at her neck. Obviously keenly alert, the man seemed actually to be pricking his ears while he strove to send his gaze piercing through the surrounding foliage. He was immobile; there wasn't the faintest of movement even of the five black-tipped green feathers standing from his headband. Tiana tried to be as still—ostensibly, while she tested the bonds at wrists and ankles. The thongs were tight; the dagger snugged against her throat in warning. The Woodling chieftain stared into the forest.

It was not from the woods that his bane came, though, but from the pack of Tiana's mule. She saw, and the back of her neck crawled.

From the pack, like spiders the color of old parchment, crept the severed hands of Derramal.

Her heart commenced to thutter. *The hands! One sought to save itself in the temple of Theba . . . I am its savior! Will it seek to protect me, then, to preserve itself?*

Yes. Dropping to the ground, the hands froze while even that slight noise attracted the Woodling's attention. He must have assumed the mule had stamped, and turned his gaze back into the woods without having seen the ghastly menace in a clump of slawgrass.

The hands advanced on the squatting man. Though his senses eventually warned him, his eyes naturally sought higher for a foe. He left Tiana to glide a pace aside, half-rising into a crouch, his ax up and ready. In vain his gaze roved in quest of the advancing enemy.

When at last he saw the hands, they had spidered nigh to his feet.

Even then the Woodling's speed and agility could surely have saved him, but astonishment and horror were ice that froze his legs. Scuttling obscenely forward, the hands closed about his ankles. Tiana saw them begin to squeeze. The man's dyed skin drew and wrinkled above and below the grip of dead fingers.

"*Hunh!*" Sweat popped out on the man's chest and forehead and he swung his ax in a well-aimed blow delivered with all the power of an enraged and horrified barbarian.

The ax struck the left hand—and rebounded as if it had hit a smith's anvil.

Dead fingers—Undead fingers—slowly constricted, crushing his legs.

A brave man, Tiana's erstwhile captor fought to the last, raining blows on the hands even as they squeezed trickling, then spurting blood from ruptured flesh. The woods barbarian made no sound until both his feet were completely severed from his legs with a splitting, spurting, crunchy sound. Only then did he voice a ululating death cry. He fell, kicking footless legs that gouted blood.

Tiana stared in horror while the hands *laved* themselves in the scarlet splashes. Then they went still. So did the Woodling chieftain.

"Brainless idiot. Drood-begot *hands!* You could have freed *me* to slay him—now when his band returns, they'll run all the way home in panic!" *But I'll wager one tarries long enough to slit my throat first—or free me from this pole by chopping through my ankles!*

In more than a little haste, she writhed and contorted and doubled herself to set about attacking the binding thongs with her teeth. For all their woodcraft, the savages were not sailors, and had bound her merely by making loops and drawing a loop through. The knots yielded easily to tugging teeth. Though it seemed to take hours and her jaws and gums ached, Tiana freed herself. Staggering a little from long inactivity and interrupted circulation, she recovered her weapons from the corpse that had not used them. The hands were quiet, and she assumed she could recover them later.

Now, she thought, teeth gritted and a desire for spill Woodling blood as high in her as anger, *where are those other naked green-and-brownies?*

Her rapier *wheep-wheeped*, slicing air, as she considered. It seemed logical that they would have suspected followers. In that event they'd most likely creep back parallel to their own trail, to ambush the stalkers. What she should do, naturally, was mount up and betake herself elsewhere and with alacrity. But the indignity of having been captured and so ignominiously carried was too fresh in her mind. Urgency was on her to seek out and slay those who'd demeaned her. It blotted out the inner voice of reason that should have convinced her she was no match for barbarians in the forest that was their home. She had ignored such sensible thoughts in past; she was alive.

Working at it, Tiana managed to glide nigh as silently as her foes. She was nearly upon the first before she saw him. He crouched beside a large tree, with his back to her.

Waiting in ambush, she thought with pleasure, and she saw naught but justice in leaping at that naked back, rapier extended. The slim blade sank deep before it jolted to a halt against a frontal rib. When she withdrew, he toppled over to lie face up. She stared.

From behind, it had appeared that the Woodling wore three feathers in the plaited hide encircling his head. Now she saw her error; he wore but two feathers in that chaplet. The third decorated the end of a slender wooden shaft that stood from his forehead.

Tiana's cursing was passing quiet, but altogether sincere. Some mangy mongrel had got to her quarry first!

"Some people have no manners or consideration," she muttered, and almost with the words an angry bee buzzed past her ear and a thud sounded behind her.

Tiana whirled. She faced a Woodling, his ax raised on high for the death blow, and she shuddered at thought of his coming upon her so silently. The blow would not fall, now, but no credit to her; the man's eyes were already glazed in death. The bee that had streaked so closely to her face was an arrow, now lodged just left of center in the Woodling's chest. He fell.

It occurred to Tiana in a wave of bitter humiliation that someone was using her as a stalking horse!

Controlling her rage, she slipped on through the woods. She appreciated now the host of subtle factors that could betray one's position in the forest, and she sought the harder to avoid such errors. Accordingly she paused at the edge of the small glade in whose center sprouted a little clump of turkeybush. The bushes' base sprouted a Woodling's lower body. The man lay prostrate, with an arrow in his side. Tiana skinned back her lips, but curbed

her hiss. This was maddening! All her rightful victims were
being stolen from her.

Beside a huge-boled tree, she studied the body.

Hold! That didn't appear to be a death-wound . . . it wasn't!
The arrow wasn't even *in* the man. *Faking, then. Bait for
ambush!* Her eyes narrowed. *Where are his two comrades,
then?* Aye, she mused, thinking back. Two of the devils had
carried bows—but neither this one nor the two she'd . . . *found*
dead had done. *So. This is the decoy. They'd choose a blind with
a commanding view of this glade. . . .*

There was only one such spot.

*By the Cud! This tree They must be directly above me! But
why haven't they killed m—* Then she knew, and she clenched
teeth and lips. Insult added to insult! The Woodlings had set this
trap for bigger game, a foe they considered more dangerous than
the woman they'd captured so easily, with her skinny little
sword. Doubtless they now hoped she'd just go away without
noticing them.

It was worse than galling—she durst not even voice her rage.

She drew her dagger from its oiled sheath without a sound. It
was out and ready even as she bounded to one side. Her arm had
begun the throw before her gaze found the target squatting just
where she'd expected, on the broad branch above. The blade
rushed to him like a homing bird so that she made an impressed
face. Struck in the stomach, the Woodling groaned and pitched
headfirst from the tree. He landed asprawl, face down in a way
that did a lovely job of grinding the dagger in until the hilt broke
his skin.

As the other green-and-brown man shifted position to gain a
clear bowshot at Tiana—who was scurrying for cover—his
movement disturbed the branches, only a little. Nevertheless,
with his bowstring cheek-drawn and the shaft centered on
Tiana's back, the man's spine was smashed by a heavy, big-
game arrow.

Tiana heard the thud, heard his gasp, and turned in time to see
his arrow skitter wildly away. The Woodling crashed to the
ground.

Nearby the faker jerked as if starting to rise and Tiana realized
she had one last chance to exact her own vengeance. She leaped
in a fury. Her dagger was gone, nor did she draw her sword;
she'd slay the savage with bare hands and feet highly skilled in
the vicious art of unarmed combat. Let him essay to match

agility with one accustomed to fighting on the ever-moving deck of a ship!

The last Woodling did not rise to meet her charge. Only after she had broken his neck did she spot the arrow that projected from his other side. Her unseen ally had killed the bait with a low shot through the grass before she'd succeeded in salving her dignity with a partial revenge.

I'm beaten, she thought glumly, *by a score of five to one . . . saved like a sniveling girl by a pair of dead hands and an archer I've neither seen nor heard!* She could only do that which came far from easily to her: congratulate and thank her unseen ally.

At that moment he stepped into the glade. Young he was, light-footed as a panther, a bit shorter than Tiana—and a superb physical example. His was a tight, closely knit body covered with hard lean muscles. In Martania of Thesia he'd have been one of their public fighters, surely, in the middleweight class. Then she recognized him, the not-unhandsome, lean-faced and boyish man with his curly hair.

"Bandari!"

He smiled. "Incredible. You are Tiana, aren't you?"

The finest cat burglar in Reme, Bandari the Cat had taught Tiana considerable subtle points of thievery—years and years ago. She'd had no notion he was a master bowman, as well.

"By the Cud—Bandari! What are you *doing* here?"

"Reducing the number of Woodlings," he said casually, and went on with a serious answer. "Life in the cities was too easy and boringly *safe*, Ty. Three years ago I returned to my home village Stromvil—where the real action is!" As the young man spoke, his eyes roved admiringly over her magnificent body; his own was even more on display, in soft red buskins, a sleeveless tunic cut very low, and naught else save weapons and hip-slung quiver. "But I have heard of *Captain* Tiana—what are *you* doing here, looking like a temptress in a temple in Shamash?"

"Reluctantly congratulating and thanking you on cheating me of my revenge on those barbars. They were taking me to their village, I suppose, after they . . . finished some business near Mount Erstand." She concealed the pleasure she felt in his gaze, though she stood with her shoulders back and hip flaunted. She'd been an awkward teenager, more nuisance than woman, when last she'd seen Bandari the Cat.

"Hmp! Better you knew not, Tiana. Assuming they were

following their normal tactics, they'd have found a good spot for ambush and crucified you there—then killed any who came in quest of you."

She blinked, swallowed. "None will. And now I doubly congratulate and thank you on getting four of them to my one."

"Oh, I—*one!* What about their warchief?"

"That is a rather long story . . . and I must go and collect my mount and pack mule."

"Just let me retrieve a few arrows, and I'll be for going along."

He did and, as they re-entered the woods, he felt it necessary to caution her to remain wary. While they made their way through the dark domain of trees and greenery, she told him of the mirror, of the bargain with Lamarred, of Woeand, of the hands and the Woodling chieftain's eerie death.

"And so now I must climb Mount Erstand. It isn't really impossible, surely."

"Tiana: it is. Last time I was atop old Erstand, I surveyed carefully. From the top I saw plainly that the slopes are unscalable—even to Bandari the Cat!"

"Then by the Back—how did you get up there?"

The lean face smiled under its unruly cluster of dark curls. "There is a way. And it too is a long story, lovely Ty. Do you know aught of Stromvil—that we are called those who hurl the lightning and ride the thunder?"

"I've heard the phrases. Surely hurling the lightning refers to Stromvili archery—that I have now seen! The other means . . . Stromvil is way up on a cliff so that thunderstorms sometimes pass under it, doesn't it?"

"Yes. But it's literally true, Tiana." He grinned, shook his head. "Captain Tiana! Who'd have thought it, back in Reme! You, ah, developed late, Ty. . . . Well. We ride the thunder—uh, careful with those branches! I will teach you such skill of it as words can convey. The weather looks for being favorable tomorrow, and we have preparations to make. You'll want to watch, and that only—we live on the edge of death, Ty."

An upward glance of Tiana's sea captain's eye told her tomorrow would most likely bring a thunderstorm—that was favorable weather? "But . . . getting atop Mount Erstand . . ."

"We ride the thunder, Tiana. In a month or so, you should be ready to essay it—if ever you dare."

Challenged, she compressed her lips firmly. Then she said, "I dare tomorrow, Bandari. I haven't a month to waste." And to preclude an argument as well as to prevent another such embarrassment as she'd endured today, she added, "Bandari. You must teach me woodcraft."

He snorted. "Oh Tiana me girl—woodcraft is a matter of experience!"

She shook her head. "No. Being well coordinated and observant come with experience. I am both; what I need is to know what to observe. How might I have known of the presence of those Woodlings—how knew you that one in the tree wasn't merely a bird or a squirrel?"

Tiana wanted to learn; Tiana hence became a charming pupil. Charmed and flattered, Bandari took up the lessons her impatience had caused Caranga to break off. Soon she realized the complex aspect—but to learn to avoid only the obvious errors and ambushes would be highly valuable. She listened until they reached her animals and the corpse of the Woodling war chief.

The hands were lifeless. Horse and mule, challenged by an entire forest, determinedly cropped grass and now and again sampled leaves from a branch. She collected and repacked the hands. Bandari was happy enough to ride the mule, which grumbled. The animal Tiana called Disciple because he followed, was not comfortable now, man-laden and leading—but Tiana was not about to mount him and let Bandari have Windsong. They rode close, and the lesson continued. It ended abruptly: the trees and underbrush stopped as if sliced by a giant ax, and a crystal lake of shining blue sprawled directly before them. Beyond it, featureless rock reared straight into the sky.

Tiana could only stare up in awe. Erstand's steep broad shoulders towered over the countryside and turned trees into pygmies. At some twenty thousand feet, Erstand was not the world's tallest mountain—but it was the most vertical.

"It . . . looks as if one could toss a stone off the top and it would fall right into the lake." Tiana's voice betrayed the fact that she was most impressed.

"Not quite," Bandari told her. "About midway up, just below the snow line, Stromvil perches on a wide ledge. It is accessible. But above—old Erstand is straight up and down."

"Hmp. And the other side?"

"The north side's not so steep—but the highest half-mile or so is absolutely vertical: ice walls."

She stared, frowning. "Ban, if every side is perpendicular, how can Erstand have a summit?"

"Doesn't. Flat as a table on top. There's even a small lake up there, on the mesa."

"But—" Tiana heaved a great sigh. "Then how do you propose to get me up there?"

He turned to gaze at her from the back of the mule, who was anxious to get to the lake. "Ah. I am for being in charge of getting you up there, Tiana? You are once again my pupil, and will do as I say?"

Tiana met his snapping black eyes for a long while. At last she heaved another sigh—a purpose, for she knew how to make a man's eyes drop from her face. "Aye."

Bandari shrugged, nodded. "Good then. To Stromvil first. As to scaling the rest of Erstand—we won't. We fly."

Though they'd reached the lake at midday, the sky was fading from the brilliant red-orange-pink of sunset to the blue-gray of dusk when they at last reached the ledge on which Stromvil lay. Disciple had proven too nervous, and they arrived with him plodding behind Windsong, who now bore Bandari; he wore the sort of sleeved vest he had collected partway up the time-etched trail.

Stromvil was an odd sort of townlet, stretched out along the ledge with each frame or partly stone building tucked back against the nigh-vertical mountainside. A host of noisy young men and women came rushing to meet them. Tiana, considering them boys and girls every one, learned that these youths were the Highriders, and that Bandari was their leader. All were built much as he was; lean, compact, hard-muscled. None was tall. The males looked marvelous, Tiana thought, while the girls—all around twoscore years of age—looked adolescent, underdeveloped. Tiana towered still, when she had dismounted, and she was well aware of the admiringly appraising looks she received from the males. The female gazes and dark glances, she thought, were only appraising. Envy? Jealousy?

Apparently, for when Bandari began to explain that he was taking her to Erstand's summit, one lean girl acted astonished. Tiana thought she'd caught her name as Nadya.

"*Her?* You're insane, Banday! You can't be for taking her highriding—look at the excess *flesh* on her! When this overblown slut lands, she'll splatter like an egg!"

Wiry little Nadya's final word was not quite out before Tiana was upon her. After an initial squeaky sound, the Stromvili fought back in the traditional style of biting, kicking, scratching. She was strong, Tiana swiftly learned, as she lost her somber cloak in a way that came close to strangling her. The eyes of the onlookers widened at the way her tight silk shirt and short breeches molded and revealed her luscious formations.

It was an intense encounter, and swiftly over. Not only was Tiana the stronger, she fought with warrior's skill and lack of inhibitions, coupled with a natural knowledge of the female anatomy. But for Nadya's surprising ability to absorb punishment, the fight would have been even shorter. As it was, Tiana knew in a few moments that her opponent had enough—which did not prevent the highrider from receiving one more kneejerk high between her wiry thighs. Then Tiana was standing astride the groaning little boy-girl, and flaunting her deep full chest with arms akimbo.

"Any else thinks I am *overblown*, rather than un-skinny—like this?" She spurned her defeated detractor with her toe.

Obviously none did, and Bandari intervened swiftly, handing Tiana her cloak.

"You see, Tiana is considerably stronger than she appears. We'll just have to be wrapping her a bit tighter, is all." And he led Tiana away from the others, who either gazed after her or clustered about Nadya. "The redhead temper remains, I see." He gave her no time for a heated reply. "I must prepare for tomorrow's highriding. As for you—tomorrow you watch, and learn."

Tiana halted. "Bandari," she said with an intensity of voice that matched her gaze, "tomorrow I join you. I haven't time to *watch*. And after my reception by that *boy*, I will *not* let them think I hold back."

He did not smile at her characterization of Nadya, but returned her gaze levelly. "It may mean your death, Ty. Like—pardon me, but—like a splattered egg. And that has nothing to do with your build. The—"

"Bandari. I highride on the morrow."

Bandari firmed his mouth, considered, agreed with a jerky nod. "You highride." Suddenly, he grinned maliciously. "Custom demands that you spend the night before your first time in the chapel."

"Talking with a priest and sleeping on a bench?" She whipped her cloak about her and fastened it at the shoulders. "I can stand both, so long as he has somewhat to eat. A chapel bench has more yield than a ship's deck—where I've slept many times. But—my instructions . . ."

"Tomorrow," Bandari said, and nodded. "There is the chapel." And he walked away.

"Hmp. Peevish, is he—mayhap he *likes* the boy-built girl," she muttered, but showed more pride than resignation in walking, alone, to the chapel.

It was not much, a cavelet laboriously hollowed out of the mountain to the depth of thirty or so feet. Carpeting of woven plant fibers, nine benches, tables for candles, a tiny shrine and altar, and a wall of wood with a door. Priest's quarters, she assumed, and a sudden mischievous impulse made her flip back her cloak. It was cold, with night coming on here just at Erstand's snow line. But—most orders of the Theban priesthood were celibate, and Tiana of Reme was hardly above teasing even a priest.

He emerged from the door in the wall of wood at the chapel's rear. They introduced themselves; he was Father Golub, almost a comical figure. Like the others of Stromvil he was rangy of frame and limb, but he had acquired a substantial pot belly. The man looked, simply put, pregnant. Tiana watched his gaze sweep her appreciatively—yet without apparent desire. Catching her frown, he smiled.

"Daughter, you may as well be for protecting yourself against the cold, for you can't tease me. My two wives keep me most happy indeed."

Tiana blinked. "What? Most priests are celibate—and you have *two* wives?"

"Aye, my strapping child. My order believes that a priest's primary vow is that of poverty. To enforce this vow rigorously, bigamy is essential. You seek absolution?"

Tiana swallowed her surprise, then her chuckle—and refrained from pointing out that both Golubwives must be superlative cooks. "I am here only because it is custom, for tomorrow I highride, Father. All my life I have been honorable."

"I see, I see." He bobbed a jowly head on which there was less hair than shining skull. "Commendable, commendable. Call me Golub. Hideous name, isn't it? Honorable all your life! Commendable, commendable. I've put a small supper on the board, my child. You'll be for joining me—highriders do not break fast."

Tiana felt as if she were on one foot and was happy to be ushered into a large room with nice hangings and to be seated before what Golub called a "small" supper. *Now if I can keep my mouth full and he'll eat rather than babble or ask questions. . . .*

But Golub asked, "What is honor, my child of Reme?" He shook his head. "Reme. Whew."

Tiana chewed elaborately while her brain worked. "My name

is Tiana. Ty-anna. My foster father, Caranga—whom I call father—taught me that honor is to take no note of small offenses but never to leave a greater one unavenged; to be loyal to my friends in danger and trouble—and to hate my enemies.''

"A strong, simple code," he said, bobbing his head. "Tell me, Tiana, what do you do?"

"I joined the family business with my father."

"Ah, ah. Commendable, commendable—and what is your father's business?"

"We're pirates," Tiana said, and stuffed a large helping of mutton stew into her face.

Golub stared. "Pirates!?"

"You know, sea-thieves," she nodded, chewing. "I am Captain Tiana, Father Golub. Of the ship *Vixen*."

"But my child—piracy is not honorable!" Golub was nearly stammering.

She waggled a two-tined Narokan fork at him. "Don't call me child, please. And why not? Nothing in the code says I shouldn't rob and slay those I don't like."

Golub drew a great deep breath and seemed to forget his heaped plate. "Daughter . . . what did you last . . . steal?"

"A bottle of wine from the nunnery near a village called Woeand." She reconsidered. "Two."

"Well . . . that's not so serious, though a *convent*. . . . How did such a strange theft come about?"

"It was easy," she said, sipping a bit of his watered wine, which was ghastly. "The nuns were all in their chapel, so I nailed the door shut and set the place on fire."

"Theba intercede! My, my . . . Tian——Captain, what did they, to receive such treatment?"

"They were *vampires*. Literally, I mean; the thirst of those demonic nuns had nigh onto depopulated the countryside."

Golub was silent for a time, though he regarded his food more than he partook of it. At last he looked up; Tiana was eating with gusto. "Daughter, this was surely no dishonorable deed. Nevertheless, do partake through me of Theba's absolution. I had much trouble gaining permission to absolve highriders."

Now that was interesting, Tiana thought, gravying hard brown bread. "Why?" she asked, and popped the large morsel.

"Some members of the bishop's council had heard distorted rumors about highriding, and suspected it involved the black arts. When I was for explaining the purely natural means involved, there was new opposition, on the grounds that there is no absolution for suicide."

That interrupted Tiana's unconcerned eating. "Come now, Father," she said after a long, surprised stare. "I don't know yet just all that highriding entails, but it can't be that dangerous. All the young villagers do it."

"Only a few, and some do not succeed. Have you looked off the edge of Stromvil cliff?"

"Aye. It's a drop of ten thousand feet straight, if it's a finger's breadth."

"My child, to go highriding, one *begins* by leaping off the cliff, and that is generally accounted the safest part."

Splatter like an egg. . . .

Tiana was awakened by a heavy boom of thunder followed by its long aftergrumble. Though the building shook with each succeeding bellow of nature, light streamed in the open door of the little chapel. Wondering, she rose, stretched tall, bent to place her hands on the floor and kick back her legs one by one, rose to stretch again toward the rafters. Then she left the chapel and its hard benches to investigate the anomaly of stormy thunder and clear skies.

The mystery was simple of solution, once she'd advanced to the cliff's edge. Tiana stared *down* at the thunderstorm.

All else was invisible. Below, a black seething mass roiled, troubled and amorphously unstable even for a moment and shot through constantly with intolerably brilliant streaks of lightning. Intense winds blew up from the storm, so that she backed, lest a sudden shafting gust carry her over cliff's edge.

She could not take her eyes from nature's rage. At sea, storms were an ever fearsome danger that kept all hands frenetically busy lest their ship capsize or be rent plank from plank. Here, she could look with safety into the very heart of the monster.

Its violence and power were beyond belief. Here were all the gods, surely; here was the power that could destroy the world. The force with which it attacked land and sea was but a tiny fraction of those that ravaged the sky. Those blue-white bolts of lightning that felled the tallest trees and shattered man's proudest towers were pallid shades of the blinding white titans that here blasted from cloud to cloud with splitting crashes of thunder that she could *feel*.

With a shudder, Tiana realized that some religions defined Drood's dark demesne as a place much like this titanic prowler of the skies. . . .

"Ho, Tiana!" It was Bandari. "A bonny day for highriding— you're favored! Come, you must be readied."

Clutching her cloak close so as not to sail away, Tiana hastened to Bandari and the little group of highriders with him. When she would have spoken, he cut her short.

"Time is short, Ty. I'll instruct you whilst the girls prepare you and the lads ready me."

Even as he spoke, the others were commencing to enwrap her and Bandari with broad bands of hard, only slightly elastic leather.

"These instructions I'm for giving but once. Your life depends on your heeding them, Tiana. Make one error, and none on all the broad back of the world can help you. The time to change your mind is now."

Tiana glanced down to meet the unfriendly gray eyes of Nadya, who seemed vying with another for the task of wrapping her upper body. "I go. You could instruct me a thousand times, Ban, but you remember I know how to listen, and to act on it. You have taught me much; teach me more, Bandari the Cat. Ow! Here—is that necessary? Must that be so tight there?"

It was not Nadya who answered, but another: "Yes, and you'd live."

Bandari smiled—and sobered instantly. "Attend. The human body—even a weak one, which yours and mine are not—is well designed. Very well designed, with great innate strength. We bleed so readily and are so easily slain that we have no notion of the punishment our bodies can withstand if we use our full strength and resilience—intelligently. Highriding uses this strength. The highrider must exert all that strength, and endure the greatest possible stress a human being can survive."

"Best you but watch, beautiful," one of those wrapping Bandari said, and he grinned. "I'll be for holding your hand."

Tiana kept her gaze on Bandari.

"Tiana," Bandari snapped, "be still for your wrapping. Be glad you're not a man whose stones must be half-crushed in the wrappings! Davri—hush. Keep your attention on readying me, or I'll come back and haunt you. Now. Highriding was born centuries ago when a boy named Longo dived off this cliff to the lake below." Bandari paused while a particularly horrendous crash of thunder subsided into a long rumbling. "He was being pursued by a cliff cat. Longo was clever, even then. Jumping, you see, is safe—the danger is in hitting the water! If one hits headfirst, the head is driven up between the shoulders and the spine is severed—snap! Feetfirst, and the thighbones are driven up through the soft stomach into the chest."

Tighter, Tiana directed mentally, though already her breathing was slightly restricted.

"Longo spread his arms *and* legs, wide apart, and fell flat—also hanging onto the cloak he wore. He reasoned that thus he would be as a sail that caught the air, and be slowed. Too, the shock of impact might be less dangerous when spread over his entire body."

"You mean—he actually survived a fall from this cliff?"

"A *leap*, Tiana. And . . . no," Bandari told her. "But an examination of his body showed that Longo Stromvilo had the right concept. The Stromvili became interested—fascinated! They tried this and that, though none ever thought of leaping into a *storm*. Then, well over a century ago, a child was standing at the cliff's edge, watching a storm. Its mother saw, and cried out. The child turned, slipped, fell. I bear an auspicious name: the child was called Bandari."

"Spread your legs," Nadya said.

Tiana knew some trepidation, remembering the several nice kneelifts she had administered to the girl, but she obeyed. Both Nadya and her companion were now wrapping her legs, having cocooned her torso.

"The horrified mother ran to the edge," Bandari said. "Tighter there, Davri. She saw her son not falling, but *flying*, his arms and legs outspread, being carried along eastward rather than down—and then suddenly he seemed as if hurled *upward*."

"The winds," Tiana breathed.

"The winds. By now many saw: that long-ago Bandari sailed high above Stromvil, his limbs outstretched like a great bat. And then—he fell. He landed on the ledge, from a height of many feet. It was as if a miracle had spared him."

"He *lived*," a bright-eyed highrider said breathlessly.

"He lived," Bandari nodded "A cripple for life. His mind was good, though, and it is Bandari who is called Father of Highriding. *He* devised the method. We've only been for improving on it, for over a hundred years now. These leather wrappings are later developments: they decrease the chance of collapsing one's lungs. The long silk streamers the girls are now attaching to your arms and legs provide extra air resistance. They are a great help."

Tiana's heart was pounding. Bandari went on. Tiana listened, knowing she could not back out now—and wishing she were not so prideful and impetuous. When he seemed finished, both he and Tiana had been completely encased in leather that flashed with enamel. Well-padded leathern helmets enclosed their heads, while their arms and legs trailed multicolored streamers of the silk from the spiders of Il-Zadok Marsh. At Bandari's stomach they had attached a large sack, filled with small bags of salt.

Below raged a storm; here, Tiana was hot in her wrappings beneath a clear bright sky.

"Questions, Tiana?"

"A thousand. But I see no reason to bother."

"Then . . . let's go," Bandari said.

The others lifted a great cheering cry of "HI-I-I-IGHRIDERS-S-S-S!" that Tiana assumed was ritual. And Bandari leaped from the cliff.

She stared after him. She swallowed. Instructions? Obviously he and his companions were insane. To jump that way was surely suicide—but to remain was cowardice. With a short running leap, Tiana threw herself off the cliff.

Following Bandari's instructions, she spread her arms and legs. Furious wind howled around her, and she found he was right; she was able to steer into it. The wind shrieked, her leather creaked, the streamers flapped and rattled—and she realized that she was indeed falling more slowly. Elation was a surging swell in her.

It's true! Bandari had said that in a thunderstorm there were updrafts strong enough to carry a person—and it was true! She was being buoyed. It was wonderful; she could stay up here forev———without warning she slipped into a down-current and fell like a plummet toward the dark heart of the storm.

Maneuvering desperately for an updraft, she was thrown suddenly into a roll. Tears were wind-blasted from her eyes. The sun above and the storm beneath flashed dizzyingly past, changing positions—and then she pulled out. Again she rose. A yellow streamer fouled and she began to spin. The terrible natural force stretched her arms and legs as if she were on a rack, and she remembered with horror that this was what Bandari had warned was the gravest danger. She had to straighten that streamer—and if she misjudged her maneuver, the resultant snap would break her spine.

Gritting her teeth, she exerted all her strength to force her arm back. Her fingers plucked stiffly in their protecting gloves, however supple. With maddening slowness, she unfurled the streamer. Still she spun. Then that long strip of yellow silk leaped out with a cracking sound to join the others of blue and green, and instantly her spin slowed.

Again she was flying free.

The sensation was akin to that of running before the wind on a good swift ship—no, it was *being* that ship, arms and legs the sails, the streamers her proud pennons, on an ocean unbelievably turbulent. Yet freedom was absolute, and—her eyes were drawn by a hissing movement to her right. An avalanche of hailstones shot past. Bandari had warned her; the soft raindrops to which all on land were accustomed were stone-like pellets in the upper skies.

Suddenly the entire sky was filled with a blinding light that emanated from just beneath her, and her body was struck as if by a gigantic hammer. After a moment of fear, she laughed; Tiana sat astride the lightning; Tiana was riding the thunder.

And . . . *I'm* . . . *I'm* rising!

She was. It was true; she was lifting, and a vast sensation of exaltation surged through her.

It was then that her stomach expressed its opinion of this new kind of sailing. What little remained of Golub's supper was soon dispersed to the sky.

Bandari sailed into view on her right. His hand signal indicated his satisfaction with her flying. Now he would seize control of nature, salt the storm to drive it around the mountain and up the north slope to the top, to what they called Longo's Mesa. Gently, surely, he sank into the roiling dark heart of the storm. In that unstable hell, cracklingly alive with thunder and violent wind, lay the secret of control. "There lies the whip I use to drive the monster to do *my* will," he'd said, "and that whip is the lightning itself." He would unleash the bolts himself, with his little bags of salt.

Tiana watched him sail down into the seething witch's cauldron of the storm.

Even though she was hard put just to survive, she realized that she would love to go down with him into the dark maw of the monster, to share the danger and the adventure. At first she had been in peril of falling through the storm into the lake at the forest's edge, though Bandari had assured her that if she fell properly she could survive even that. But now they were higher, and passing over the rocky slopes of Erstand. Were she to fall now, she'd be but a red splotch on the rocks.

Nature would not leave her alone. A new attack came.

First a scattering of hailstones passed to her left—and then an avalanche of the little iceballs was upon her. It was as if an army of disembodied fists beat her. They rattled loudly on the leather wrappings with their shining coat of enamel. They and the helmet provided some protection, but the merciless assault felt as if she were being sledgehammered repeatedly. A red haze danced before Tiana's eyes. She fought to retain consciousness and continuing control of her flight. Neither rising nor falling now, pinned in midair by up-driving wind and down-pelting hail, she started to slip into a spin. She corrected; she sailed, pelted. Now spearing darts of lightning struck all about her as if a corps of godly archers was loosing salvo after salvo. Each vivid, arrowing blast jarred her body, and rattled her brain. But an odd sensation in her ears prevented her hearing the sizzling cracks and roars.

How long Tiana fought the storm she never knew. The hail diminished. Slowly it pierced her mazed brain that her leather cocoon was being pierced by the cold. Abruptly without strength, her limbs scarcely responded to the demands of her will. Breathing had been difficult; now it was far worse. The trick Bandari had explained, using the wind to make one breathe, was no longer possible. The air was too thin. What little she could suck in cut her throat, burned her lungs. Her vision began to gray. Then for an instant it cleared, and she saw that she had been slipping downward. The powerful maelstrom that had carried her was dying. Tiana fought panic.

Had she reached her destination? If so, she might come down safely in the mountaintop lake; otherwise she was dead, for . . . she was . . . falling.

Through the fading, ragged thunderclouds she plummeted, into the rain. Desperately she willed herself to a limb-extended flatness. She had to wrest her eyes open. Relief was dizzying; she was directly above a shining little mirror of silver—the lake atop Mount Erstand.

A sudden insupportable thought clutched her brain. The lake! Far above the frost line, it must be frozen as hard as the silver it so resembled. And it was growing so rapidly, lengthening, broadening as she rushed down. Despite her new fear, she maintained the correct flat dive. The shining mirror grew and grew and grew until it was ALL THERE WAS . . . and then there was an explosion of pain and a million lights that were gulped by total blackness.

Tiana regained consciousness.
She was floating.
A burning taste assailed her mouth; salt! No wonder the lake hadn't frozen; it was brine!
No longer cold, her limbs tingled and were filling with a glowing warmth. In new horror, she knew that was impossible;

the icy brine was freezing her. Forcing movement only because
her will was forged on some prenatal anvil, she swam. It was like
propelling herself through flourbean soup, and that after having
overeaten. She swam. She saw nothing. She swam. Then her
gloved fingers were pawing wet stone—and then Bandari was
helping her climb and slither and drag herself out of the mountaintop lake.

She tried to speak. She had no voice. No; she could not hear
herself.

Squatting before her, Bandari pantomimed. Weakly, she
rolled onto her back, forced herself to sit up. Her stomach's
muscles complained bitterly. She imitated Bandari: Tiana sucked in a great breath, the leather straps hurting her chest, and she
swallowed. Again. Then, holding her nostrils well pinched, she
tried hard to exhale through her nose. Pain assaulted her ears—
but they did not pop. Resigned, she gritted her teeth and staggered up. Their leather-clad bodies clacked as she hugged Bandari. Her world remained shrouded in eerie silence.

Over his shoulder she saw the little cairn, just west of the lake.

Soon they were there, and Bandari was tossing stones aside—
all in silence. Just as she started to join him, Tiana saw that one
flat white rock was inscribed. She dropped to her knees. The
words were in three languages; Nevinian, and Narokan, and a
third she could not identify:

> Beneath these stones is imprisoned the right arm of the
> demon Derramal. His soul is evil and reigns in evil beyond
> the silver plane. He can not be slain save by a countless host
> of swords striking from beyond infinity. Leave the arm!

Studying the strange words thoughtfully, Tiana glanced over
to see Bandari using a stone to smash the lock of a box of dull
metal. He opened it. Within was a human arm, handless. Its hue
was that of very old parchment. Unlike the hands, it showed no
sign of outré life.

With a glance at Tiana, Bandari plucked it forth and without
ceremony stuffed it into the sack in which he'd carried the salt
bags.

Realization struck Tiana then that she was atop unscalable old
Erstand . . . with no idea as to how to get *down*. The storm was
gone. They had no mountain-climbing equipment. She looked
questioningly, in the silence she feared was total deafness but
refused to think upon, at Bandari.

He mouthed a suggestion; she read it on his lips and smiled, but shook her head. With a shrug, he put carnal thoughts aside and led her to the mesa's north cliff. He sat down with his legs dangling, motioned. Joining him, she saw that this northward face was as he'd said: a straight drop for at least half a mile. Below that, the flashing ice wall began to taper, seemingly smoothly, into a broad flat slope of snow, sparkling as if frosted with sugar. She looked at Bandari when he slid an arm around her, at the shoulder.

"Draw a deep breath," he mouthed, and she did, and then he pushed the both of them over the edge of the cliff.

For a few seconds they plummeted past the vertical icewalls, until there was jarring impact and they were sliding downward at an appalling pace. When the slope's steepness lessened, their momentum pressed the adventurers harshly to the ice. Tiana first felt warmth in her leather-clad bottom, and it was pleasant—until it intensified to a definite burning. There was no way to relieve it. Side by side, seated like children, they rushed downward.

From above, this slope had appeared perfectly smooth. It was not.

As the incline grew less steep, boulders took shape. Several whisked by, well out of their path, before a great rock loomed directly before them. Hanging onto her shoulder, Bandari pulled hard. They swerved, whisked past the massive obstacle by a narrow margin. Immediately another boulder appeared, racing up at them. Bandari leaned hard against her. They appeared to be missing this one by a hair's breadth. But as they hurtled past, Tiana felt a sharp jolt to the man's body. His face writhed in pain, though the Cat's strong will kept him alert and clutching her shoulder. Tiana had no indication as to how badly he was hurt.

Though now they sped over smooth clear ice, ahead loomed a formation of rearing boulders like the teeth of a lurking giant.

The grouping was far too wide to steer around, and so thickly pressed that going through would mean being crushed by those molars of stone. Closer they rushed, and Tiana knew they were death.

To have come through all this, she thought in anguish, *to have* flown, *then fallen* leagues—*and now to die this way, like children on a toboggan! Must it be so . . . ignominious?*

She strove to pull free, seeing that Bandari was aiming precisely at the largest of the blockading boulders. His arm and hand tightened. Tiana set about relaxing. *He's insane with pain*, she thought. *And I can't escape anyhow. We die together then, Bandari—and I'm sorry I didn't say yes up there.*

The largest monster of rock rushed toward them, growing, growing, and she saw that it showed them a face packed with smooth, sloping ice. Even as she realized Bandari's wild plan, they were there and that natural ramp was under them and they raced upward and shot through clear cold air over the other clustering boulders.

Snow caught them. The impact was nonetheless a teeth-clacking one that wrenched them apart. They rolled, sprawled, somersaulted, crashed together into a huge obstruction that turned out to be a snow-covered evergreen bush. Grasping each other, they shot through it without so much as a scratch, in what had now become leathern armor hardened with enamel.

A snowbank appeared in the distance, grew, loomed. They plowed into it.

Tiana lay motionless, enveloped in snow. *We—we've made it!*

Now for a nice long nap. . . .

She had to talk and fight herself into moving, force herself to push her head to the surface. She stared downward. It was over! A group of highriders waved wildly, and she could see that they were shouting. As they came running and floundering to her and Bandari, Tiana allowed herself to collapse . . .

. . . and awoke under a great blanket of fur, in a candle-lit room. She turned her head.

There was another bed, another covering fur. Beneath it: Bandari. The fur moved; he breathed. He was alive. She was alive. They had the arm. Too, she was aware that her ears were functioning, though there was little to hear. She snorted, grinned. She heard it—though her ears felt afire.

Tiana took inventory of Tiana.

Her backside seemed to have been scorched, while that strange sensation in her hands and feet might well be frostbite. Though no bones seemed broken, every nerve twitched and every muscle ached from prolonged strain and exertion. Surely not one inch of her body but bore bruises. *I'll be as colorful as the streamers I wore!* Her mouth burned from the brine. Her stomach was most unhappy.

I will live. I will be fine. I'm not crippled, and I can hear!

She blinked her eyes, and the girl Nadya was bent over her, smiling.

"You overblown pirate—you're magnificent!"

Tiana grinned. "My thanks, Nadya Highrider!"

"I am naught but honest, Tiana Highrider!"

She savored that. From Nadya, it was better than being called Captain. Hostility could not survive mutual respect. "And—Bandari?"

Nadya shook her head. "A cut where we sweet darling females should not discuss it—but he'll be fine, and given to much standing rather than sitting."

Tiana sighed. "It was glorious, Nadya! Promise me we'll all go again tomorrow!" And her body, heeding her orders to be fine, put her to sleep.

7

Bird of Prey

Two days after Tiana Highrider's departure from Stromvil, the
solitude of Mount Erstand's Mesa Longo was again disturbed.
Three great Arctic hawks circled the summit briefly on black
wings of preternatural spread. They landed, beside the scattered
remnants of the cairn. They seemed to study it and the empty
metal box for a moment, before drawing together for several
seconds, as though mere birds could confer. Then they flapped
again aloft.

Two of the outsize birds of prey continued in the high air,
riding currents that would take them far to the west.

The third swooped down to glide above the forest, the broad-
sweeping ragged edges of its wings nearly brushing the treetops.
It flew in broad circles until it crossed the trail by which Tiana
had left Stromvil.

Then the great hawk turned and began its pursuit.

Silver and pink and streaky with orpiment, this dawn found
Tiana deep in Dark Forest. Windsong's chestnut coat was nigh
black among trees into whose press the sun had not yet fingered.
The towering trees of this wood east of Erstand cast great pockets
of deep shadow, magenta and indigo and jet. Already she had
found the overturned wagon and the four skeletons beside it; a

man, a woman, two small children. Dark Forest's name held new meaning.

The Woodlings would surely never fare so far south and east, into Nevinia. These cruel murders were the work of the bandits who made the wood their own, so that sensible travelers wended wide of it, like ships in need of a canal where none existed. The appearance of the wagon and other shattered remains indicated that these victims had been poor—yet the bandits had slain them all. She had little doubt that they'd attack her if they saw or heard her "interloping" into "their" shadowed hunting ground. She was a mere novice at woodcraft, at least with the advantage, now, of knowing it. The murderous bandits would be more expert, if less so than the forest-bred Woodlings.

Much of woodcraft, she knew, lay in seeing things as they were, not as one expected them to be. And one must take nothing for granted.

Such as the sudden shrilling of birds all about her.

Squinting up through the trees, she saw that it was that enormous bird she'd seen afore. Now she recognized it as an Arctic hawk, far south of its normal demesne. A cold finger traced out her spine. The same bird. . . .

It had passed over her earlier. It had turned, flown westward; ten or so leagues she now judged—and here it came back, *as if to reaffirm my position?* Birds of prey could be trained for the hunt—but to hunt *humans?* There was the feel of sorcery about such, and more than nervousness touched her.

I must be thrice wary.

Without sudden movements, she strung the long fine bow Bandari had given her. Bird-vision prevailed; ere she had an arrow nocked, the hawk was flapping away,—westward again, as if it knew precisely where it was going. Briefly her fingers curled into claws. Frowning, squinting up through the trees at the receding bird, she considered. Then she swung down and placed an ear to the ground.

Her hearing had not yet returned to its former keenness, but she'd surely be able to discern hoofbeats. She heard nothing. Well, she'd repeat the action again and again, hopefully to be ready if attack came. And she'd be mindful of the skies, too, and that outsized bird. If it returned yet again. . . .

Tiana rode on along the well-defined trail in Dark Forest's fragrant coolth—which had suddenly gone very dark and menacing indeed.

8

Incident in Dark Forest

Maltar of Banarizur in Collada fancied himself the lord of Dark
Forest, and not without reason: he robbed and slew most who
passed through it. The Lord of Dark Forest had no castle, nor
even a tent. Yet he slept, under the trees, in the calm security
denied a king enthroned. His security lay in the knowledge that
the dozen men of his band were the finest cutthroats of five
several lands. When danger arose, they warned him—or showed
him the corpses in the morning.

Maltar the bandit slept well.

This night his slumber was interrupted by a tiny pain that
persisted. He awoke, confused and annoyed, knowing only that
something sharp was pressing at his throat. His eyes focused and
his heart nearly stopped. A large yellow eye stared into his. On
his chest perched an Arctic hawk of unusual size. Shock froze
Maltar's blasphemous tongue.

The pain left his throat; the bird balanced easily on one foot
while it held up a long slim needle for Maltar's inspection. Most
of its length was shiny, reflecting the firelight. The point, however, was green.

Realizing that the needle was smeared with poison, Maltar
drew breath to call out to his men. The needle leaped forward and

pressed so hard as almost to pierce his skin. Maltar fought for self-control. Forcing down his panic, he slowly and silently released his breath. The needle remained at his throat, but the pressure eased slightly.

Maltar whispered, "What do ye want?"

The needle moved back a fraction of an inch.

"Well, speak up."

He felt the needle's point once more.

"I . . . must guess."

The pressure eased. That brightly golden avian eye stared into his.

"I'll, uh, repent, change my ways . . ." He broke off at the needle's advance. "I'll . . . give ye all my horde—uh!"

Maltar realized that one more bad guess would surely finish him; the skin just to the left of his Adam's apple was dented, creasing and stretching around the needle's point. Xanthic eyes glared with human intelligence and Maltar was one to know that the hawk's apparent cruel willingness to slay for failure to understand that which had not been stated, was truly human. A thousand worms seemed to crawl over the bandit's flesh.

"There is . . . some service ye—want of me." The needle was pulled away, just a little.

"Ye want . . . someone murdered?" Maltar asked hopefully, and the needle retreated, then advanced. "I'm . . . partially right," he essayed, hoping for a free one. He received it, in the needle's retreat.

"Ye want someone . . . robbed and murdered." The needle drew back the more.

Maltar smiled. "It is my trade! Ye want something of his?" The slightest of retreat of the needle; an identical return. Maltar tried a different trail, sure he was close, now, safe and merely wanted for that at which he was not only expert but in which he took great joy.

"Ye'll lead us to him?" The precise retreat and advance again. "Hmm—ye'll lead us to them—uh! Ahh . . . *her!* Ye will lead us to her, whose death ye want and from whom ye want aught?"

The needle was drawn back, well back. Maltar expelled a deep breath. How to query whether she was young, worth a bit of sport as well as killing? Thinking of no way, he pursued a new trail.

"Of the loot, ye'll take but what ye want and leave the rest to us." Now the needle had left his throat entirely. "Our share will

include . . . silver, gold?'' That hopeful question was answered
by the hawk's putting away the needle so swiftly that Maltar saw
not where the deadly sliver was tucked.

"Friend hawk, we be well met. All Nevinia—aye, and Zadok
and Bashan, too—well know that Maltar un-Banarizur and his
band would slit their own mother's throats for a gold coin!''

With one silent rustling flip of its wings, the hawk departed his
chest; whereupon Maltar sprang up. In the firelight he was a
maleficent giant; eyes hard and black and glinting in cold opaci-
ty, his beard totally unkempt and equally black, his body tall and
thick and dark with its fleecing of jet hair. But little of that great
bulk was fat; most was hard muscle. Nearly as long and hairy as
a Simdani gorilla's were his legs and massive arms, and the latter
soon clad him in a dull round helmet, mailshirt over the filthy,
discolored leather leggings and haubergeon in which he slept.
He buckled on the thick broad supple belt he'd got off a fine
escort captain of Escallas years past. From it dangled a ridiculously effete jeweled dagger, slipped from the girdle of a merchant's fat wife of Slee years agone, and a heavy Korese sword
he'd brought with him from his native Collada a dozen and two
years ago.

He was calling up his men even as he dressed and armed
himself.

"Up, up ye sleepy churls!" The hard toe of his soft buskin
kicked surly Gerenna of Banavinbonro in Sarch—a man who
had indeed been a herdsman ere he'd raped his sister, slain his
father and then a militiaman, and fled over the course of a year
across Sarch, Morcar, and most of northern Nevinia to join a
lord worth following—the Lord of Dark Forest, crowned by his
own hand.

"There's gold to take and a pretty throat that wants cutting!"
Maltar called. We ride! Jogu, you dark pig of Ig—up, up and
into helm and saddle!''

They were soon up and a-saddle, a column of men grim enow
to bring pause to a squadron of Escallan cavalry. As they left
their camp, dawn turned the sky silver and pink shot through
with orpiment streaks.

Winging low over the trees from the eastward, the hawk
reached Maltar and his band. Maltar leading, they rode single
file at a steady trot down a gloomy little trail that would intersect
the main east-west one. The hawk passed over them, amid a
chorus of frightened birdcalls, wheeled, dropped to land on

Maltar's mailed shoulder. The bandit grunted at the great bird's weight, but said nothing. It gave him no sign of dissatisfaction, and Maltar assumed that their prey was but a short distance along the main trail. To others it was Forest Road; to Maltar and company, it was . . . the game trail.

They reached this path's end, turned around the truly monumental crentree with its spiderweb lacing of feathermoss, and emerged onto the Forest Road. Maltar glanced at the bird. It stared ahead as if in high anticipation. Maltar grinned.

The Lord of Dark Forest was not perturbed at being errand boy for this weird mage-bird; the chase and the slaying were his joy, the spoils pure dessert. And mayhap in this case there'd be a bit more of the sweet, an she were not too old and hideous. . . . The hawk had indicated the unknown prey had gold and silver, and here were her tracks, indicating she possessed a horse and a mule as well. Maltar grinned anew.

They rode.

Around a bend in the wide trail they filed—and ahead was the camp of the intended victim! Ah, the innocent; the horse's saddle and the mule's pack lay aground whilst the beasts cropped grass, and there in plain sight lay the stupid darling, cloak-enveloped and sleeping movelessly.

"In and take her!"

The hawk's claws clamped in between the links of Maltar's mail, but the man had already clapped spurs to his mount. Too late to halt the charge of hungry, anticipation-driven men. With shrieked cries from an assortment of lands, the band spurred forward. They were nearly to the little camp when Maltar realized that certain yells were missing—Gerenna's bass Sarchese roar, for one. Gerenna was ever rear-guard, when they rode thus.

Maltar glanced back to see that the last three horses bore empty saddles. Before he could speak, earringed, vulture-nosed Serl of Port Tilonbi pitched screaming from his horse with an arrow in his back.

Without changing direction, the charge became a panicked rout. Across the camp the band galloped, knowing the fastest way out was straight ahead. Though he was in the lead, Maltar was swept along; nor was he able to halt the others until they were a good league past the camp.

"HOLD, ye snapping tail-down dogs!" he bellowed, reining in so that his big bay reared. Maltar wheeled him and waved his sword. "So the little bitch tricked us and can shoot! From

Varban back—dismount and spread out! Vols, Hangman, Radev—a half-league down to Blasted Cren trail—ride swiftly and we can trap her between us! It's only a WOMANNN! On on on—ye want *our* gold to escape us?''

The three went on; the six fanned and returned through the forest to the encampment. They saw no woman, and rangy Varban in his Bashan chaincoat soon showed them that the "sleeping woman" was merely a handsome black cloak draped over arranged branches. When a snarling Maltar ordered his men to move on, the hawk objected.

Grumbling, they searched the camp. They found naught to interest the grim bird, who could not tell them what he sought. Sotor and Chotor of far Aradot were working together as ever, when a flash of metal caught Chotor's eye. Aye—there on the ground lay a fat leathern sack and, spilling from its mouth— gold! He sprang for it, but Sotor was ahead of him. The twins wrestled; Chotor gained the bag—and stared in horror at the rope attached to it. He tried desperately to fling himself away from the vast black shadow that fell over him amid a sound like windswept branches.

Maltar looked their way in time to see the falling saytree crush the twin ax-men from Aradot in Bemar. He rushed into the maze of leafy branches, not to see to his men, but to snatch the sack that had cost them their lives. In moments he was cursing in two languages. Despite the several gold coins of excellent Bashan mintage that had been scattered before its mouth, the sack contained only stones and clods.

"The slut's cost me half my men! She'll not escape—and then it will be the turn of that Drood-sent bird!"

But Maltar only muttered the words, for the fell hawk was there. With his remaining trio of men, the challenged Lord of Dark Forest pushed on with the three he'd sent to circle the intended prey they'd never seen.

The three lay in a little glade beside the side-trail.

Apparently having sighted her and charged into the glade, they had run afoul of the silken rope still stretched there, at the height of a mounted man's neck. It had slain two of them, breaking their necks. Radev the Short had escaped that fate—but lay dead, with his sword in his hand. Yet blood smeared that blade, and a trail of dark splotches led into a clump of red-bush.

"Yaaaahhhh!" That hillman's warcry from Varban of the high country in Gray Lands, and he rushed the scarlet-berried bushes with his excellent Sinhorish sword carried low and deadly.

Varban's booted left foot sprang the hidden twig-and-cord trigger that brought the sapling springing up to drive a sharpened, foot-long stake into his body. His awful cry of battle changing to a gurgling one of agony, Varban stood shuddering. Then he was silent, and fell backward off the dripping stake, nicely wedged into a daggered-out hole in the sapling.

With definite trepidation, two men exchanged looks. Then Alnick of far-coastal Shamash stalked past dead Varban. A stalking cutpurse and cat-thief had been Alnick, before he was caught and jailed and sent into some lord's arena, where he had killed his man, and then his lord, and turned up here three years later. Now he followed the trail of blood, which led to a dead body.

"It's a ra-a-a-a-a-abit!" he bellowed in an outraged tenor.

Of Maltar's twelve, but Alnick and Barrenton of Lieden-town remained. Stating that he'd had enough of this bootless pursuit of a demonic phantom, long-maned Barrenton mounted and fled along the narrow trail his former companions had named Blasted Crentree. Almost soundlessly, the hawk winged after him.

It scarcely touched the man in the bluesteel helm as it passed, but it was a touch of death. Convulsions shook Barrenton. He toppled from his horse to lie quivering and jerking on the ground. Then he went motionless. The hawk returned to Maltar.

The Lord of Dark Forest flourished his sword with its silver-chased hilt. "Now, friend hawk," he said, for he dared not attack one that slew with a touch, "it be surely time ye were doing your part! Do ye fly high now, and spy out our shadow-foe."

To his and Alnick's considerable relief, the winged fiend acquiesced.

The fell bird was hardly out of sight when there was a little rustle amid the bushes crowding the bases of a cluster of saytrees. Alnick glanced at Maltar, then paced forward in a weaponeer's crouch to investigate. He returned promptly, nor did he speak of what he'd seen. No word came from his drooping sorrel mustache, and only a wet gurgling sound emerged from the new red mouth in his throat.

Staring at Maltar, Alnick fell prostrate as if in theistic adoration.

The shadow-foe stepped from behind the straight boles of the saytrees and strode callously over Alnick's body in her advance on Maltar. Maltar stared. Aye, she was young. Her lithe, dancegirl-shaped body bore no wounds save an occasional pink scratch, though her shirt of sheeny green silk was torn so that a brace of large firm breasts pushed half forth to draw his eyes. In her hand was a sword like a stick—a rapier, of all things. It was stained the scarlet of her burning hair, and her eyes seemed ablaze with green fire.

"Tell me, Butcher of Babies and Lord of Naught, will you make answer to a few little questions before I kill you?"

Maltar's opaque black eyes roamed the lovely figure, but with the dispassionate interest of a farmer inspecting a pig on slaughterday. Those exquisitely formed features, the rounded thighs crowding her snug short breeks, the full perfect breasts so displayed—all, he knew, comprised a death trap. The finest dozen cutthroats a man ever gathered from five nations lay in bloody proof. No doubt many a fool had failed to perceive the strength her beauty hid.

This time, it's she who's made the fatal underestimate!

From his great size, she must surely deem him slow. Oh aye, she was doubtless the swifter, with her whippy switch of a sword. At an opportune moment in the duel to come, though, he'd give her a brief demonstration of how fast a big man could move. With his hidden speed, his more than a foot's advantage in reach and his far greater strength, Maltar was wholly confident.

"Surely," he replied at last, "if ye'll answer my few questions before I kill you, fiendish slut."

"I am Tiana Highrider of Reme, Captain of *Vixen*, called Pirate Queen—by survivors. I do not split the skulls of children. So much for your questions. The hawk—is it a trained creature?"

"A demon, methinks; I know not whence it came. How did ye evade my men so easily?"

"Every bird cries and every animal in the forest hurries elsewhere at sight or scent of a hawk. Ye might as well beat a drum. It has not been long with you?"

"It has not. Ye have treasure, but ye carry it not. Where be it hid?"

"You attacked a camp with a pile of branches covered with a cloak, in the belief that I lay there. After such a disappointment, who would bother to thrust aside the branches? —My wealth lies beneath them. And I have no other queries, pig-faced murderer of children."

"Why don't ye just put by that steel switch and spread your legs like a good girl, and mayhap I'll not kill ye so slowly."

"That was your last question."

They came together cautiously, eyeing, testing with tentative little thrusts and tight slashes, for each had respect for the other and must take measure. She was fast. The rapier sang like a mosquito and now and again he could actually see, for just an instant, her blade's silver-gray wake in the air. Cautiously, Maltar began his attack. He kept his blade ever in good defensive position while he struck short, powerful blows. The flamehaired pirate dodged and parried easily, but the continued impacts were surely weakening her arm.

She's no more accustomed to buckler than I, he thought, *but only half as strong*. He did not show her his smile of confidence; she was too dangerous for him to mock.

Steadily she gave ground—and then with a sideward dance into the glade's center, she launched her own attack. Now the silvergray blur was constantly before his eyes. Steel rang on steel again and again as he parried an inordinately swift flurry of strokes. None breached his defense, but he was glad enow when she fell back, looking disconsolate—a trick! Leaping past him like a cat, she whirled and cut at his ankle. That hamstring stroke Maltar only just evaded, and was nigh skewered as he was off-balance. He caught the stroke, pushed strongly, and was recovered.

I was nearly slain! Maltar was not accustomed to such shocking possibilities. But now he allowed her to rain blows on his never-still defense in a series of *wheep-clang* sounds followed by the skirl of metal sliding off metal.

"Ho, that prance and cut-at-the-leg never failed you, hey? I am supposed to be down and helpless!"

She smiled, mocking. "A test of your speed, pig-breath. Deceptive for your size, isn't it?"

By the Cud and that whore Theba—she *had* tricked him! Now she knew his swiftness. What a magnificent slut! What a shame; together they could *own* forest or sea and their coupling would be heard for leagues! And he must put death to such a woman—a *woman worthy of me, by Theba's nest!*

She eased up; he attacked. Back and back across the sunlit glade he forced her, and it was not easy to keep his eyes off the jiggle and bounce of her half-displayed bosom. He had chosen time and location with care. The sun was to his back now, while he drove this astonishing woman toward a great spikebush,

abristle with its long, curving thorns. To his right sprawled
Radev's corpse; she'd try to break past him on his left. One fast
stroke and he'd make two of the wench. A shame; he'd not even
be able to use the corpse. But . . . he dared do naught else. She
was too good. Twelve dead men! His entire band. How did one
even begin recruiting?

*Careful, careful, the mind must not wander, nor the eyes.
Give not away the plan; that tight arse nears the spikebush. Ah,
she knows—she's set to jump—now!*

Tiana's knees bent, straightened, and she jumped—

Maltar put all his body behind the leftward lunge. His blade
keened with terrible force. It sheared through air only, and he
had an instant to know that she had jumped *in place*, that his
entire right side was exposed to her, his arm far to his left. He
heard the *ching* of her slender point's striking his mail just below
his armpit, and he felt the blow.

The blade slid in. Maltar's corpse pitched sidewise, trapping
her blade and tearing it from her grasp. As Tiana knelt to recover
it, a small bird squealed in fright. She flung herself aside. The
diving hawk missed her by the breadth of three fingers. It
slammed forward great wings, banked, shot upward, wheeled,
dived.

Though the forest promised safety of a sort on either side,
Tiana fled through the center of the glade, toward the trail.

The hawk leveled. On only a slight downward course, it was
rushing at great speed straight for the back of the fleeing woman's head. There was a hideous cracking sound when it struck
the silken rope still stretched across the glade. Tiana heard the
leafy shiver of the tether-trees on either side, and the flutter. She
whirled to see a mass of broken bones and feathers fall to earth.
The flopping, broken creature underwent a writhing convulsion
that was unnatural even in its dying.

As she watched, its shape changed. Hawk became man. The
broken body was wrapped in black robes now splotched with
scarlet. In agony, with blood pouring over his chin from his
mouth, he forced out words with the will born of total malice.

"My curse on thee, meddling fool. Though I fail, my brothers
will slay thee. Best accept that, lest thou share thy brother
Bealost's fate."

The dying were-man fell silent. Before the horrified and
vindictive Tiana could snatch Maltar's sword and chop him to
bits, his body shriveled, dried. A little puff of smoke huffed up,
and then fire sprang forth.

The body was consumed in seconds, with Tiana backing from intense heat. The grass of the glade was not so much as scorched.

On a table far to the north rest three little figurines in the shape of hawks. One is burning.

9

In the Tomb of Kings

The members of the ruling house of Nevinia attempt to extend their luxury beyond death. Near the capital, Calancia, at the edge of the Turbanis River, they have established the most beautiful and luxurious cemetery in the world. In vaults hundreds of feet beneath the earth the dead, buried with their most precious jewels, rest in rooms of marble and jade and lapis lazuli. The tomb is guarded by three squadrons of the Royal Guard, naturally the pick of the Army of Nevinia. Within the tomb, in front of the casket of King Nestor of old, rests the left arm of Derramal.

—the map of Lamarred

Tiana awoke in total darkness with the taste of defeat like ash in her mouth.

An attempt to raise a hand to her pain-throbbing head brought only a clinking sound and more discomfort. She was stretched on a cold stone floor, naked, arms back over her head, legs obscenely wide apart, both wrists and ankles manacled to chains set in the chill floor. Her nose told her the place was filthy and had soaked up much blood and urine.

Despite the pain, her mind was clear. She recalled the disaster.

Early in King Zohar's reign, the monarch had been embarrassed by a successful robbery of the royal graves. He had taken the strongest measures to prevent a recurrence of the desecration. Now the royal cemetery was guarded by both soldiers and ferocious dogs, the famed mastiffs of Sigilata in far northeast Bashan. The approach was limited to two bridges spanning an artificial lake . . . which was stocked with crebas, maneating fish first imported from one of the many Kroll Islands. Thereafter attempts at theft had been rare. An unsuccessful thief who survived the immediate dangers received the harshest punishment devisable by the prodigiously fertile mind of Zohar's charming queen.

Tiana based her plan on the simple fact that guard duty was dull. Once again she used the fact of her womanhood. Discovering which brothel sent girls to entertain the bored Dark Guards was not difficult, nor was bribing herself into the red-haired whore's place. An amorous Dark Guardsman still wore his grin of desire when she hid his unconscious body in the bushes. Thus she won to the very door of the royal vault, where it seemed a simple matter to pick the lock and enter.

It was not. Instantly the tumblers were disturbed, there was the swish of a weight's slipping within, followed by the clangor of an alarm bell. Perhaps she should have continued with her work and entered anyhow; instead, she spun and fled. Twice dogs overtook her. The first obligingly spitted himself on her needy sword. The second provoked a desperate fight at the edge of the lake, into which she was eventually able to hurl him, still alive. With the fish thus distracted, Tiana ran a few yards along the bank and plunged into the artificial lake. She swam across. She hadn't succeeded, but at least she'd escaped to plot another try, she thought as she pulled herself out of the water. Then she had seen the pair of buskined feet, and the spear butt had come down on her head, hard.

In which of Calancia's several prisons she was now chained, she had no idea.

It didn't matter. Death would be horrible, slow and unbearable. Her pose alone suggested a number of torments; so did the little noises she heard—a rat. Well, he'd stay well away for a while, until he was sure she was unable to defend herself. Perhaps that was to be part of her punishment; they'd just let the lanky rats of Calancia gnaw awhile, before they came to demonstrate a few interesting devices. It was in Calancia that the device called the Lion's Teeth was invented; even the Narokans had been impressed.

I need one hand free. Perhaps a chain was weakened by rust or set in cracked mortar. Knowing better than to hurl herself against her iron bonds like a wild beast, she applied her strength to this limb and then that. There was not the slightest yielding, even when she used the full strength of her superb body.

Tiana went limp to drain the tension. She could only wait for such opportunities as chance or someone's carelessness might bring. Rested, she'd meet them better. Accordingly she applied her will, chased from her mind all thoughts of rats, torture, slow execution—and went to sleep.

Sounds awakened her. The darkness in which she lay was grayed by faint light that crept around the edges of the door. Metal clinked against metal; rusty iron slid, grating. Lovely; the door opened so that its shaft of light would fall directly between her wide-forked legs. Surely this was the torturer coming to ply his trade, and this might well be her only chance to win free. If he underestimated her strength and guile, she'd escape.

The door groaned, grated back. Tiana squinted at the rectangle of light; this lifting of her head was good for the muscles of her stomach anyhow. A man stood gazing at her, a man tall and lean with gray-shot hair. He was clad in silk and ermine. For an unpleasant moment his face looked hawklike, and she remembered the were-hawk's promise of vengeance from his brothers. But when he advanced his torch, she saw that he was more ferret-faced, with ridiculously curled mustachioes.

"Know you the charge against you?" His upper-caste Nevinian accent came in a toneless voice that held neither threat nor promise. A tenor.

"Of course. Grave-robbing—royal."

"Not so. You are a whore who sought to peddle your wares to guardsmen on duty. They virtuously refused and arrested you."

"Lying hogs! I should have castrated that—I reached the vault *door*! But for that cursed bell I'd have plundered your whole boneyard!" Tiana was livid at the guards' perfidy and her being executed on a lesser charge.

"The door! Small wonder the Dark Guards lied. His Majesty would double-decimate them if he knew a robber came so close to success. Can you guess why I come to you?"

"I told you I'm a thief, not a whore! Try to use me and I'll bite your throat out."

"Hm!" He moved the torch about. "Naturally red hair, too. It is obvious the guards did indeed lie when they claim to have refused your body.'' He entered, circling a little to the side, holding the torch out over her.

''I look even better standing up.''

''Not to a man, Scarlet! But—do you still covet the royal cemetery?''

''Oho! Certainly—for an equal split.''

''Oho yourself,'' he said, just as equably. ''A fourth, my dear. As the torturer Faeho will be along shortly, your bargaining position is . . . poor.''

''A third, then. You'd not be here if it were easy to find another.''

The tall man sighed, then smiled. ''A third, then. You drive a hard bargain, my dear.''

Was there mockery in that smile? Had he agreed too readily, or was this fancy noble above such haggling? ''My name is Tiana, not your dear. With the torturer coming, shouldn't we remove these chains?''

''Ah, a pragmatic mind. Freedom first, then concern to your lewd nudity, eh?'' The richly attired man bent to remove her left manacle. He was in his late forties, she judged. Without a day's work in his entire past. Turning to her right ankle, he spoke. ''I am Count Brehar, ah . . . Tiana, and you may call me 'my lord.' There is little need for haste, really. I . . . exaggerated about Faeho. I bribed all the guards—Faeho is with an expensive little masochist from Naroka.''

''Is he now, milord?''

The voice came from behind Brehar, who whirled to face a big, heavily muscled man who seemed to breathe from his great stomach. It was much in evidence, he being bare to the waist, though his head was black-masked. Short sword poised low, the torturer advanced on the noble, who wore no weapon belt.

''Milord, ye be a fool. Ye really thought I'd sell so lovely a piece as this? Ho—His Maj himself will attend such a show! It be those who do *not* love pain that *I* love, my lord.''

''Come, Faeho. When she talks, she'll send a dozen of your cohorts to their deaths.'' Lord Brehar was backing slowly to Tiana's left.

''Their problem,'' Faeho the torturer said. He paced slowly after the noble, a great cat confidently easing in on his mouse.

He was now within reach of Tiana's freed leg. It came whipping over and up to jar home at the base of his torso, between his legs. Faeho grunted, bent; a knife appeared in Brehar's hand as if by magic; a moment later the torturer wore the finger-thin blade in his jugular.

"We all miscalculate," Brehar said in that same neutral tone, while with some haste he opened Tiana's remaining manacles.

As soon as she was free, she snatched up the late Faeho's sword and let Brehar see its tip. "Now my lord, I'll thank you for your fine cape of ermine. You can have it back as soon as I have aught else to wear."

The rest of the escape was uneventful, though she did lose the heavy shortsword while swimming the prison moat. The city's guard was lax; the two were soon in Lord Brehar's stately, strangely empty manse. He poured two silver cups of tension release, blood red. Tiana took the one he didn't offer.

"We must hurry, Tiana. You need considerable preparation, and the guests will soon be arriving."

After she'd drunk deeply of the excellent wine, she asked, "What guests?"

"Mourners—for your funeral."

"That's nice of them I'm sure, but I am not going to die to oblige them." Noting that he also drank, she pushed out her goblet for more wine.

"Ah, but that is the point. The last syllable of my name marks me the king's kin. He has both the crown and the wealth, you see. You will soon be buried in the Royal Tomb—alive, of course."

"My *dear* Lord Brehar! How clever you are!"

"You are my niece, my dear poor little Dinharu, who's lived so long with me. Hurry now, you can't be buried in an ermine cape. I've seen you already, remember?"

"Ah, but then I had no choice. I'll change clothes alone. Just a *bit* more of that lovely wine, dear Uncle Brehar."

A bit more it was, and a fat roll to soak it up in her stomach. In a small room with draped windows, he had laid out a full set of rich, elaborate clothing. It was hardly to Tiana's piratical taste, but if Calancian fashion decreed that aristocratic young ladies called to Theba be buried in such, she'd submit. After coolly gazing at Brehar until he departed, she hurriedly pulled on the indigo underpants, which had tape attachments inside the mid-thigh legs for the pink hose. Wrapping the length of matching pink silk six times rather tightly about her fulsome breasts was distasteful, but she knew that bosoms were out in Calancia this season. Next came the four underskirts—white, pink, white, too-yellow—and the buckled shoes of red leather with their thumb-long heels. The dress was high in back and cut not deeply in front, heavy green velvet with so much brocade and pearls at the bodice that it stood stiffly from her. *Excellent; when I'm flat*

*on my back in my coffin, these awful bindings and this iron-stiff
bodice will disguise my breathing!*

Brehar was cheating; she noted that the magnificently jeweled
carcanet consisted of brass, glass, and paste.

"Oh my," she murmured, "you absolutely raving beauty! A
perfect fit, too—what a fine figure Lady Dinharu has. Had. Poor
thing had to tie her breasts down all the time, I suppose. Milord
Count!"

He came, bearing a tray of paints and creams; Nevinian
nobles wore copious cosmetics and painted absolute masks on
the dead. *Civilization's proudest purebloods and the savage
Woodlings both paint their faces,* Tiana mused; *how deliciously
absurd! Still, it makes the impersonation possible.*

Once he'd smeared and carefully brush-drawn the hot stuff all
over her face, Brehar led his animate corpse into a carpeted,
black-draped room filled with chairs. On a covered table at the
front of the room, away from the heavily draped windows, lay a
handsomely finished chest of Colladan mahogany. Its interior
was softly cushioned and lined with a lovely silk of leaf green.
Tiana said not a word until she had inspected the concealed air
holes and the inner releases for the coffin's locks.

"Good enough. I go out in high fashion and good style—how
do I return?"

"Under the casket's floor lining you'll find the robes of a nun.
Tomorrow, accompanied by a nun, I shall come to sprinkle
water and wine and drop a totatten leaf on your grave. Other
mourners will require the good sister's comforting, and you and I
will be well away ere the guards realize that more people left than
arrived."

"And if there are no other mourners?"

He smiled. "Shall I describe those who will arrive just before
me?"

Returning the smile, Tiana said, "Clever Uncle Brehar!
You—what's that?"

"A carriage outside. The first of the guests. Hurry, drink this
and into the casket." He extended a silver goblet of wine, which
she had not seen him pour. "A mild sedative. You will have
need of it, to remain motionless during your final rites."

"Uncle! But you didn't want me to have more wine, lest I fall
asleep and snore." Accordingly, she let just the tip of her tongue
touch the wine—and hurled the scarlet fluid into Brehar's face.
"Poison! You'd poison me before our theft?"

Brehar sighed. "There is to be no theft, my dear Tiana. Nor
any visit, nor nun. You see, there is no escape from the Tomb of

Kings. You must die after all. You have called me clever; my niece is heir to a considerable property, which I hold in trust. On her death, I inherit. Unfortunately, the slut's just run off with a wright's son, and forfeited the trust. Therefore, I had to find a girl who resembled her—and bury her.'' Once again his hand held the knife that had sent Faeho into the domain ruled by Theba's daughter Hella.

"Clever, clever Uncle Brehar,'' she said, watching him start to close on her and reflecting that he'd have to stab her in the back that her wound would not show. ''But oh Brehar, you have chosen the wrong person. I am hardly just a girl . . . see?''

Too many skirts rustled with her rapid movement. Her hand was inside the wine goblet, and she used it as the tiniest of targes, batting away his knife-hand. Her other hand was already moving in a great roundhouse that slammed an open palm over his ear. His eyes went huge and his face writhed in the agony of a burst eardrum. Tiana did not want to leave marks, either. Accordingly, she gave Brehar a kneelift in the crotch, which both assured his silence save for a tearful gasp, and bent him into position for the back of her elbow, which slammed down on the back of his neck. Count Brehar stretched his length.

"Brehar?'' Male voice, in the entry hall.

"I hear something, Shibenhar.'' Female voice; entry hall.

"Rat dung!'' Female voice, very quiet; Tiana's. She glanced about. Trapped in a room with a warm corpse and no place to . . .

"My lord Count Brehar?'' Male voice, definitely priestly.

When the door was tentatively opened and a hooded priest in death-black robes entered just ahead of several nobles, there was a body in the casket, as expected, and another on the floor, definitely unexpected. No dagger was in evidence.

Poor Brehar! He must have suffered a stroke in his grief. He was patently dead, and a pair of relatives moved him elsewhere, muttering about his and *dear* Dinharu's property. But—all arrangements were made, and it was Dinharu's turn, and Brehar would wait until his turn, tomorrow—poor man.

Tiana greatly enjoyed her funeral. It was unfortunate that she couldn't participate more actively, but at least she could hear what was said, which was likely more than she'd be able to do at her own final ceremony. The best part was the priest's oration as to what a wonderful child she'd been, so kind, so dutiful, so chaste and obedient to her loving uncle. The paean was hardly marred by someone's stage-whispered, ''Probably poisoned the round-heeled wench so she wouldn't run off with one of her lowborn studs.''

After the funeral, the guest of honor wrestled mentally with a difficult decision. On the one hand, this seemed a —literally— golden opportunity, not to mention a silvery, pearl-besprent, and gemmy one. On the other, Brehar had assured her that there was no return from the Nevinian Tomb of Kings.

While she debated, the decision was made for her.

Before the last mourners had departed, a squad of the Royal Guards Dedicated to Theban Hella—the Dark Guardsmen— arrived. They sealed the casket, carried it to a wagon, and soon the box and its supposedly moribund contents had been conveyed to the final resting place. There was no opportunity for escape.

Wishing she'd at least had another of those perfectly lovely fat wheat-rolls, Tiana heard the groan of a great iron door's being opened. She was carried down and down a long flight of stairs, during which her head was uncomfortably propped against the end of the coffin. She was carted along a level again, though she was in position to be sure her honor guard mounted a slight incline. She was set down on a level surface. She heard rope-noises. Her coffin swayed down, jarred to a halt on a level. There was the buzzing sound of ropes being drawn from beneath her box.

Brehar was indeed related to the royal family, and he was indeed poor. Tiana had expected a niche in a chamber; she received a hole in the ground.

The first shovel of dirt rattled over the top of her coffin. One of the guardsmen was remarking on what a good piece she— Dinharu—had been. Tiana fought panic; she was being buried alive and could still raise so much fuss that she'd be hauled up.

And accused. Attempted seduction of the Dark Guards. Illegal entry to the Tomb of Kings. Murder of the royal torturer. Murder of a royal relative. Attempted robbery of the dead. No, she'd take her chances. Death by torture would be long and long; here she had a chance—and death by smothering took not long at all.

She listened to the fall of earth on her coffin. Very swiftly, her air began to go stale. The sound grew more muffled. The air worsened. Earth stopped falling.

The shirking scum buried me shallowly enough, she thought—and moved swiftly. Already she had opened the coffin's inner fastenings and knifed open the one that held together the two halves of the lid. She pushed upward. There was the very faintest of yields, and she knew that she must get her back and legs into it. Scrambling over onto her stomach and forcing her legs up under herself used her vitiated air more swiftly, but it was the only way. Like a great cat in horrid *hot* darkness, she arched her back and pressed with both arms and both legs.

The scum had indeed buried her shallowly. The lid rose and dirt fell in on her. Drawing a great, great breath that surely emptied her little area of all air, she pushed with all her might. The lid gave and gave; soon she was striving to stand. The strain on her neck was terrible as she pushed upward with her crown. Her lungs began to burn—and her head emerged into air—and no less darkness.

Despite her wrappings and the pressure of gravedirt against her chest, Tiana stood in her coffin with only her head above the mound of dirt and breathed as deeply as possible. Then she began the next part of her resurrection, which was hardly easy, forcing her arms up through the pile of—fortunately very, very dry—earth and then dragging herself out.

Having emerged into total darkness, she shook herself like a dog and bent over to shake dirt out of her hair. She did not knuckle her eyes; she was covered with sweat and knew that dirt adhered everywhere.

Well, Tiana m'girl—you are where you wanted to be, in the Tomb of Kings. Dark, isn't it!

It was. She walked until she came to a wall, followed it until she came to a doorway, followed that passage. She had no notion where she was going, but she did possess steel—Brehar's dagger—if not flint. Perhaps she'd find a way to make fire, using one of these accursed underskirts and someone's coffin wood.

Reminded of the skirts, which were both hot and resistant to her strides, she leaned against a wall of cool earth and began stripping. She removed all but hose, shoes, underpants and the wrappings—which she decided to keep to arrest her natural jiggle and sway. Making the fine velvet dress into a sack, she thrust two of the underskirts into it. The subterrene air was cool on her upper body, most of which was bare.

She was just starting to resume her blind walking when she heard the sound. Surely it came from the large chamber she'd recently quitted. Her nape prickled. Was she not the only restless "dead"—or even dead—here? Very still, she listened.

Someone was digging in the earth, and with hands alone. She listened. The sounds ceased—and there came the sound of a couple of terrible slamming blows, accompanied by the splintering of wood, followed by a howl of rage.

Tiana did not smile at the frustration of some grave robber who had discovered her not at home; she trembled. All she could think about was that this was the demesne of the dead, and . . . the Woeand vampires. *Why did someone or something want a recently planted corpse*—and not one likely to be accompanied by great wealth?

Hopefully it was merely another thief—who was now coming, with strange steps, her way. Without light. The only certainty about those rolling, semishuffling footsteps was that they were two-footed. Another thief, surely. Tiana tried to make herself very small, edging along the earthen wall until she was against a supporting beam.

The footsteps neared.

Now Tiana heard breathing—heavy and raspy, like the snoring of a giant. Cold sweat covered her; she actually felt wet dirt sliding down her body. She was glad that Calancian noblewomen did not wear underclothing of white. Her hand was wet on the hilt of Brehar's slim, triple-edged dagger. She scarcely dared breathe. Nearer came the unnatural footsteps and the huff-snort-puff breathing.

They passed. As they did, Tiana's nostrils were distressingly assaulted by the odor of death; corruption. *Do I believe in ghosts? —Of course; I am not, after all, a fool!*

The footsteps faded into the distance along the corridor; the foul odor lingered. Tiana's arms itched; they were covered with gooseflesh and every little hair stood erect. He—or It—was gone, and she was Tiana; curiosity overcame fear. Stepping out of the heeled shoes, she began ruining the soles of the pink silk hose by retracing her steps—and His/Its. Aye, it was her grave she'd heard dug up anew—and the coffin was not only unearthed, but smashed to kindling. Tiana shuddered. That coffin had been well made of the hardest Colladan mahogany!

More than human strength was needed for this destruction, she thought, taking up a goodly chunk of cleanly broken wood.

This time she made certain that the pitch black hallway she entered was a different one. *You go your way, Thing, and I'll go mine.* With her eyes useless, her ears were keenly alert. She heard

nothing. Beneath the earth, darkness was absolute. She roamed. On, and on. And eventually blinked—that was a glow, in the distance! She blinked, for though it was but an indirect glow of light, her pupils had surely grown so huge as to accommodate a fingertip.

She came to the crypt of a noble family. In its center, a small oil lamp rested on a pedestal of ivory; some aristocrat had earned—or demanded—an eternal flame to guide his way to

Hella's domain. That unfortunately did not imply an attendant she could await and overpower; an inch-wide pipe of gold carried oil to the lamp, which was mounted permanently in place. *Odd*, she mused, but it wasn't; gold would last forever, whatever that meant, and the pipe's thickness was doubtless to prevent its becoming clogged with sediment.

Ah, you selfish kings of Nevinia! With that pipe I could buy all Reme and make it into a lovely port for every pirate on the Great Blue Sea!

There was more; a broken, tenantless coffin had been wrapped with endless yards and perhaps leagues of silver thread. Humming, Tiana spent many, many minutes rewinding it around her mahogany stave and securing the other end to the lampstand. Meanwhile, she noted the niche-lined walls of the crypt.

The slabs had been torn from every one, and every coffin had been smashed. None of that was surprising; she knew grave robbers had been here afore her. What was . . . disconcerting was that the previous despoiler had left a tidy fortune in jewels—while taking every single corpse.

Tiana considered that mystery while she squatted to collect scattered jewels like a maid gathering berries. With those stowed in her fine velvet sack, she pieced together a torch: a large chunk of the newest coffin, wrapped with strips of underskirt, oiled. Linking two ornamental silver chains that had dropped or been torn from stolen bodies, she slung the sack of loot from right shoulder to left hip.

"It may just be useful to extinguish this torch," she muttered, and twitched at the sound of her voice, and shut up. *And I may want to relight it*.

Unfortunately no one had thought to bury a relative with flint. Only jewels. She tried for a spark from an extremely valuable ruby of great size, but the stupid bauble broke into fragments. A large diamond, though, seemed as if it would work nicely. Lighting her torch from the lamp, she set off to find the tomb of King Nestor and the left arm of Derramal.

She'd read surely a hundred names on crypts, all of which were untenanted but so full of plunder that she'd long since become choosy. Ships had been sent to the bottom for less than she'd judiciously plucked up and popped into the velvet bag that had been Brehar's niece's dress. Only one crypt contained a skeleton—the bones of which had been cracked and were clean of marrow, powder or otherwise.

That discovery made her reconsider her torch, but she decided she'd rather be able to see, even though it might attract. . . something. She would never forget the constant horripilation and awareness of death on that Narokan ship while a cobra sought her in the dark. Besides, she had found the subterrene cemetery's plan, and King Nestor's tomb was now but a few turns ahead.

The silver thread paid off. With a sigh, she glanced back at the tiny argent trail she'd left. *Well, I'll have no trouble finding it and, with it as guide, I can run to the lamp chamber, at least!*

Rounding a turn, Tiana came face to face with the Thing.

It was obscene in its totally hairless, pasty whiteness. Naked, it was a monster, an anthropomorphic horror, an awful travesty of the human form. General shape and long, powerful arms and barrel chest placed it midway between man and—totally hairless—gorilla. The genitals were trebly obscene for being a lovely pink. A squat, misshapen head crowned the tall and rangy form—and yellow eyes blazed with hunger. The mouth drooped open to reveal doglike fangs. It drooled.

The horrified Tiana now understood the missing corpses and the marrowless bones; the noble Tomb of Kings was a warren of semihuman ghouls. Of course it had been enraged to find her coffin empty—it had missed its dinner thereby.

The Thing advanced, long arms swinging up. Remembering how the coffins had been ripped asunder, she backed. There was no way to strike a mortal blow without entering the unusually large circle of arms thick as her thighs—and long as her thighs and calves combined.

"Nice monster. You like fire?"

It was not bestially fearful of it, she discovered upon extending her torch; the thing batted it away, seemingly casually—and with sufficient force to tear her low-burning brand from Tiana's hand. It struck the wall with a bright spatter of sparks and gobbets of burning silk. One bit of burning cloth sailed against the advancing creature's shoulder, and it snarled and jerked its head toward an attack it could not understand. On the floor, the torch flickered into death—and Tiana dived.

The ghoul's left hand-paw was at its singed right shoulder, and Tiana went low, on its left. Before it could swing a long arm down for her, she was past, grunting as she hit the earthen floor but thrusting herself up and spinning in one superlative movement worthy of a gymnast. She had stabbed the Thing twice in the back before it swung for her—she followed, staying behind and squatting to slash an ankle.

The ghoul fell, hamstrung, and took the knife in the neck. A flailing arm failed to clutch and succeeded in saving Tiana by tumbling her against a wall. The torch died just before the monster did. She heard the last shaky, raspy breath.

The torch still glowed, and a panting Tiana knew it could be rekindled readily. But if there were more than one of these creatures here, it now endangered more than aided her; she knew where she was going. Working her arm where it had been struck and rolling the opposite shoulder, which had first impacted the wall, Tiana stood in darkness. She pressed her ear to the ground, noting that it was damper here. She heard no footsteps, but there was another sound . . . water.

This section of the tomb must be under the river, she realized, though that gave her only a sense of direction.

She advanced, knife ready in one hand and dead torch in the other. Around another turn in that chthonic dark she eased, to see another glow. She smiled. Certainly King Nestor's tomb had an eternally burning lamp! She hurried toward the glow—silently.

The tomb of Nestor, anciently King of the Neviari ere they formed Nevinia, was a magnificent chamber nigh as sprawling as the throneroom of his successors, though hardly so lofty. Pearls clung like dewdrops to walls of jade. The floor was a blue lake of lapis lazuli. The eternal flame flickered like molten gold above a gold-banded ivory stand—and beside it, in a place of honor on a chrysolite table, lay a handless arm the color of old parchment.

Before that uneaten arm, almost in an attitude of worship, fully a score of deathly white ghouls squatted on their obscenely hairless haunches. They were busy with a grisly feasting.

Once again a part of the evil is the center of worship for creatures of evil—and now I must rob twenty ghouls the size of gorillas!

She must distract them. *Fire served me well in the convent of vampires. . . .*

But there was nothing combustible here, save the enormous pile of bones in a discard pile that totally obliterated one wall. Tiana's eyes widened.

Oil.

She ghosted away, back along silent corridors of velvet blackness. Her stockinged feet easily reassured her from time to time, treading on the silver thread. She returned to the other vault with its eternal flame. Cutting even soft gold was slow and hardly silent work, but the ghouls were preoccupied in the cracking of bones and smacking of reeking lips.

Thin oil began to pour rapidly onto the floor. It stank, but Tiana smiled. The tunnel before this tomb definitely sloped downward to that of Nestor's. Leaving that corridor, Tiana slipped rapidly back to the entry of the ghouls' dining chamber. She waited. Once the oil had formed a nice puddle around the squatting monsters . . .

Roaring flame should distract the filthy corpse-eaters!

She waited. At last she saw the approach of the oil. She frowned; most of the flow she'd started was missing. Was the supply finite after all? She watched the trickle turn soundlessly into the vault, and Tiana noted a trembling in the air between her and the flame, beyond and above the streamlet. The oil was evaporating! How dare it adopt such a course when she needed it so desperately?

Does evaporated oil burn? Who knew? As one could not drink evaporated water, evaporated oil was probably useless. Gritting her teeth, she knew she'd just have to wait until enough fuel had accumulated, then strike fire and light it herself. Lest one of the beasts glance around and see her before she was ready, she withdrew along the corridor and tried not to listen to the drooling, lip-smacking, marrow-sucking repast. She chided herself for being reminded of her own hunger. How horrid! Her stomach lurched at the thought, and . . .

Her wait ended. The sound from the chamber was like unto that on the day of her highriding. First the tremendous clap of thunder, then roaring flame, billowing out the door and following the oil-trail up the tunnel. The rushing air was full of flying fragments of jade and lapis lazuli and bone and ghoul. Even well along the corridor that ran past the vault's doorway, Tiana was tumbled heels over head.

Evaporated oil, she thought, *burns*.

The flame had already subsided and she staggered up to race to Nestor's chamber. The lamp was gone, but burning pools of oil nicely illuminated the ruined vault. The walls dripped gore, and shattered corpses were all over—but where was the arm?

Moving, of course, inchworming along to save itself. It resumed lifelessness the moment she stuffed it into her bag of jewels. As she bent to a burning pool to relight her torch, a loud crack sounded from the explosion-weakened ceiling. Tiana pounced away. Thus she narrowly missed being buried beneath large pieces of ceiling. They were followed by an avalanche of rocks and silt. Then, rushing noisily, came a torrent of muddy water. The River Turbanis was entering the Tomb of Kings!

Tiana regained the shelter of the tunnel ahead of the falling stones and mud, but she was hardly safe. The rushing river followed her, anxious to fill all this wonderful new space. Tiana *ran*.

Hunger and weariness were forgotten. She did not have to coax what was surely a record speed from her supple strength. She ran. The river pursued. The race was unfair; at each turning she must choose the proper direction, while the rushing waters of the Turbanis took every direction, every tunnel. It gained steadily. By the time she had passed the other eternally lit vault she was splashing in water that rose faster than she ran.

She burst into a large chamber and cursed only briefly after stepping into a hole and sprawling in filthy water; the hole was her own grave! She remembered being carried down that flight of stairs—and uphill. Several exits left this chamber, she saw as water reached her knees and kept climbing. Only two went away downward, and one was behind her. Tiana plunged into the other—and was in water up to her neck.

Despite the dragging sack of loot, she lunged forward to swim.

She was not aware of being borne up until her head thumped the tunnel's ceiling. She realized that death was close, as close as the stairs and the door to the outside. Swiftly seizing one enormous breath, she dived and tried to hurl herself forward through inky black water. Tiana swam blind. There was no measure of time or distance, save for the growing ache in her lungs. Her bag of plunder dragged at her, slowed her; she'd not leave it, not now. Though she loved life, she was not particularly fearful of death. Too, until the onset of the panic that banished reason, she cherished the hope of leaving here with both the arm and wealth. Her arms grew heavy, even under water. She stroked and kicked, on, on. Lungs afire, she made what speed she could through the black water. Now she had to have air and, with one hand up to protect her head from slamming into the ceiling, she kicked herself upward. Her lungs were in agony and her arms begged to be left alone. She rose.

She did not even know her hand had left the water until her head broke the surface and she was gasping, exhaling and sucking and snorting. No wind had ever tasted better than the stale, subterranean air of the Tomb of Kings.

But it was not stale—and she saw above the level of her head a horizontal line of light. Grinning, she stroked with new vigor toward what she knew was a door backed by daylight. Her knee barked on cement—the steps! Huffing, quivering all over, she rose streaming from the water to climb the stairs to the door.

With weary gratitude Tiana sank down on the landing at the top, just inside the entry to the Tomb of Kings . . . and the exit.

Sunlight and escape from this tomb of horrors lay just on the other side of this great slab of steel.

So did armed guards and vicious dogs and a moat full of carnivorous fish.

Elated by her successes, Tiana knew she was far from safe. This problem was more instantly deadly than the previous ones. She had been on the other side of that door, fresh, fed, better armed and unburdened—and she'd been captured—after having to fight off two dogs. Now she felt half-dead, and her first attempt would insure that the Dark Guards would be extremely vigilant.

She could see that the water was no longer rising; it lay at the fifth step down, and it was almost still. The Turbanis had found its own level, having totally flooded the Tomb of Kings.

She had to have rest . . .

She did not dare take the chance . . .

She had to. She did: Tiana went to sleep.

When she awoke, stiff but at least rested, it was with a semi-sane plan in her mind. Her fingers examined the lock and learned that it was easily opened from within. This cord probably went to the alarm bell; she cut it. Slowly, with care for quiet, she unlocked the door, eased it back and peered through the crack.

Before the door, a body length away, stood six Dark Guardsmen in their cuirasses and greaves of black leather and dulled helmets with white-gold plumes.

Taking a deep breath, Tiana opened wide the door and called.

Six men turned to stare in shock at sight of a bedraggled, indecently semiclothed young woman who stepped *from* the tombs. They made incoherent questioning sounds, followed by words, "Ghost!" and "Lich!". And then, almost incredibly: "Cow's dung! 'Tis an aristocratic young lady in the undergarments of burial, somehow interred alive. Isn't is so, my lady?"

"You," she told that guardsman beside his white-faced captain, "are a clever and brave man. Please do come here."

They came, slowly and with pale caution. "By the Cud!" the captain exploded in horror. "The entire tomb is *flooded!*"

"Aye," Tiana purred, "and if you are silent about my presence here, all will think this a natural catastrophe or visitation of the gods. And . . . you'll not be blamed and double-decimated."

The captain's skin proved it could achieve a greater degree of pallidity. "It . . . is not a . . . natural . . . disaster?"

"No," Tiana said, feeling her strength rise with her spirits, for she was enjoying herself at last. "I was plundering, you see, and accidentally blew a hole in the ceiling with one of those perpetual lamps." She shrugged deliberately, watching their eyes go appreciatively to her breast bindings, which were plastered wetly to her; she'd slept only long enough so that she no longer dripped, Theba be praised. "Arrest me and His Maj will doubtless behead you all for allowing me to perpetrate the crime of crimes."

"God!" and "Oh—mother!" and the corpse-pale captain: "But . . . if we let you go, we are guilty of this . . . heinous crime!"

"Captain," one of the tomb-guardsmen said hurriedly, "wait—if she departs, and good riddance . . . we are surely entitled to a share of her . . . profits." His nice blue eyes, which should have been greed-green, were fixed not on his captain but on a smiling Tiana.

"Why share?" demanded another. "Why not sword the bitch and . . ." He had been looking at the captain and of Tiana's lightning-swift action he saw only a flash of steel close beneath his chin.

His fellows looked at him in startled horror.

Through there had been only the slightest quick pain, he could feel warm liquid trickling down his throat.

"Don't worry," she said smiling, the red knife in her hand, "your jugular vein is little more than scratched. You won't bleed to death—unless you talk too much." To the captain she added, "If we're going to haggle, oughtn't we go where we won't attract . . . undesirable attention?"

She was standing poised at the entrance to the Tomb. One false move, he knew, and she would be gone.

What then? His men were glorified night watchmen. If he summoned help, they'd all be executed. If he led them into the Tomb to catch her, they'd be fighting this tigress in darkness and water.

Why hadn't he taken his mother's advice and joined the priesthood?

As a matter of fact . . . with his share of the loot . . . he could buy himself a fine position in the priesthood!

And thus they went to the brothel that Tiana knew. All services were bought with one string of unusually valuable pearls—and a large jeweled comb for the overweight proprietor of that temple of pleasure and service to mankind.

*   *   *

On the morrow Tiana awakened in an inn some distance from the house of pleasure. Her temper was as bad as her headache. After breakfast—which the shriveled little innkeeper served to her as timidly as if she were the king's pet lion—she went to the stables.

Her horse and mule were safe, and all she'd left with them was undisturbed—including the hands and other arm of Derramal. She even had her rapier and thief's kit, the sergeant of last night having appropriated them after her previous capture; she had repurchased them at the price of a valueless piece of green glass. Aye, for before the drinking reached prodigious celebratory levels, better light and clearer eyes had shown that many of the jewels were worthless imitations. Apparently, many of the occupants of the Tomb of Kings had been robbed even ere they took up residence.

How fortunate that there was a pair of emeralds and the sergeant too drunk to know which was real . . . or . . .

Instantly she pulled open her sack and held her emerald to the light—only to hurl it from her.

"Cow Dung and Turtle Droppings!"

As she checked her sack, she swore the more. Why should those lazy barracks rats get more than half the loot? All they'd done was hold out their dishonest hands.

It wasn't fair.

Yesterday she'd been chained naked, buried alive, assaulted by a ghoul, half-drowned and had come just short of being knifed, poisoned, blown to pieces, and publicly tortured to death. A hard day's work. She'd earned the jewels.

After taking a deep breath and letting it out, she thought of the captain. He, at least, had paid for his share of the spoils.

While she and the Guardsmen haggled over each exact share, there had been much whispering among them, whispering, winking and exchanging of knowing leers. Not surprisingly when the business was all seemingly settled, the captain had insisted that Tiana accompany him to the rear gardens—to see something "truly extraordinary."

Apparently he had poured considerable courage from his wine bottle.

Tiana could have forgiven him if, maddened by her great beauty, he had tried to force his affections on her. The captain, however, made it all too clear that rape was a mere incidental in their plot to rob and murder her. As commander, he was taking the first turn.

Perhaps instead of recovering her weapons and share of the

spoils and then fleeing, she should have stayed, given the men some of what their officer received.

As for the captain—if he recovered from his wound, he might treat women with a little more respect. If he did not recover, she felt vaguely sorry for him. Still, if he was going to enter the priesthood, it shouldn't make any great difference.

The sun was high, the morning well spent, and she several leagues down a road that wound through peaceful farm country. The wind that tossed her burgundy hair had for the moment swept away all angry thoughts. She had gained four parts of Derramal and, far more important, she felt she had most of the clues she needed to solve the evil riddle of Derramal and Lamarred.

10

The City of Shadows

Caranga to his beloved Tiana, by way of the log of *Vixen*:

Though the spiders of Serancon's isle had slain none of my
men, the effects of their venom faded but slowly. I strove to
let them recuperate, and did but wallow on to the coast of
what you benighted members of the pale race call the Dark
Land. Even then, having wasted days upon days, I had but a
score of men able to make the overland trek to Killiar. As
delay always costs more than it repays, I dropped anchor in
a sheltered bay and left most of the crew to recover while I
and the twenty marched inland. The trek was long and fairly
hard, but without incident.

When I and my eleven men reached Killiar—oh. No. I
did not allow nine to die. They were part of that group of
galley slaves we liberated off the Narokan merchant ship
that started all this. As it fell out, each had left several wives
behind, with numerous children. In the villages we passed,
those asses were so foolish as to bray boasts of their adven-
tures. The jungle drums carried the story, and soon their
wives arrived to drag them home. Back to slavery for them,
and I doubt they'll gain freedom this time!

Lamarred's map gave information about Killiar, as follows:

No nations are there on the great southern continent called the Dark Land, but areas controlled by various tribal groups. Once this was nearly changed, by the great warrior Nagranda. By his conquests and several advantageous marriages, he built a sizable empire and established a capital, Killiar. The empire disintegrated on Nagranda's death. The city prospered until eight years agone, when the citizens fled. The deserted city houses both the feet of Derramal and a fabled treasure, the Egg of the Phoenix. This is a cut and polished diamond of ten thousand facets, egg-shaped and large as a man.

This was most interesting of a surety, Tiana, but it raised questions. If the sweet treasure was unguarded, why had no one stolen it? Indeed, why had such a proud city been abandoned?

The villagers had no useful information. All did know the legend of the origin of the egg. Over five centuries agone, a fantastic bird flew over Killiar. Its wings were a hundred feet across and of shining bright colors. Three times this sweet, feathered rainbow passed over the city ere it landed. Its great size frightened the people, but it proved to be peaceful, and ate the grain given it. The bird continued in the city for seven days—when there was a mysterious fire.

Afterward, the bird was gone without trace and the gigantic diamond called the Egg was found.

The same men who were ready to swear to events of centuries long fled could not tell me what happened but eight years past. The people had fled from the city in panic, yet no one knows why. Their ruler had been frightened to the point of being permanently afraid of the dark. When the new greathouse was built, he ordered lamps to burn all night on every wall. One oldster swore that this king feared not darkness, but something else: that he ordered the constant illumination because he feared *shadows*, having none of his own!

Apart from such nonsensical tales, it was known with certainty only that men entered the city from time to time. If they went by day, they generally returned having seen nothing out of the ordinary. Those who entered Killiar by night were never seen again.

It was late afternoon, daughter, when we arrived at the rubbly outskirts of abandoned Killiar. I had caution enough not to enter. While the men set up camp outside the walls, I climbed a hill overlooking the city. As I had been told, it was a strange mix. Many buildings were those normal throughout most lands, huts with palm-thatched roofs and tightly woven walls of grass and reeds. Most were simple two-room structures. Others were elaborate mansions with many rooms and fronted with elaborately carven planks that were inlaid with many different shades of wood—beautiful, in truth.

Naturally, every building was decayed from years of abandonment.

That is as it should be. My people—my former people— know that a hut is a nearly living thing. Its roof breathes so that the interior is cool despite the sun's blazing heat. Even without windows, the interior is filled with a soft light that diffuses through the walls. It is natural that such a structure saddens and dies when it no longer serves man. The huts were built by my fellow blacks, while the other buildings were found there when my people came to this land.

They are alien structures, and they rise like specters among the huts. Tall and of black stone they are, and completely without windows. Though they had stood un-told ages, time had inflicted few scars on them. As I gazed down, I knew that the interiors of those towers must be black as the pit and hot as kettles on the fire. Why would anyone build such structures? The only creatures that like hot dark places are serpents and their kin.

I watched the sun set. The city became a maze of shifting shadows with no sweet sign of life. There was no sound and, though I was downwind of the city, no odors came to my nose—which you know, Tiana, to be keen as a hound's.

I had imagined that some great monster guarded the incredible diamond. If so, it did not perform the usual functions of nature!

Full darkness fell. As I was about to return to camp, lights sprang up in the city! They were here and there on the walls of the black buildings, sometimes inside. I returned to my men troubled, and did not tell them of the lights. Ere I retired, I reminded Susha the Voluptuous that I was home and hoped she was watching kindly.

Next morning we entered to explore Killiar. Quickly we passed the empty huts and began to move among those looming, darkly brooding structures of black stone. There was no sound save our voices and footsteps. Dust was thick everywhere, and I noted that the only footprints were ours. The city *was* deserted—and yet when we came to a lamp set in a niche, I knew that it had burned last night. How then that it was wreathed with cobwebs and could not be lighted without disturbing them?

We exchanged looks that I admit were fearful. (The men's, I mean. You know me to be without fear.)

At midday, we found the skeleton.

Its rotted clothing was that of a city dweller. Probably he had not fled when panic emptied his city, eight years agone. Whatever had caused his death, he had no broken bones. When one of the men lifted parts of the skeleton to prove this, I noticed a thing more than odd about those bones—they cast no shadow.

Apprehension hung on us now like a shroud while we continued our unfruitful search.

It was late afternoon when we made our first contact with the dwellers of abandoned Killiar.

Klain of Port Thark had separated himself from us by tarrying to examine something or other, and suddenly he cried out. We drew steel and rushed down an alley and around a corner . . . to find his corpse. There was no blood, none, but there were peculiar discolorations on his skin. Though the skin was not broken, the marks resembled sword wounds. But where was his killer? Klain had still been screaming when we entered the alley. Mere seconds had passed. There was no way past us, nor was there aught other way out. We banged the walls in search of secret doors. We called out challenges. We stared upward along those ugly black towers, seeking steps or windows.

We found nothing—until I myself spotted the enemy. He was standing behind the corner of a building, so that I saw only his shadow. I whirled and leapt at where he must be, and I assure you my sword was high and ready to slay.

Tiana . . . there was no one there.

Suddenly, Narata made a choking sound. Aye, old everjesting Narata! He stood in our midst with no enemy near him—*and yet he was being strangled*.

I have heard tales of invisible men, and directed my sword to where such an attacker should be. I must have looked insane, beating the air while Narata's life was being squeezed away. It was when I glanced by accident at the ground that I saw the horror; Narata's *shadow* was being strangled by the shadow of a man who was *not there*.

So I acted insanely again. I stepped into the sun and thrust so that the shadow of my sword thrust into the attacking shadow. Tiana, I swear—I felt resistance to my blade! And that phantom shadow writhed, lay still as death . . . and slowly faded!

Not a man of us but whose hair didn't stand straight up. Mine was uncurled for an hour, I swear by Susha's own curls.

Narata had hardly regained breath when the host of shadows came upon us. Small wonder the sweet people of Killiar had fled in panic—their shadows had rebelled and taken up independent life! Independent, and total hating of normal men! Now this eerie umbral host came to slay us, gliding grimly along walls and ground.

'If they slay our shadows we will die,' I yelled, and heard my voice high. I fought it down. 'They can be slain only by the *shadows* of our blades!'

Our men understood, and in such a weird combat we proved superior to the attackers. Swords flashed in the sunlight like silver wheels, but it was their dark shadows that did the work of death—bloodlessly. Steel rang not against steel and, had any watched, he'd have thought us ridiculous prancing fools. But the battle was deadly. Though many shadows writhed and faded into naught from our thrusts and slashes, we too suffered strange and painful wounds. With our backs set against a wall, we stupidly supposed we could not be attacked from behind—until a man yelled and pointed, and I saw the shadow of a club raised above the head of my own shadow.

I *moved*! Unfortunately, I was not swift enough to avoid that blow entirely. After that, *all* was in shadow for your valiant Caranga!

I awoke in chains. My head throbbed. My back muscles ached, so that I knew I'd lain there many hours. When my eyes focused, I saw my men chained beside me, still unconscious. We were in a vast room that was lighted by a single little glim. This, I knew, was the dwelling place of the disembodied, Susha-abandoned shadows of Killiar.

Here, they moved not merely along walls and floor, but through the room. I could see them, almost solid, tangible forms. I saw their eyes, dead and soulless, mere gray ovals like ash. These . . . things were irefully destructive not from conscious cruelty, I realized, but of their own evil origin. Some would pity them.

I had no time for that; I was their prisoner, and they'd proven somehow substantial enough to chain me and my men. Now we were but seven.

There was no furniture in that black-walled room, only an altar in its center.

On that dark stone lay a pair of mummified feet and beside it a large object, like a giant's head covered by a black cloth. The Egg of the Phoenix, I was sure. We had succeeded in finding all we sought, but there was the inconvenient detail that we were in chains and surrounded by bodiless enemies.

I considered. They had taken us alive for some purpose. Since this place had the look of a temple, I felt they meant to use us in some grisly sacrifice.

Naturally, I examined my chains. Ah, the pleasant surprise! They were indeed set in ancient mortar, and it was indeed weak with age! Obviously, the Susha-abandoned shadows could not judge strength, mine or the chains. Nor had they maintained this building. I saw a pillar that was decayed with age, partially eaten away at its base. Years had rotted those ironwood timbers, and either their transformation from humanhood had affected the shadows' brains, or those insubstantial wraiths paid no mind to such tangible matters.

Yet how could I make use of these errors on their part? If the roof fell, we would most likely be crushed, while—can a falling roof slay shadows? What *were* their weaknesses? I gave this much thought.

As they had not attacked us until dusk, they surely could not stand bright sunlight! As they burned lamps, they surely could not function in complete darkness! Shadows preferred the shadows, then. Ah, Tiana, what a mind is your father's.

I footed the man beside me and bade him wake the others. "When the shadows are distracted, we must wrest ourselves free. If I can extinguish that lamp, we'll be safe for a few minutes."

Scarcely was my last man awake when the shadows

gathered about a spot to the left of their altar. The bodiless things appeared to be waiting reverently for someone or something, and I delayed our bid for freedom. Perhaps there was a hole in the floor where they congregated? Something was coming, something I would have to brace in complete darkness. I wanted to see the thing these unnatural things worshiped before I made my try at putting out the lamp.

It came; I heard it. Slowly the thing of night slithered into the chamber.

It was huge, reptilian though not a serpent. The eyes were old, *old*—more ancient than those buildings. And I had thought them only grim legends, about the Old Ones who had been here before the fathers of man! Their time was long past, by Susha's eyes, but they had not departed in peace or with grace. With fire and steel and much spilling of their own blood of valor had the heroes of thrice-ancient times won the world for us from these fell creatures. Now this one, surely the last survivor of those enemies of human-kind, had at its pleasure seven of the thieves who had stolen the world from it and its hideous kin. Small vengeance, for the loss of a whole world—to eat us seven!

It was time. A mingling of terror and resolution wrenched my chains loose in a spattering shower of mortar and bits of stone.

The shadows turned on me and unshining swords of darkness whirled up. I snatched up a goodly chunk of stone as I sprang up and, in the doing, I narrowly evaded a shadow-thing's thrust. I ran *at* them, for the lamp threw my own shadow behind me, and then I was where I had to be. My heart was pounding furiously and my hands were wet with a chill sweat. I knew that I would have but one throw of my piece of stone, and that I must not let panic rob me of that throw—everything depended on it!

For just an instant I forced myself to stand motionless. Then I made my throw. The stone flew. A shadow came at me with his sword. It thrust, and I could not evade it. I was to die—

The stone struck the lamp, straight and true. The lamp toppled, and died. The enemy and their deadly umbral swords were now truly invisible. Shadowless, I could not be slain.

The sound of clanking metal and rending stone told me my men were breaking free. The Old One, though, was mine alone, and I had only my hands and the lengths of chain dangling from the manacles on my wrists—which were both bleeding by the way. I glided in the dark, holding my chains silent. I found the weak pillar I had noted, rotted ironwood beams. I felt out a piece of strong timber, and gave but a moment's thought to the fact that the roof might come in on me—better to die like a warrior beneath tons of rock than to be swallowed alive like a rabbit eaten by a python!

I tore the timber free—and the sound brought the monster to me. It came in complete silence. A faint musty odor warned me, and with all the power of my limbs I swung that ironwood club. It struck true, with a heavy impact and the sound of crunching bones—and then the thing was upon me.

Its ophidian flesh was cold as ice, its breath foul. I whipped it with my chains without seeming effect. What seemed tentacles without number gripped me. Paralyzing cold fire ran through my veins. I was forced down in the absolute darkness. The thing's great bulk was an overwhelming weight and I felt a cold soft wetness sucking at my feet. Susha's scarlet mouth . . . I think, Tiana, that I began to gibber then. Aye, I Caranga, admit it.

Slowly, helplessly, I was being pulled into a toothless mouth entirely huge enough to encompass me!

Dread clutched my heart, for I realized the Old One's true mouth would be in its belly . . . teeth or searing, melting acids or stones, perhaps to grind me—or my body, as I'd have smothered.

I was being swallowed alive.

Slight scratches on my legs burned from the creature's acid juices. It was agony. Desperately, I flailed, but my legs were afire—and I knew that had there been light I'd not have been able to see them—they were in the beast's maw.

It was then that the rumbling began. There was a roaring crash, like thunder. The ground shook as if struck by great sledgehammers. My chest felt crushed by the heavy blow that fell onto the creature atop me. Every tentacle snapped loose and flailed in spasms. The Old One writhed, convulsed and, with a mighty final convulsion, it went limp.

Only time had been holding the place together. The one timber I had torn loose had been sufficient to create stresses that ancient rotted timbers and the weak pillar could not meet. Down it had come and, strangely, it was the sweet creature itself that saved me, by being atop me!

It was dead, and I gathered my strength and clawed my way out from under the dead bulk—into bright sunlight. The temple floor was littered with three-foot blocks of stone. Most of the roof had come down—and one of those blocks had slain the Old One.

The walls stood; my men had been against a wall, feeling their way—they were all alive, blinking in surprise!

Yet now the shadows were back. Sweet Susha's paps, but they were enraged at the slaying of their god! They moved along the walls, weapons in hand, hatred in those soulless ashy eyes. We stood unarmed, in the room's center now, in the bright sunlight where they dared not come. It seemed a standoff, but then came new horror—they produced shadow-bows and a shadow-arrow came streaking at me!

I was stupid to fear it. The shaft faded to nigh-naught when it entered the bright sunlight, for it was not a real shadow but the shadow of a nothingness, a shadow without a—well, I know what happened, and I saw it and think I can understand it, but I can't explain that sweet set of paradoxes and impossibilities!

At any rate, when that pallid stick struck my chest in the bright sunlight, it was less than a bee-sting. Yet Narata was this time less fortunate, for he squatted beside a jumble of blocks, in shadow—he was slain by a volley of the shadow-shafts.

Hide amid the stones as we would, the host of foes ever found vantage points and loosed volleys. The sun would not long be overhead; when it died or even dimmed, we'd all die of invisible arrows. I must bring light to slay the shadows that cowered near the walls . . .

I sprang from cover and ran to the altar. Oh, they saw my intent aright, and they unleashed flights of their umbral shafts. I was staggered from a score of stings. Even falling, I hurled myself forward and my hand was just able to snatch away the veiling cloth that was my goal.

I was already squinting; I heard men cry out as sunlight struck the Egg of the Phoenix and all its facets blazed up like ten thousand torches. Every color imaginable rayed the walls in a blinding splash of fiery light. Shadows writhed, vanished.

But I had invoked greater aid than even I knew. Spears of *living* color leaped from that Susha-sent egg. When they struck the shadows, the creatures glowed red and twisted, writhed as if they were *afire*, by Susha's lusty blood! Living light fought those things of darkness, and light prevailed. We could but squint and shade our eyes during that silent war. No—massacre.

Soon, Tiana, the army of shadows was slain. All of them were gone, gone forever. We had won both the feet of Derramal and the marvelous, the unbelievable Egg of the Phoenix!

And now, beloved daughter, we sail home, home to Reme, and I am the wealthiest man in all the world. By the Cud of the Cow and by Susha's circumcision, I hope you are safe and well, with naught to do but rob a tomb and some silly old fool's garden!

11

The Garden of Turgumbruda

In Escallas, capital of Bash-an, dwells a gardener of considerable repute. He is Turgumbruda, and he is also a wizard of black knowledge. Sinister plants are sold from his garden to men of dark desires. Others he grows for his own amusement. In his garden rests the torso of Derramal.

— the map of Lamarred

"How may I serve my lord?"

Dorbandura bowed low before the man who had just entered his inn. From his posture of obsequious welcome, the innkeeper furtively examined the customer with cold calculation.

The man was as tall and thin as Dorbandura was short and fat—bloated, really, with rat eyes stuck amid the meat of a hog face. The tall man was hard and lean, like an animal or a bird of prey, with penetrating, pale eyes in a dark face in which every bone was prominent. His black robe, ungirt, completely covered his feet, which made strange clicking sounds as he entered the establishment of Dorbandura of Escallas. Without speaking, the robed man seemed to examine the entire room and its furnishings.

"My lord, be assured that nowhere in Escallas can good accommodations be found at so good a price as at my inn."

"Call me Thor-Nack. There is good reason for your inn's modest rates. Thou dost robbery and murder on any lone traveler with valuable possessions." The accusation was delivered in a perfectly calm, matter-of-fact tone—by a man who seemed to possess no weapons.

"Good Thor-Nack! I fail to understand your—humor. Please be seated and let us discuss your business."

Blackmail, Dorbandura thought; he'd dealt with such men before. He motioned, and the robed innocent complied, leaving his back exposed to the kitchen doorway where lurked Dorbandura's son, Shorbanthuda. He had caught his father's tiny signal, and waited now to see if there would be need of his ax. Hopefully not; Dorbandura filled two mugs with wine and as he handed one to Thor-Nack, his ring dropped in the poison.

Thor-Nack accepted the mug and drank deeply. "Rather clumsy, fat man. Better to keep a poisoned mug handy than to play the obvious game with the ring. Too, this is a poor venom, easily tasted. Thou are too tight with thy money, fat man. Better to eschew this dithba, unless it is to go into something spicy, and spend a few more coppers for Naroka's Sweetbird." He finished the wine. "Tell your half-wit son to set aside that ax."

Shorbanthuda took that as his cue to lunge forward. His ax swished through air only, to bite deep into the floor. An instant later he was flat on his back with the robed man standing over him.

"Do not move, fat man," Thor-Nack said in the same calm tone. "*This* needs an object lesson."

Thor-Nack's arms were motionless at his sides, his feet and the youth's throat and upper body concealed by the robe. Shorbanthuda struggled briefly, apparently strangling. Then, with a snap, his head twisted at an unnatural angle. Thor-Nack stepped off—*click*—leaving the youth's neck marked by the imprint of a huge claw.

"A worthless boy, host. Yet do precisely as I say, and thou may have him back. Fail, and he *stays* as he is—dead."

Shaking, his lips blubbering incoherencies, Dorbandura went to his knees.

Thor-Nack resumed his seat, helped himself to more wine. "Now to business. Among thy guests is a young woman, a flamehair of considerable beauty. She is a thief. In the room thou hast rented her are even now precious jewels, gold and silver— ah, thou knew not, eh, and would have slain her ere now! Thou may keep all that bright metal and stone, she has certain *other* things I desire."

Greed displaced fear in Dorbandura's face, where grief had not yet appeared. "My lord! We have but to rob her room ere she returns!"

"Thou art stupid, fat man. She must first die."

"I shall poison her tonight!"

"Thy crude methods would but earn thee a rapier in that gross gut, Dorbandura. Though thou shall spring the trap, I must prepare it."

Thor-Nack bent to the corpse of Shorbanthuda and held his wine-cup to its throat. The boy's father went all over gooseflesh. He saw no knife, yet suddenly blood flowed into the cup. When it was half full, Thor-Nack took it to squat on the floor near the fireplace. He began to paint on the floor, using the warm blood of the youth he had just slain. Dorbandura watched, petrified with fear. The drawing was merely a crude fingerpainting of a face. It became less crude. Rapidly it took on fine detail and horrid realism. When the face of a horrific demon stared up at him, Thor-Nack drew a wide pentagram around it. He rose.

"Now, partner, learn thy part," he said in a calm tone of command. "Today I shall search the city for her. Should I fail in my quest, she will come here to demand supper. Thou will have covered the pentagram with dirt—have a care not to mar it!— and placed a table within it. All other tables must be occupied by guests or piled with dirty dishes. When she seats herself, open this." Thor-Nack drew a small box from his robe. "Throw the contents into the fire. Obey, and thou shalt be wealthy and thy murderous son restored. Fail, and . . . join him."

Thor-Nack strode from the inn, clicking.

The first rule of theft was to know the place and the victim. In the present instance, that meant Tiana's learning the layout of Turgumbruda's home. She examined the walls, which were some eight feet tall and covered with ivy. There was but one door. Only when she banged on it for the fourth time was there a response. The door opened but a crack. The face within was hidden in shadows.

"What do you want?" The voice was blurred, strained, rather as if the speaker suffered some disease of lung or throat.

"Apprise your master that a customer with gold would buy his wares."

"Nothing here is for sale. Begone, wench!" The door slammed.

I do not believe it, Tiana thought, looking about. *Perhaps I'm somehow recognized.*

Accordingly she walked away, looking back twice as if disconsolate, and spent several minutes coming around behind the house. That wall, she assumed, surrounded the garden. The wall was closely grown with greenery-including a huge saytree snugged close to the stones. It was quickly climbed; she was as quickly astonished and disappointed. Turgumbruda was a gardener; she had expected his garden to be sinister, yet beautiful and, above all, perfectly tended. She looked down into an ugly mess, weeds overgrown and run riot. In the center of that unkempt eyesore stood a small stone building attached to a greenhouse. The former was in good condition; the latter was not, with several windows broken and all of them filthy. Directly before the stone building burgeoned a great thick mass of ugly bushes. Why anyone would want to grow such or suffer them to thrive, Tiana could not imagine. They bore neither fruit nor flowers, though they looked revoltingly healthy, far more so than anything else in what appeared to be an abandoned lot. Vinaceous tendrils sprayed out like green-leafed tentacles.

The small stream was strange, too. It ran into the greenhouse but did not emerge. *A sewer drain inside*, she supposed, though she still wondered. *I need to know a lot more than this!*

Climbing down, Tiana betook herself directly to the District of Roses—otherwise known as the thieves' quarter. A few discreet inquiries, one bribe, one threat and a promise led her to a decrepit little hovel of leprous stone. Its door was ajar; she boldly entered a large dark room.

"Marderun the Wise—will gold loose your tongue?"

"The tongue of an old man is always loose," the lean oldster said, from behind a counter strewn with handsome crockery. He was soft of white hair and face—from which stared two bright, black eyes. Marderun wore a faded blue tunic under a leathern apron stained with clay and dyes.

Tiana tossed a jingly little goatskin bag from hand to hand. "Of all men in Escallas, Marderun, you are surely the most knowledgeable. What know you of Turgumbruda?"

"I am nosy," Marderun said. "It is my weakness. You are from Reme. Your confidence is high, and you are beautiful. Well I know a man of Reme, a man the color of raven. So, I think, do you."

Tiana blinked, then smiled. "Marderun, I see that you are wise indeed. Caranga fares well. I am his foster daughter, Tiana Highrider."

"And you have designs on Turgumbruda, nor will my urging you against it be to aught avail." Marderun sighed, gestured, leaned on his counter. "My excellent mugs are priced at three coppers; examine them. A strange man, Turgumbruda, grown the stranger of late. His strange and usually vile business long ago bought him the favor of important men, yet now he turns away all who would buy. Time was when he was seen at any slave auction that offered comely girls. Through the years he bought more than fifty. Once within his house, none was ever seen again. There was such an auction but ten days ago; Turgumbruda was not there. Too, he has ever bought horsemeat for his guard dogs and food and wine of the finest quality—for one."

Tiana dropped three coins into a blue-striped mug; silver coins, not copper. "And none ever did aught about it? *Perhaps the girls at last revolted and he is their prisoner—no no, they must have food. By the Back—he's slain them all!*

"As I said, Turgumbruda long since won the favor of important men, who are known to suffer at times from blindness concerning some matters. Lately, though, he may have gone too far."

"Ah. How so, friend of my father?"

"No no, no more silver, generous Tiana; you are Caranga's foster daughter. None would take you for his natural one! Well, Turgumbruda has stopped spending altogether. He no longer buys food for the dogs or himself—he buys nothing. He has now neglected to pay his taxes."

"Ah, the final sin! But what of that peculiar servant who slammed the door in the face of a customer with gold—me?"

"None ever saw him, before this change came on Turgumbruda."

"I didn't *see* him either, Marderun. Tell me of his home—and the greenhouse."

"I do wish you'd give it up, Caranga's own flower!" Marderun sighed. "All was built years ago. I have not been in the house. An aqueduct channels the stream through the greenhouse. He had the workmen dig away on either side, so that the greenhouse is sunk a bit. Thus he may take as much water from the stream as he wished and divert the excess to the sewers."

"Odd. When did that process begin?"

"It happened gradually. And Tiana—a man seeks you. I cannot keep it from one so beautiful, and Caranga's own. He is tall, hawkfaced, in a black robe."

Tiana was given pause. A brother, surely, to the were-hawk she'd slain. "An assassin. Thank you. This pot would be en-

hanced by a gold coin—there. Has anyone sought to rob Turgumbruda—recently, I mean?"

"Two," Marderun said, affecting not to notice the golden
eagle she'd dropped into the brown-and-gilt pot. "Three, really.
The first two climbed the wall—and vanished. I do not advise
it."

"The third?"

"A tax collector. Yesterday he forced his way past that
obnoxious servant." The old potter gestured. "He has not
emerged. The Dark Gardener's influence has run out, for the
king is disturbed. He has ordered a troop of soldiers to arrest
Turgumbruda. I would say . . . at sunset, today."

"I would believe it, if you said it. Marderun. Excellent health.
I will speak of you to Caranga. That hawkfaced man . . . is there
a back way here?"

"Through this curtain. Farewell Captain Tiana Highrider
hero of Dark Forest."

Tiana hastened through Marderun's living quarters and out the
rear door. *He does know all!*

Walking among other, far less talkative denizens of the Rose
District, she pondered. Turgumbruda's house would shortly be
plundered, first by soldiers and then a mob; such was the way of
the world. She would be part of that mob. Her sudden smile sent
the hand of a rat-faced passerby to his hilt, but she went on—

Until the sound came, from behind her. Harsh it was, re-
sounding, intense, as if a great army of hawks was screaming in
unison. The volume increased until she felt the street quiver, she
and scores of others—who saw great cracks leap through the
walls of the building she had just quit.

Marderun! She started back—and the cracks became gaping
fissures. With a thunderous crash, the home of Marderun collapsed. Dust rose from a heap of rubble.

Surrounded by the most unsavory of Escallas's populace
Tiana spoke loud and clear.

"A baneful werehawk has done this, and slain a good man. I
Tiana Highrider who slew Maltar of Dark Forest, swear to
avenge him." *As soon as I have Derramal's body.*

A troop of red tunics under shining steel corselets and sur-
mounted by black-plumed helms filed through the door of the
house of Turgumbruda. Already a mob had grown, sure of
plunder but cautious of the king's soldiers. The last of the
troopers was through the wall's gate just as the sun set. As if in

warning omen, it died in a sky that went the color of blood ere it grayed.

Never still, never silent, the crowd waited without patience. Twilight deepened. The house gave forth no sound. Words went about; the troopers had surely found rich booty indeed and were busy gathering it. Plenty, though, would be left. . . . As twilight gave into night, the people of Escallas grew steadily more uneasy. Many slavemaidens had vanished into this house of the man called the Dark Gardener. And two thieves—and a tax collector. At last darkness was complete. No soldiers, no sound. A wave of panic ran through the muttering mob like a wind through corn, touching every stalk. It grew to a gale—and the good townspeople fled in all directions.

One remained, a redhaired woman in clothing that was obviously new. She stroked an alley cat she had caught up. She glanced around. Pacing to the side wall, she tossed the blue-barred little beast over. Silly, perhaps, but Tiana cherished the hope that she could learn something thereby—from a good vantage point. As if in invitation, a bushy tree thrust a branch out over her head. Easier to climb the bole, but she felt energetic; she squatted, leaped, caught the branch, swung up. She moved back toward the trunk until she reached a fork, where she sat. It was an excellent lookout, made the better by the bright silver coin sailing up across the sky. More light poured from the windows of the greenhouse to turn the garden into a maze of shadows in mauve and bottlegreen.

Nevertheless, Tiana could not see her feline go-before.

She waited, but still her keen-eyed seeking went unrewarded. A whirling arose behind her. The tree rustled in a breeze; a giant Arctic hawk landed on the ground only a few feet away. Hardly breathing, Tiana watched it follow her trail to the wall, hopping along; and then, with two swift noisy flaps, it was atop the wall.

The unnatural bird peered into the shadows of the garden. It waited, poised and staring, the consummate hunter. There came a slight movement in the shrubs, and with an earsplitting scree the hawk launched itself. It rose rapidly, dived to hurtle like a living arrow into the shrubs. The cat squawled—and Tiana's eyes shrank from an eerie flash of flame that turned the bushes momentarily into a minor sun.

On a table far to the north rest three little figurines in the shape of hawks. One is a charred ruin; another is burning.

*   *   *

"So much for avenging Marderun," Tiana muttered.

The pirate was not, however, happy. Though she was glad to be rid of the menace of the werehawk, the manner of its death made her theft appear far more dangerous. Turgumbruda's defenses were . . . extraordinary. Yet the robbery must be tonight; she was certain that on the morrow the Bashan army would attack in full force. If all else failed, they'd bring up siege engines and extirpate Turgumbruda, house and all, with fireballs. Her need to act was desperate, and she'd learned nothing—save that all who entered this ireful place did not return.

While the house could probably be approached via the sewer system, she'd had enough of dark tunnels for a while. Her eyes narrowed; a smile touched her lips. She'd use the stream! Dropping from the tree, she plucked a long-stemmed dandelion and snapped off its golden head. She went directly to the water and slipped in.

The streamlet was swift but shallow, so that she crawled more than swam. From time to time she remained underwater, using the dandelion stem to draw breath. Nearing the greenhouse, she noticed the creeper-shrubs. Long, arching branchlets dipped into the stream on both sides, though the center remained clear. As it was dark, she did not avail herself of their excellent cover. Purely by chance as she neared her goal, she brushed one tendril-like branch. It quivered like a drowsing beast.

Tiana was careful not to touch another as she slipped under the greenhouse wall and into an aqueduct of smooth stone. It tottered a little; a rotted support? Warily, she raised her head to peer over the edge.

The greenhouse below was a fairyland of beautiful blooming plants.

A small portion of this stream, she saw as she inhaled a blend of myriad fragrances, was automatically diverted to irrigate the plants. The rest did not drain into the sewer at all, but left the greenhouse via the aqueduct. Puzzling; the stream bed before the house was dry. Where did the water go—and why?

The fragrant, frutrescent wonders here drew her attention, and she set aside the new mystery.

Tiana climbed down to inspect the marvels of Turgumbruda's garden. Though neither lamp nor candle was in evidence, the greenhouse could not better have been lighted by day. Scattered all about, obviously by design, were tall flowers whose large blossoms were a brilliant white. Their uncanny glow illuminated the garden.

The colors of the first grouping of flowers she approached were reversed; the blossoms were a dull green, thrusting from leaves and stems that were a riot of colors. Nearby, plants that were otherwise unprepossessing put forth odd structures rather like the pipes of a shepherd's flute. On impulse, Tiana blew across them. She was rewarded by a burst of cheerful music. As if in response, a faint sweet tintinnabulation arose on her right. She examined the plants from which that dainty ringing tinkled; their little silver bells were equipped with clappers! Amid the tiny bells squatted a bush of medium size whose fruit was fascinating indeed—gold coins of varying mintage! Tiana squatted to discover that the soil from which the bush sprang was rich gold ore.

A promising achievement, Tiana mused piratically, *if a bit beyond the average gardener's means!*

Judiciously dropping the coins into the pouch at her belt, she moved on to a table on which grew little potted flowers of varying colors but similar shape. It was a pleasing effect, and she couldn't resist the temptation to smell each hue.

The first variety was a hot crimson. Upon inhaling it, Tiana became aware of how much she wanted a man's arms around her, his hard body against her, how she needed to submit to his desire, urge him to do with her what he would. Trembling, she broke away, pushed her nose down to the pink-and-blue blossoms. *Ah, if only I were married! What a fine wife I'd make! I'd take tender care of my man, cherish him, obey his every wonderful whim. . . .* Sighing, she moved on to the blood-red blossoms.

"What am I thinking? All men are swine! Better to slay than let one touch this body—I've slain many and I'll slay more, more!"

The scent of flowers of greenish yellow sent fear to lay an icy hand on her heart. *I knew it was madness to come here; this is my bane! Here in this vile place of unnatural flowers I will meet a nameless and obscene death.* Flowers of deep blue: Ah, fate. She'd come here for the sake of her brother; now she knew he was gone forever. Tears streamed from her eyes as Tiana bent to blooms of pure soft white. Ah, everything was fine, good and right! She faced no danger in this place of calm serene beauty. It was so relaxing—why, she felt like easing right up onto the table among the lovely, lovely flowers to sleep in peace and forget all her resolves, her bothersome mission. . . .

Only with a great deal of effort of will did Tiana force a step back from that beguiling table.

By the Back, what a brilliant and fiendish accomplishment

this is! Everyone *is prey to a devilish wizard who can force upon him any emotion he pleases, merely with the nice gift of a little plant!*

The baneful nature of the spear-leafed plants on the next table was more obvious. These bore not blooms but small, doll-like figures about the length of her forefinger. Most were vague and unformed, but she saw crystal-sharp images, too: the King of Bashan was here, with several of his nobles and various other people of import. A few of these perfect images were pierced with long pins, while several tiny human skeletons dangled from the foul branches.

Monster! Tiana withdrew every pin.

An assortment of stunted fruit trees pushed up alongside the wall. All were heavy with lush scarlet fruit, obviously ripe, begging to be plucked and eaten. All were perfect, none even slightly green or overripe. She had learned to be suspicious. Drawing her dagger, she prodded a fruit lover's dream. Instantly sharp spines leaped forth.

Poisonous, no doubt, she mused. *How popular these would be in bloody Shamash!*

Tiana glanced about that house of beauty that was a chamber of horrors. Beyond the fruit trees, a small section of the greenhouse was partitioned off. Plucking one of the light yielders she already thought of as a glim-flower, Tiana entered the little room the partition formed.

Here the irrigation system must have failed. Everywhere drooped red flowers, going brown; withered they were, and completely dry. Her curiosity carried Tiana far into the room before she recognized the danger. Fireplants! The flowers were so called because of the extreme irritation their pollen induced. The victim did not survive, and showed every sign of having been burned to death. Tiana had walked into a trap, not dreaming this virulent plant could be grown so far from its native home. To her horror she saw that every flower was dehiscent, ready to discharge deadly pollen at the slightest disturbance.

She froze, looking about, then staring at a tree in one corner of the death room. It was not out of place here; those barren branches looked like skeletal arms . . . and some were! The twigs were small, finely formed . . . bones. With a shudder, Tiana thought of vanished slavegirls. Choosing each step with great care, a suddenly prickly-hot Tiana escaped the plants that would have slain most intruders.

As she approached the steps leading out of the greenhouse, she blinked at two barrel-size pods to her left. They were not hothouse plants, for their stems passed through breaks in the wall. These were outside shrubs, invaders. Tiana felt no desire to disturb them. Halfway up the stairs, she remembered the little stone building she'd seen from outside.

The hidden door required but a few moments to find. Inside were no plants but numerous pots of earth, racks of bottles and jars, and a bewildering variety of strange instruments and apparati. In the room's center squatted a narrow table, six feet long and sinisterly equipped with numerous leather straps. A stand beside the table bore an array of surgeon's tools; the table was dark-splotched. Despite her revulsion, Tiana was surgeon of *Vixen* and had to examine these instruments. She marveled at their excellence; with them it would be as easy to sew a limb back on as to chop it off. And their *sharpness*!

She paused, considering, attempting to plan.

The neglect of the fireplants, added to other evidence, tended to indicate that Turgumbruda was no longer master of his house. Either he was dead or a captive. In the latter case, he could be a useful if hardly trustworthy ally. Moreover, there was a most important question he could answer. *Now suppose that* . . .

Wearing a tiny smile, Tiana plucked a scalpel from among his instruments, squatted and went about the table, slicing nearly all the way through every strap, where they were fastened to the table's underside. No one would notice, not the gardenermage's captors—not even Turgumbruda himself. Perhaps some future captive would surprise someone!

As Tiana left the hidden room, there was an agitation within one of the enormous pods. It partially opened, to spill forth a limp figure with a little *plup*.

"Ah," she gasped, "why does such monstrous horror *exist?*"

The misshapen thing ejected by the outsize pod was—or had been—a man. Every inch of his skin was covered with minute red wounds. Rather than pinpricks, they looked as if roots had been pulled out through them. The pitiful creature was still alive, all floppy and boneless looking, with each shuddering breath an obvious convulsion of agony. Awful eyes opened, saw Tiana. He, or it now, forced out words in a blubbering, barely understandable voice.

"Tell the king not to send soldiers."

That warning, made the more pathetic by its concern and misfortunate tardiness, exhausted his last reserve. The man Tiana assumed had been the tax collector ceased breathing. She forced herself to feel the body to confirm what her eyes told her.

Gooseflesh ran the length of a fearless pirate captain, then; aside from the tiny wounds, the man's skin was unbroken. Yet every single bone had been removed from his living body.

This time there was no warning whatever. The seedpod split wide and a man pounced forth—a green man.

Though his eyes were but black holes in his head and he possessed no genitals, he was more than man-shaped, and he could see. He advanced on Tiana with clear menace. Her rapier sang its way into his heart—or to the spot where his heart should have been. He twisted, jerked, and the sword was torn from her grasp. It slid from the wound to clang to the floor. No blood marked the blade; none oozed from the creature's torn flesh.

Fading back, Tiana drew her dagger, observing the while that the creature's height and general build were the same as the late tax collector's. . . . Though clearly strong, the green body was clumsy as the newborn. Tiana easily evaded its rushes, while slashing it repeatedly. It should have lost a gallon of blood; there was none. Nor did its awful wounds reduce the thing's vitality.

The woman made a small error in timing; the green man caught her. Abnormally chill fingers closed about her throat. They began to squeeze the life from her. With her hands together, she jerked her arms up between its wrists and broke the strangling grip. Up and out went her linked, balled fists while she pivoted, and in they crashed, into the thing's neck. The snap was loud in the silent greenhouse. His head toppled to an odd angle—and still the green monster sought another strangle hold. Tiana snatched his right arm and twisted, again pivoting, to throw the creature over her hip. Before he could rise, she twisted his right arm behind his body and pushed up hard. *Crack!*

His neck and right arm were broken. And the plant-green man continued to attack.

Grimly, she broke the other arm, and both legs. The monster continued to writhe in ineffectual maleficence.

Tiana tried hard not to look at him/it while she regained her weapons. Viciously, she hacked his foul womb, then slashed open the other one. Within that second pod were a shapeless green mass-and a man. She was careful in cutting him free of the great tangle of green tendrils surrounding him. None had penetrated his skin, which felt like glass. She drew him from his prison, a ghastly botanic womb in which a man was boned to provide the skeleton for his heartless, bloodless plant substitute.

He showed no sign of life, but seemed not so much dead as in a suspension of life. He was thin, old, and wore a gardener's green smudged smock. His nose was enormous and his teeth were bad.

The hair that straggled past his shoulders was limp as old corn-silk. When the cold steel of her dagger touched his skin, he awoke.

"Turgumbruda?"

"Yes . . . who . . . what has . . . happened?"

No time to answer; the windows were smashing all around them to admit long vines and branches. The foliage slithered and snaked with malevolent animation that seemed brain-guided. Tiana jerked the old wizard to his feet, fled up the stairs into the house. It smelled—green. She slammed the door behind them. They were in a pantry, and Theba be praised there was not a plant to be seen.

"You provoked them to desperate violence in cutting me free, young woman."

"How was I to know you'd outdone yourself? Your shrubs have revolted and taken over the whole place, haven't they?"

The door thudded and shook under the impact of slamming branches. From other parts of the manse came most unpleasant sounds; the shrubs were entering via the windows.

"We'll not be safe here for long. Why came you here?"

"For the trunk—I mean the body of Derramal. If I help you subdue the plants, will you give it to me?"

His voice was growing stronger by the moment; he sounded no older than thirty, as though he possessed more knowledge of life than mere plants. "Aye."

"I would go in peace as well, wizard. Swear."

"I will permit you to go in peace. This I swear on my power. If I break this oath, may my name be changed and my power lost."

Tiana nodded. "Done. Now how do we destroy the plants?"

"My beautiful young . . . lady, I have no idea."

"Oh, wonderful. No use trying to burn them; the werehawk was consumed without harming the shrubs. Ah! The water from the stream! Turgumbruda—the main group of shrubs in front of your house is sucking up all that water. No wonder they're so green and healthy. And they are huge, exerting themselves—they need more water than an army of horses!"

Without hesitation, Turgumbruda's piratical savior pulled open the door and pounced onto the greenhouse steps. A whistling slash of a long, triangular blade sent three large branches flopping, and she descended into a hellpit of snakelike vines and writhing, whipping branches.

Dodging the heavy blows aimed by the larger branches was not difficult. The vines, however, enwrapped her and were deadly. Wherever they struck her flesh, they quickly sank rootlets that probed like needles and could not be pulled loose. She kept dagger and rapier in constant play, cutting and slashing, weaving a deadly web of steel around her, for there was naught here but the silent enemy. Imbedded tendrils dangled, severed but clinging. She would rather have been surrounded by swordsmen; these living, *cerebrating* plants were ghastly and their only sound was the constant sinister rustling.

She had almost reached the aqueduct when two branches swung at her in eerily perfect coordination.

She sidestepped one blow, rolled with the other—and was knocked flat amid tendrils and branches like a snakepit.

A swift-snapping vine pulled the dagger from her hand. Others began to enwrap her legs like so many green serpents, and she was glad of the jackboots she'd bought with the rest of her new clothing, after the stripping back in Calancía; at least these things could not sink roots through leather that rose to her thighs! They attached themselves to her arms. She whimpered in pain. It was as if she were attacked by scores and scores of needles. They entwined her body, sank their rootlets through expensive blue silk, tore it.

All the while she forced herself forward. Through she was being enwrapped like a mummy, she gained her goal—one of the wooden beams supporting the aqueduct. Nor had she remembered awrong; this was the quivery one, rotted at the base by overmuch dripping water.

Wallowing, burning with needly root-probes, more than half mummified in green, Tiana drew back her legs and with all her strength drove them at the brace. Pain bit the soles of her feet and leaped up her legs—and a section of the aqueduct collapsed. Down-crashing stone narrowly missed her; water gushed freely.

Now the stream was diverted into the sewer, denying the ruling shrubs outside so much as an ounce of water. More of the weird, the eerie, but this time it was in her favor: the activity around her changed immediately, becoming less coordinated and more frantic.

A wave of proud exultation swept her. Though she was wound about so that she was nigh moveless, she had surmised aright. The plants' great activity necessitated a prodigious consumption of water, which meant a great and constant need. *They*, the plants themselves, had diverted an enormous quantity for themselves and proliferated accordingly. Now they had none.

"Die, damn ye all," Tiana groaned, wallowing and hacking. "Dry and die—*rapidly!*"

She struggled to free herself from the weakening vines, wallowing and tearing.

She heard Turgumbruda come running in from the stairs. As he approached, the botanical wizard dodged contorting branches and questing vines with an agility surprising in a man of so many years. He drew a paper tube from a pocket of his gardener's smock, bent beside Tiana, and blew pollen into her face.

Vivid flashes of color erupted before her eyes. She saw nothing else—until the gray came rolling in. Then everything converged into the ultimate color: black.

She awoke strapped to the operating table. *Oh*, no—*naked again!*

Turgumbruda smiled down at her.

"Before you complain, note that my salve has obliterated your hundreds of puncture wounds; thus have I repaid *your* saving of *my* life. Now, my dear lovely rescuer, I shall keep my promise. See—there beside you is the torso of Derramal. Ugly lump of flesh, isn't it? As for letting you depart in peace, I shall . . . you will soon be asleep with my peaceflowers. You didn't really suppose that Turgumbruda would let such a choice subject as your lovely self escape?"

She glared up at the Dark Gardener. "Hardly a show of gratitude—what about your oath?"

"Ah, darling girl. A wizard's Power is based on deceit and unconcern with . . . niceties. When he swears on his Power, the promise is always literally true, but its fulfillment is sure to be a disaster. If you would know the true meaning of a wizard's promise, imagine the most evil meaning the words can sustain."

"So I suspected," Tiana said, and burst the straps she'd earlier weakened. Turgumbruda whirled to flee. Tiana again thought of the slavegirls who'd been brought to this house never to be seen again. She pounced. The wizard was an old man, and his bones broke easily.

"Now," Tiana muttered, standing naked over the broken corpse, "someone's taken action on behalf of all those innocents."

Sergeant Militor of the Nightwatch touched hand to sword pommel at sight of the weird vision. He stared at a signally shapely girl pushing a gardener's barrow along Escallas's Queen Ina Street. She alone was surprising enough, for she was clad only in a gardener's smock, skin-tight black boots that vanished up beneath it, and a weapon-belt. More shocking was the wheeled barrow, which contained a male torso without head, arms, or legs. Yet there was no blood; the disgusting thing looked *old*, like an unwrapped mummy. Too, it was a bad day for investigating the strange, what with a whole company of his comrades having disappeared into the garden of that infamous sorcerer. Militor bit his lip. Then he turned hurriedly down a side street in quest of aught unusual or suspicious. . . .

Tiana was tired, but well satisfied with her second day in Escallas. She'd stolen not only Derramal's torso—after this night she'd never refer to any part of a human body as a "trunk" again—but she'd got various other spendable valuables (for new clothes, *again*), and Turgumbruda's extraordinary surgical tools. More importantly, she was sure she knew now where her brother was hidden. Poor Bealost! And she *understood* the riddle of Derramal and Lamarred, and knew what action she must take.

First, she mused, *I'll have to brace that last werehawk and gain Derramal's head. But, right now—supper and sleep!*

Oddly at this hour, the door of her inn was open and the common room was lit by both a fat candle and the fireplace—as though it were necessary! She pushed the wheelbarrow in, seated herself with ladylike aplomb at the only clear table, smock and all, and banged with her fist.

"Dorbandura, you lazy steer! Where's my supper?"

He called from the kitchen: "Immediately, dear lady. I've kept food warm on the stove."

"Why, that's service befitting a queen!" she called, and muttered, "of pirates."

The innkeeper, belly and chins jiggling, bustled in with the food he'd kept warming for her, all but praying she'd return. Setting the dishes before her, he stepped back a pace and opened the small box Thor-Nack had given him. His eyebrows rose. It was a mandrake root, but hardly the normal one with its approximate man-shape. This one was the perfect image of—something dreadfully not human.

Already Tiana had noted the open door, the burning candle, the fire here in the common room; and remarked his apparent delight at seeing her. And of course all those messy tables. Too, though the floor had obviously been swept, dirt gritted beneath her booted feet. Aye, the floor had been swept . . . into a rough circle around this table where she . . . had been forced to sit. . . .

No, it's not a circle . . . more a rectang——Pentagram!

She was out of her chair and vacating the dirt-outlined formation even as he tossed the demonic mandrake into the fire.

"No!" Dorbandura cried, and the murderous pig tried to push her back within the five-sided drawing.

Agile pirate was far too much for fat taverner. She punched, tripped, shoved hard. With a cry of that same single word, "No!" he sprawled within the pentagram.

In the fireplace the mandrake root blazed up, and every wisp of the resultant billowing smoke fled directly into the pentagram. In stark wide-eyed terror, Dorbandura scrambled to leave that sorcerous formation. He could not. It had become a prison; empty air formed five walls of glass against which he beat his fists without avail. The smoke was growing thicker, and now Tiana saw a blood-red demon's head rise from the dirt that had concealed it.

While Tiana watched, horror-frozen, table and chair and innkeeper vanished within roiling smoke. Shrieks emerged from the sulphurous, swirling mass. Then came the ghastly snapping and crunching sounds—followed by the unmannerly noise of great teeth chewing ravenously.

As the smoke commenced to dissipate, there was a distinct belch.

The only sign of Dorbandura, innkeeper and murderer, was a few drops of blood.

Tiana would never admit that the ghastly incident frightened her. She merely decided that she was no longer hungry. She would gather her belongings and depart Escallas now, in the middle of the night. Woe unto him who sought to deter her! Hopefully in Lieden of Collada she'd meet only human foes who were easier on the nerves—and stomach.

She did take a leathern sack of excellent Narfish wine.

12

Siege of the City of Light

Prince Eltorn Bihal of Collada looked in most respects like a storybook prince. Eltorn the Fair was tall, lean, hard of muscle—the perfect knight. At present, however, his broad shoulders were slumped, his mild blue eyes bloodshot and his handsome features drawn with care and worry. Stretched over a decision cruel as a rack, he paced the flooring of his pavilion while his generals and advisers repeated the same arguments for what seemed the hundredth time.

"Our dilemma," General Narthur was loudly declaiming, "is the result of a capital mistake by our ancestors. Not content with one nearly invulnerable defense, they built another."

"The fault is ours, not our ancestors," General Fersen grumbled.

"Oh, aye," Narthur shouted. "Ours for trusting fortifications that were adequate for our great-grandparents instead of building new ones to meet present needs."

"The cost of the fortifications you proposed was and is prohibitive!"

"Will it be cheaper to replace our king and queen, our capital city and all its people—in fact, the whole *nation of Collada*, Lord General?"

"My lord General Narthur," the prince interrupted. "I asked

you to review how the present situation arose, not how it could have been avoided. You will not be interrupted," he said, and his blue eyes fixed their gaze on portly Fersen.

"But—very good, Your Highness," Narthur said, and his bass voice had come down somewhat. "Our Lieden, capital of Collada, is the fairest city in the world. A center of learning and art without equal, graced by superb marble buildings and peaceful parks. It is justly called the City of Light."

It came into the prince's mind to call for more facts and less oratory, but he held his tongue. In agonizedly troubled times it was all too easy to fight one's friends rather than the enemies one could not reach.

"It has been our responsibility," Narthur said, rumbling now, "to guard this jewel. We have failed. Part of the city's beauty is provided by the crystal blue waters of Lake Belanda, which surrounds it on three sides. Our ancestors provided the city with a good set of walls, and similar conventional defenses. In addition, they dug away parts of the peninsula and erected stone ramparts. What they built thus was a hunter's shooting blind. Any army approaching the city must ride along a narrow strip of land with water to right and left. The entire length of this strip is within easy bowshot of the ramparts, so that any invader would be cut to pieces by arrows ere they reached the plain before the city. It was *planned* that those invaders who reached the plain would be destroyed by a charge of heavy cavalry. In that too the defenders have the advantage; they'd be charging downhill into disorganized men just emerging from the narrow land strip. One could ask for no better opportunity to slay the helpless."

Narthur paused to turn his gray-eyed stare on each man present. His voice lowered still more. "Unfortunately, Duke Lokieto, brother to the King of Thesia, sailed across Lake Belanda and landed a large army behind the ramparts. The attack was completely without warning; the city was completely unprepared. His spies had served well the duke, who struck when the regular army was on summer maneuvers and more than half the city guard was away, dealing with a minor emergency in our province of Lugania. Thus it is *we* who are in the role of attackers, and we are outnumbered three to one . . . in addition to the impossible disadvantage of position."

The prince was nodding, his lips tightly set. "General Narthur, in all your criticisms of the old fortifications, did you ever say that Lieden was vulnerable to direct frontal attack . . . or any attack we might now launch?"

"Your Highness—I did not."

"Can you now see any weakness?"

Narthur shook his head.

Eltorn looked at a spindly old man whose pot was hidden within his deep-blue robe. "Counselor Orld, is there any hope that Lokieto will grant surrender terms?"

Seated at the map table to Eltorn's left, the old man shook his head. "None, Lord Prince. When his demand for surrender was refused, he vowed that *when* he took Lieden, his men would publicly rape every woman and then, beginning with the smallest infants, slay every human being and domestic animal in the city. It is his boast that he will level the entire city save for one tower. That he will leave standing as a memorial to his victory. This . . . is to be believed, Highness. They describe the duke's behavior to several villages and small towns."

Eltorn closed his eyes. "General Fersen, Lokieto must bring his supplies by ship. What do your spies report?"

"Highness, his men *feast*." Burly, paunchy Fersen spoke grimly indeed.

"And what is the condition of our city?"

Fersen shook his huge head. "The people have—have caught and eaten the last rat. The guards on the walls are unable to stand, let alone fight. Lokieto of Thesia could take the city with ease. That he delays implies either that he lacks spies in the city or that he prolongs the agony of our people out of sheer cruelty."

"My lord Kandor, can the navy take supplies to the city?"

The young genius who served as admiral of inland Collada's Lake Belanda fleet spoke rapidly as ever. "Your Highness, since the last battle with the Thesian ships, our fleet consists of one racing galley. Though it is one of the speediest craft ever built, *Swallow* maneuvers like a turtle. It is useless in combat and cannot carry cargo. It *can* convey any messages Your Highness wishes sent."

"Into Thesia, perhaps," Eltorn said, tightmouthed. "Orld— have we any hope of foreign assistance?"

Orld shook his head with its sparse strings of ash-colored hair. "No, Highness. Agreements and alliances have become running water. No one wishes to aid a losing side . . . and Lokieto is called a military genius. He is *feared*."

"Can we recruit more warriors?" The prince was looking at Narthur, though without hope. He knew the answer.

"No, Highness. One admits surprise that even more men have not deserted."

Eltorn paced disconsolately "Well, gentlemen, the answers

have not changed. What do you now advise? My lord General Narthur?''

''Highness—*attack!* We shall most certainly die, but it is not meet that your royal father and mother should perish while we sit in safety.''

''Attack and die. I see. General Fersen?''

''We must save what we can, Highness. We must retreat.''

The prince held up a hand as Narthur jerked and opened his mouth. ''What little we can—the army? Can we retire to fight another day?''

Fersen regarded the floor. ''Not likely, Highness. When the city falls and Collada is a duchy of Thesia, the men will lose heart and desert. Those who remain in this land will be sought out by Lokieto's men, and slain.''

''Then what is this 'what little we can save,' my lord General? Does it include any part of our land?''

''No, Your Highness.'' Fersen's voice was nigh inaudible. ''When the head is smitten, the body dies.''

The prince lifted an eyebrow. ''And yourself?''

''Highness, I will go to my estates and seek to defend. That will cost me my life.''

''I'm sorry, Fersen,'' the prince said very quietly, and then addressed them all. ''So we should die, or save naught but my own life to spend my days in shame and dishonor, hated by all as a coward. I take it all of you repeat the same advice as yesterday's—attack and die, or run. Counselor Orld . . . Sulun Tha is in Lieden, a great old man whose wisdom and judgment have never failed. Is there any new word from him?''

Orld shook his head. ''No, Highness,'' he said, to the map table.

''Then repeat the message we had from him.''

''Sulun Tha wrote: 'I have no useful advice or knowledge. If Lokieto of Thesia has any weakness, only he knows it. Therefore, watch him closely and seize upon whatever makes him show fear.' ''

''Of course.'' Eltorn leaned on the table, spoke intensely. ''General Fersen, what Lokieto fears he must watch. Has there been unusual activity of late on the part of his spies?''

''Your Highness, for the past two weeks there has been no activity of any sort. Whatever the duke may fear, he neglects the most routine measures to observe our army.''

''For the past two weeks. Did aught unusual happen two weeks ago, then?''

Fersen made a gesture. "Lokieto showed his contempt. It was then he began flying his hawk."

"Hawk? Hawk? Tell me more, lord General."

"Lokieto has an Arctic hawk of extraordinary size, Highness. A pet. It was first seen two weeks ago, returning from its outing. Since then it has flown over our lines every day, northward above the Escallan Road. It returns some four hours later. Today it returned a bit later than usual, minus a feather or two."

"Good," Narthur rumbled. "Perhaps a peasant loosed an arrow at it! It is more than we have—*by the Back!*

The meeting adjourned noisily, with every man hurrying to the entry of the sprawling royal pavilion. It was the sound of battle they heard, the ring and clangor of sword and shield and the screams of dying men.

The army lay north of Lieden, which rose on the western shore of Lake Belanda. Now all saw the little Thesian craft high on the beach. There were no Thesians in sight—alive; the shore was littered with their dead. Running, Eltorn grabbed a soldier and demanded information.

"They were *mad*, Your Highness! Their galley put out normally, and then, without warning or reason that we could see, pulled hard for shore. The ship came *fast*, Highness, and scudded high up on the shore as you see. Enemy poured out—but we were on them in seconds."

"Good. And did any survive?"

"The ship was not yet stopped when fifteen men plunged off, on horses. We slew three, Highness; the others rode into the woods." The man pointed.

Eltorn squinted at the woods, and ran down to the shore.

Admiral Kandor was examining the beached galley. "Its keel has been modified, Highness. They intended this; this ship is useless for normal plying or combat."

"Highness!" Narthur bawled. "Fear! Lokieto has shown fear! These men were sent only to give their lives while the knights landed and rode to some purpose!"

Eltorn's eyes were narrowed; now his face lighted with realization. "Aye—some purpose within two hours' ride—along the road to Escallas, I'd lay wager! Twenty good men, half armor for fast riding—and the best horses."

Narthur nodded, grinned, and began shouting. Fersen, frowning, asked, "Two hours, Highness?"

"Aye, my Lord General, half four hours—as the hawk flies!"

*   *   *

There was great joy and high excitement in leading mounted men in hot pursuit, particularly after their long helplessness and too much talk of it. Yet now they'd cantered two full hours, and Eltorn grew both nervous and self-doubtful. Surely he was right, and the hawk was a somehow intelligent spy. Lokieto sought some menace along the road from Escallas of Bashan to the north. As he needed no reinforcements, it must be something he feared. Now Eltorn realized that he should have ordered pursuit at all speed, to overtake and kill the dozen Thesians—all, perhaps, but one. *Then we could have ridden on to meet— whatever they ride to meet.* Sacred udders, he'd given them too great a start, and he may have cost the kingdom its only hope.

These thoughts niggled as he topped a long rise—and looked down upon the enemy.

There were but ten, not twelve, and they were turning off the road into rough country. Clapping spurs to his horse, the prince waved for the gallop he had already begun. The Thesians were out of sight behind a grove of trees below, and he was sure none had looked back. His horse thundered down the long hill before his followers reached its summit.

As he neared the spot where the foe had turned, Eltorn saw that the other two had not ridden ahead as he'd feared; they lay dead at the point of turnoff, and his knight's eyes told him even in passing that their wounds had not been made by a broadsword. He reined rightward in pursuit of their fellows. In doing so and urging his excellent mount to all its effort, he ignored prudence and the shouting voices behind him. He was well ahead of the others. But he'd not slow now; a second's delay might well cost the kingdom. Obviously the Thesians had come upon him they sought, and he'd slain two ere he fled into this rocky country.

Eltorn rounded the grove. Ahead rose a rock-strewn hill, and on it, six enemy afoot, clustered about a rockbound pocket partway up. It was the perfect place for a warrior at bay; his foes must attack one at a time. Charging now like a hound with the fox in sight, Eltorn bucketed past four arrow-pierced Thesian corpses. *It must be one man alone*, he thought, *and with six of a dozen to his credit, he is worth fearing! Lokieto you filthy crawling snake—we have what you fear!*

Eltorn loosed a wild yell to distract the Thesians from their attempted death-dealing to the cornered quarry. And Eltorn rode, his warhorse gathering itself, hurtling forward, great muscles leaping and rippling.

The first Thesian fell prey to a racing, trained warhorse. The other's head went flying and rolling ere he'd got his sword around at the mounted newcomer. And then Eltorn's horse stumbled on that ill-suited terrain, and the prince of Collada went flying headlong.

Eltorn's helm struck sparks off a small stone as he crashed to earth. Bright lights danced before his eyes, and he shook his head desperately to retain consciousness. Two Thesians came rushing, well separated.

The prince rolled leftward. His mailshirt screamed across stone. Thus he only just evaded the ax stroke of the man on his right. The other aborted his stroke in his sudden need to avoid Eltorn's vicious kick. In a trice the prince was on his feet, facing his enemies. Long and hard training had seen to it that he retained his sword. The two men separated but slightly to attack him again.

The Thesian invaders were overhasty. They should have taken their clue from Eltorn's obvious confidence and the fact that he'd clung to his sword and gained his feet without being touched, rather than from his being a prince of the contemptible Colladans. The ax-man's over-eager stroke left him open and Eltorn slit him from belly to thigh. He spun away, dodging a stroke from the other foeman. His sword tore that Thesian buckler like paper, wrenching the man's left arm nigh out of joint. When the soldier sought to parry Eltorn's vicious backswing with his own blade, the Colladan's edge carried away both the sword and the hand that wielded it. The prince was merciful; a quick slash opened the man's throat that he might die the swifter.

His follower's horses were thundering closer as Eltorn swung from two dead enemies.

Having engaged the trapped quarry, the last Thesian staggered back from the rocks with blood streaming from both a slash and a thrust precisely in the hollow of the throat. He collapsed, wide eyes fixed on the sun. Of all the dozen enemy, but one remained. This was a motionless man in a long, ungirt black robe that must have been hot in the sun; Eltorn was sweltering within his chain and its padding.

The robed man was swiftly surrounded by mounted Colladans. They looked to their prince, who held up a restraining hand.

Relief was like the removal of a great weight from Prince Eltorn's chest. He had won whatever it was Lokieto feared enough to spend a special boat and so many men in acquiring. Now the invader had failed. Eltorn had . . . whatever it was.

What? And how did one use it? Who was within those rocks, aside from an excellent warrior?

Narthur reined up on a belly-grunting horse. The burly, slabby general was boiling in anger he obviously wanted seen.

"May it *please* Your Highness, and though it does not, you are our liege and leader, with your father pent in the city. You must not hazard your person in riding ahead of us into minor battles that I and these men could easily handle. As matters stand, we have had a long ride to do naught save capture one unarmed civilian."

"General: your horse was slow as your wits. Sirrah: your tongue is sharper than your sword."

A new voice broke into that tension between the general who had been publicly chastised by the royalty he had publicly chastised.

"Be careful of that creature in the robe—he's worse than deadly."

The warning came from the rocks. Every eye fixed there, to see the unknown warrior the Thesians had waylaid at such great cost. And every eye widened.

A genuinely beautiful young woman stepped from the rocks. Her hair was flame and gold in the sunlight. Though she whipped a long black cloak about herself, no man's eyes missed the perfection of her form. The prince gazed into deep green eyes and felt that he could fall in, with ease. Under other circumstances, he'd have been captivated by the exquisite face that smiled at him.

Narthur broke the silence of astonishment. "The hellcat's beauty matches her fighting, but how can this girl be what Lokieto fears?"

She seemed on the point of making an angry retort, but the robed man stepped forward as calmly as if he were here by invitation.

"If I may be of service. I am Ter-Gon, acolyte of the mighty *Pyre*. I gather that thou art obeying some oracle to learn what my lord Duke Lokieto fears. What he fears is not this small girl, but the power that compelled him to send his soldiers in quest of her. That power is my master, Pyre. If *Pyre* commands, Lokieto will grant thee favorable terms. His army will withdraw on payment of a modest ransom for the city. In exchange for such an obvious gift, I ask only that thou dost cut this meddling wench's throat."

Though General Narthur was visibly excited by the offer, his prince's voice was cold. "There are many who ask crowned heads to do evil in exchange for promises of good to come. Ter-Gon, you seem anxious. Explain your case.''

"This girl—''

"My name is Captain Tiana Highrider of Reme and I am no more girl than you are a man, Ter-Gon. Surely was no *girl* or *wench* who slew your gruesome brothers.''

The robed man did not take his eyes from Eltorn's face. "This *woman* serves an evil sorcerer. If she is permitted to continue, she will loose a monstrous danger upon the world.''

Again she interrupted. "I serve none but myself. None.''

Ter-Gon wheeled on her. "Then why seek ye to serve Der-ramal? Know thou not what will happen if he returns to the world?''

"Certainly,'' Tiana said. "I shall kill him. Permanently.''

"Little fool, thou dares challenge him even Pyre doth fear?''

"I have the courage to fight my enemies, and without means arcane. Pyre does not, and sends you, foul creature. Pyre is thus branded coward.''

That was too much for Ter-Gon. Soldiers guarded him on both sides; without visible movement on his part, both men turned green, sagged, and fell dead. With the earsplitting scree of a hunting hawk, Ter-Gon threw himself at Tiana—feetfirst.

Her rapier was out, but it was Eltorn's yard-long broadsword that flashed out to skewer Ter-Gon. The dead acolyte's body seemed to shrivel. Then it burst into flame.

On a table far to the north rest three little figurines in the shape of hawks. Two are charred ruins; the third is burning.

"*Very* fast, my Lord Prince,'' Tiana said. "And nicely done—though I was of course ready for him and perfectly capable of slaying the beast—as I have both his fell brothers.'' A slight exaggeration; Tiana realized that she had not personally touched any of the three man-hawks.

General Narthur was staring gloomily at the charred remains of Ter-Gon. "This man offered generous terms—which Your Highness has irrevocably rejected.''

"I'd call slaying the creature an irrevocable rejection, yes,'' the prince said coldly.

"By the Great Cow's Cud, my Prince! Think you this trollop is some mighty sorceress who's going to blast the army of Lokieto for us? She—''

The general was interrupted by the tip of Tiana's rapier, which flashed beneath his thick, broad-flanged nose. Though no blood was drawn, a considerable portion of his pride vanished—with much of his bushy red mustache. Narthur stared; the steely point of the slender sword danced before his eyes.

"My name is Tiana, not trollop, *soldier*. I have said that—are you hard of hearing?" For a moment she stared into his astonished and affronted eyes. Then she turned to the prince. "Your Highness, I gather you seek aid in some grave emergency. Lieden is indeed in the hands of this Thesian conqueror?"

Eltorn nodded with a sigh. "It is."

"Then though I have no magic I will help—I have business in Lieden. Nor do I care to treat with conquering invaders."

Thoughts of Lokieto's obvious fear of this woman, combined with her incredible confidence—and the effect on him of those level green eyes of hers—prompted Prince Eltorn to explain the military situation. She asked several questions, now and again looking over at the lake and up at the sky. Then she considered, nodding, her teeth in her lip.

"My Prince—" Narthur began.

"I take it you are prepared to take desperate chances?" Tiana asked of the prince, without so much as a glance in Narthur's direction. "Even—commit an act of apparent madness?"

"It has long been apparent that there is no sane way to save the city." Eltorn said, with a sideward glance Narthur might have taken as reproval.

Tiana nodded and spoke with confident purposefulness. "We must ride swiftly to your camp. It looks as if a storm is brewing on the lake. Time is short and we have preparations to make." With a slight smile, she added, "I see I have a wide choice of mounts . . . Thesian horses."

Night was heavy on the land when they reached the Colladan army. Prince Eltorn gave immediate orders. "A few men must perform certain tasks. Let all others sleep well this night, for it is our last in this place. Tomorrow night we shall sleep either in the ground—or in our beloved Lieden!"

All were of more cheer in the morning. The long agony of waiting was over; Generals Narthur and Fersen knew they would die this day. Theirs was the responsibility for the preparations for battle. With no hope of surprising the enemy, all was public, almost a parade. Certainly watchers from Lieden must have been puzzled, and hopefully made nervous by the activity in the Colladan camp. As for the Colladans, they were glad to move at last, and enjoyed knowledge that they were confusing the enemy.

Despite the storm out on the sprawling lake that divided Collada from Thesia, the sun drenched the camp with brightness that reflected in dazzling rays from newly polished armor and shields. Though such a formation was surely tactically useless under present circumstances, the generals nevertheless assembled the knights in a long rank of glittering steel. Brightly colored banners flapped in the wind that came constantly off the lake. Thunderous cheers greeted the addition of each proud pennon to the growing line. No man but was proud to be in this noble company on this day of days. Though few men held illusions of victory, they welcomed the action and knew there would be glory in their deaths.

Behind the three thousand mounted knights were less than a thousand foot—or men the generals were willing to call foot. Behind them milled a motley sea of folk, a vast disorganized rabble. The people of the surrounding villages and countryside had come to fight and, if necessary, die: farmers in homespun and armed with hoes or scythes, afoot or mounted on plow horses or mules; blacksmiths with hammers in hearth-darkened hands; millers and bakers, artisans and craftsmen, old men and young boys; aye and some of their womenfolk as well, and the lame and halt.

In this strange land of beloved royalty whose people had a sense of what could be called nationalism, all had brought their lives to the altar of battle. Only in the peasantish company was there expectation of victory; of *course* twelve thousands of the ancient tribe of Colla Long-Arm could best four thousand mounted knights and eight thousand foot, mainly archers—*they* were after all not of Collada! The citizens saw themselves not as rabble, disorganized, undisciplined, armed only with a jumbled array of makeshift weapons . . . against an enemy of battle-hardened troops, professional soldiers of the very highest skill, and half in full armor at that.

Yesterday Narthur had publicly chastised the son of his liege and been publicly rebuked; today both affected not to remember. The burly general surveyed the assembled host of the Sons of Colla.

"Today, to be Colladan is the proudest, noblest estate a man can achieve."

General Fersen nodded. "It's true. Like her or not, yon wench has wrought some sort of miracle already. We must be shaking the enemy's nerves badly.'' He grinned, shooting a glance at the walls, where Thesian heads could be seen. ''No harm can come of our making this showy display, Narth. It need mean nothing, to worry the enemy.''

''The prince and that madwoman have already seen to that!'' Narthur gestured lakeward.

Down at the lake's edge, Tiana Highrider was carrying a sack and an enormous *kite* out to the prince's racing galley. She was a strange sight indeed; helmeted she was, swathed in hard shining leather with silken streamers attached to her legs, all of Colladan blue and gold. The rowers shoved off the moment she was aboard. *Swallow* swiftly reached deep water, turned laboriously into the wind, and headed toward the storm that darkened the entire lake.

A cry rose from shore on the launching of the tent-sized kite. Every eye watched it rise rapidly aloft—with the foreign woman hanging from its tail like a plummet!

Great lengths of silk rope played out as the kite soared into the sky. As the ship approached the glowering, grumbling storm, the dangling pirate vanished from view into the blackness of restless clouds. On through storm-wild waters raced the slim craft. After several minutes another cry rose; the cord dropped from the indigo underbelly of a roiling cloud. Slowing, the racing galley began its long, laborious coming about.

At the head of his army, Eltorn was mounted as should be so handsome a royal scion: on a white stallion. His scintillant, blued armor was chased with gold and the scarlet lion of his family's house rampaged on his blazing shield. Strong and clear, his voice quieted every other and carried to the farthest man in the host.

''Sons of Colla! I make no pretense that our situation is not desperate. Indeed, my generals say that it is hopeless—'' He had to pause then, for a great roaring shout of *No* rolled across the land. His helmet flashed fire as he nodded. ''—But there are some things they do not consider. They forget that the gods are just and visit their wrath upon the wicked with sudden fury. They forget that we are SONS OF COLLA!'' Another great roar; a cheer. ''Nor do they fully appreciate the love of home and hearth that fills our breasts. The ground to which we offer our blood is OUR soil, the beloved land that gave us birth, anciently ours. The enemy are aliens, Colladans none who are far from their homes and fight for greed and gold. We fight for what we hold dear: COLLADA!'' Pause; cheer. ''Our ancestors look down upon what we do this day—Colla watches! Whether our children breathe free air depends on what we do this day. Forward . . . to freedom or death. FORWARD!''

Shining trumpets blared and tympani rattled and rumbled. Prince Eltorn himself led the advance of the Colladan host. His public reason for leading was that he might inspire his people; hidden perhaps even from himself was his private reason: that since they could not prevail, he would die early in this battle. The direct descendant of Colla of old had no desire to look upon the defeat of his army and the fall of his land. His white stallion curveted and pranced, anxious to enter battle; the prince's blue cloak whipped out to flaunt its lining of cloth-of-gold.

As the trumpets pealed out their brave notes, there was a trembling within the storm and a black cloud broke away from the main portion as if on signal from the trumpeteers.

"The hammer of the gods raised above the earth to smite evildoers!"

Perhaps; the menacing sable cloud did move with clear intent toward the Thesian position.

Just as the Colladan cavalry charged within arrow range, the heavens opened above the Thesians. The prince and his men rode in sunlight on dry ground; the enemy archers were deluged with torrential rain. Though they tried to drive their shafts through the veil of water, the arrows were pelted astray, slowed. Their effect was minimal on the river of mounted men that surged beneath the ramparts. From that narrow path, Eltorn emerged onto a wide, upward sloping plane. Poised above him, wet but with perfect formation unbroken, was the steelclad might of the host of Lokieto; four thousand knights in heavy armor. They waited grimly, lances ready, each man seeking totally to relax the muscles of his legs against the time when he must grip the beast in charge and clash. When enough Colladans had assembled to justify a charge, it would be launched; the enemy would descend to slay Eltorn and his pitiful squadron.

Prince Eltorn, drunk with the elation of initial success, did that which no sane man would dare.

With but a few hundred of his knights gathered, he ordered an uphill charge against many times their number. Nor did they hold back, Narthur on his great black horse actually galloping past his royal commander.

That charge of madness was scarcely begun when the sky split and lightning slashed down into the Thesian host.

Bolt after bolt smashed into their wet ranks, shattering horses and men. Flames leapt up to dance above writhing bodies.

Horses screamed and reared and fell and stepped on fallen men. The very earth seemed to reel from the rapid sizzling, crashing blows from the sky. Lokieto's knights were smashed in broad groups like china figures beneath the sledgehammer of a vengeful god. Desperately, riders fought their own terror and sought to control horses that lurched into mad panic. They availed naught. In waves, armored men were thrown from their mounts and trampled beneath heedless hooves.

Into the forefront of this disorganized mass smashed Eltorn and his galloping host, lances in perfect array. Men screamed and died as lance and sword bit through armor. More Colladans came bucketing up the long incline.

The key to the battle rested not in the splendid fury of aristocrats in mounted combat but in the southeast corner of the ramparts. On paper, they manifestly defied successful assault; the protected defenders could easily inflict worse than prohibitive losses on any attacker. Yet it was this very corner that the leaderless rabble assaulted, bellowing out their rage and defiance. Scores fell for each man who scaled the walls to strike a blow—and die. To the Colladans in their berserker fury this was acceptable, and their pressure steadily increased. Hoes and scythes tore open Thesian faces and a burly, dark smith jellied no less than nine enemy heads ere he was transfixed by two arrows simultaneously. A hurled woods-ax felled one of those archers ere his string had ceased to tremble.

The defenders at that southeast corner were soon faced with a grim choice: give ground ignominiously before outraged peasants, or give their lives to save their comrades. On their position the mob had focused its rage, and there was no stemming it save at enormous cost of life. Aye, and Thesian knights were under attack by both gods and men.

There are few things at which amateurs are superior to professionals. Yet dying is one of them. The Thesian mercenaries were not willing to die. Knowing that retreat was disaster, they nevertheless gave back.

A great tide of roaring, ludicrously armed, temporarily inhuman humanity poured through the breach in what had been their defenses.

"Collada for Collada-a-a-ans!" the cry bellowed forth, and even the thunder was whelmed.

The rest of the Battle for Lieden forms a chronicle not of combat but of massacre, of men who begged for the mercy they had vowed not to give—and were denied.

Eltorn and his knights rode and swung and struck until arms were leaden and their armor ran red with the blood of others.

Blacksmiths shattered helmets and skulls with flailing hammers while the scythes of farmers reaped a human harvest. As individuals, the Thesians fought with skill, though few but sought to let his fellows do the dying. For lack of the will to die, they died all, and badly.

First to realize that the Colladans had won an impossible victory was Lokieto. With all but one of his ships afire and Lieden awash with the blood of his men, he deserted them without hesitation. Accompanied by a few favorites, he boarded the last ship and ordered it to set sail. At the water's edge, Narthur himself raged and shook a scarlet sword.

The Thesian craft was a half-mile out when a messenger of vengeance overtook them.

Commanding the racing galley *Swallow* was Admiral Kandor. The young genius was determined that the author of this suffering must not escape. Yet Kandor knew his racer was useless in conventional naval warfare. With the enemy a few hundred yards away, he ordered his men to hurl away arms and armor—and commanded full speed at the other vessel. *Swallow* had attained great velocity when it smashed into the side of the Thesian ship. Though the galley was broken into kindling, most of its crew swam away. For a moment the Thesian vessel seemed undamaged . . . and then it slowly listed and sank.

Of its armored crew and passengers, few swam to shore. Those who did, including Lokieto, were promptly slain.

13

A Wizard and a Prince

The head of Derramal is in the possession of Sulun Tha of
Lieden, the most dangerous of all wizards. He makes this
the most perilous part of the mission. Though his knowledge of the black arts is not deep, he is perfect at one deadly
art: the false appearance of wisdom and goodness. When
you meet him, slay Sulun Tha instantly. Do not give heed to
his voice; do not look into his face. Delay, and his mask of
kindness will paralyze your will. He will send you to your
death as he has sent hundreds before you, with bad advice
you will feel compelled to trust.

—the map of Lamarred

Prince Eltorn had fought all the day and was exhausted.
Nevertheless, he could not rest. Eltorn Bihal knew and felt his
responsibilities. In victory, they were even heavier than before
and during the battle. Were proper orders not given and arrangements not made, wounded men would die unnecessarily. Too,
the dead must be buried quickly though with honor, and their
families informed. Food must be brought swiftly for a city of
starving people.

With these and a host of other cares Eltorn of Collada
struggled.

His difficulties were worsened by his own omissions; having expected defeat and death, Eltorn had made no preparations for victory. The incessant call of details kept him occupied, and his message-bearing aide from him, for hours. At last the messenger burst past the guards, who followed with enraged faces and bared steel.

"Your Highness! You need come; the Lady Tiana fell from the sky, and the physicians fear she is dying."

Waving back the guards, Eltorn hastened away with his aide. Duty had forced him to gross ingratitude; that magnificent young woman had saved his city.

"I waited by the lake as you ordered, Highness," Rushil explained as they ran. "Very suddenly, she came plummeting from the sky and hit the water at terrible speed. When I pulled her out before she could drown, it was clear she had taken an awful beating. Riding *in* a storm—! I had her placed in your pavilion with Forfis to attend her and—"

Rushil broke off; they were sweeping into the royal pavilion and Eltorn was seizing upon his plump personal physician with ungentle hands. He learned swiftly:

"She has frostbite on both hands and feet and more bruises all over her body than a thief after a public stoning. Every muscle appears strained, though she is in excellent condition, my Prince. Ah—was. No bones are broken. By itself none of the dear lush girl's injuries would be serious. Whether or no a human being can survive such a ghastly catalog of injuries, though, I cannot say."

"Forfis, lay one hand unprofessionally on that 'lush girl in excellent condition,' and you will have to raise lentils to support yourself in *sudden retirement!*" And the prince armed Forfis aside to hurry to Tiana's bedside. There he knelt, the royal knee bent to the savior of Lieden.

One eye was not swollen shut; it opened and focused on Eltorn. Tiana winced at her own smile, but threw her arms around Eltorn just the same. She kissed him most soundly indeed.

"You are a handsome fellow, for a prince! Oh, it was glorious fun, Prince. Next thunderstorm, you must come riding the thunder with me."

"Ah . . . but— your wounds . . ."

"Nonsense. Everything fun is dangerous."

Eltorn made no reply; how could a prince admit that this flaming red-haired young woman was more daring than he—and she from Ilan, at that. After a long awkward moment, he explained that the racing galley had been lost in the destruction of Lokieto of Thesia.

And then the "Lady Tiana" was moved to the royal palace in Lieden.

There she spent her convalescence, in a gold-headed bed sheeted with white silk. The service was perfect, the food delicious, and the handsome prince not only made daily visits but was plainly reluctant to depart. It was all most pleasant—and Tiana's temperament soon had her up and about her business.

Eltorn's face fell when she told him what she wanted. "Tiana . . . any other man I could summon and he'd obey instantly, whether from loyalty or compulsion. But Sulun Tha . . . the man is a white wizard, and holds that it is the better part of loyalty to disobey aught of unwise counsel."

Tiana sat up, looked down, tugged at herself. "Shameless bedgarments you inflict on women in this palace."

"I like it."

She ignored him, and waited until he lifted his gaze again to hers. "Then why not use force on the man?"

"My ancestors tried that, with unpleasant results. As a white wizard, Sulun Tha is unable to use his Powers to his own advantage. But his Powers are considerable, Tiana. None can force him to assist in anything evil or foolish."

"Evil or foolish!"

His Royal Highness sighed. "You *do* want the head for . . . good purpose."

Tiana stared, and anger flashed in her green eyes. "No, of course not. I want to un-save your country, *Prince*."

A struggle took place in Eltorn's face. Though naturally a prince could not apologize, he at last nodded with an air and mien of contrition—and great resolution. "I shall summon Sulun Tha and politely ask for the . . . head. He's certain to help in any cause for good."

Tiana sighed, which made her glance down and then sigh again in resignation. *Down, impertinent appurtenances!* "What's so difficult or fearsome about that?"

"Tiana, Sulun Tha is a truly good man. He expects the same of all others. His presence is . . . most uncomfortable. Many seek his advice, but . . . by messenger."

Tiana hardly noted Eltorn's leave-taking. She'd had two warnings concerning Sulun Tha: he was deadly evil; he was too good for human society.

"It will be interesting to meet the man," she murmured.

*   *   *

It was. Sulun Tha was a thin, not tall but intensely erect man with a full gray mustache and a marvelously full head of hair, gray-shot white. His dusk-gray robe was girt, she thought, because this all-evil or all-good man was not above a bit of human vanity over his trimness. She noted also that his gaunt face appeared to have been chiseled from a block of flint. The large blue eyes that stared into hers were deep-set and full of intelligence. They were also cold and hard, like glaciers of blue ice. Having considered the sources of her conflicting advice, Tiana slew him not.

In an instant, he said, "I see that though you commanded storm and lightning to the saving of Lieden, you are no witch at all."

Then Eltorn was speaking, but Tiana could give his words no attention. Her eyes and mind were as if chained to Sulun Tha. Even his physical appearance lost importance. Though she could see and touch the prince nearby, it was clear that she faced the mage all alone, with none to aid or protect her.

Her bright swift rapier and razor-sharp dagger became meaningless bits of metal; she was completely disarmed.

Her new Colladan clothing no longer covered her; she felt naked and helpless as an infant.

Her mind had become an unfurled scroll; every thought was writ large for the world to see, and Sulun Tha read therefrom.

Dead memories rose from their graves like haunting specters. Though she fought with all her will, they would not be exorcised. She remembered a careless mistake that had cost the life of a friend, years agone; good people she had failed to rescue; times she had been unjust and cruel to friends or others deserving better of her. Memories of guilt . . . she had slain often, and now intense guilt arose; what right had she to be judge and executioner? Her entire life stood in grim review, and it was dark, a series of acts of monstrous egoism. Morals? Naught that she had done had been acceptable.

Now Sulun Tha was an infinite height above her. His gaunt face was the entire world. His eyes were blazing suns that left dark no cranny of her soul. She stood naked and helpless before a sternly moral judge whose demand for righteousness considered no compromise. Weighed in the balance, Tiana was found wanting. Desperately she sought a suitable penance. She'd take the vows of a nun and live out her life in a convent of Theba, perhaps . . . yet even that seemed hardly adequate for her sins, for the wrongs she repented.

Down from the sky thundered the voice of Sulun Tha. "Why do you want the head of the lord of evil, Derramal?"

The crushing weight of her guilt eased a little, for in this she knew she was in the right. "There is no comfort for my brother's grave."

"That is true, for your brother is not at peace in the grave, nor truly dead. Know you the danger of what you seek to do, danger not merely to your inconsequential self but to all who live?"

"How can it matter! Lamarred is a wound festering upon the world! Such wounds must be lanced and cleaned at any risk. Delay but invites disaster."

"You speak up strongly, as none do to me, and with truth withal." Sulun Tha nodded thoughtfully. "You have wrought more that is good than you believe and you repent the bad. You shall have your chance to combat Lamarred. Seldom has a gift been more likely to slay the recipient—but I shall give you the head of Derramal. After your death, I and others will have to fight this war, Tiana of Reme."

And, suddenly, a drained and sweating Tiana was alone with Prince Eltorn. On a table before them rested a box of softly gleaming ivory. It was of size and shape to house a human head, and Tiana knew she need not look within.

Pretending a calm she hardly felt, Tiana asked, "Eltorn . . . what did you just experience?"

"Memories best forgotten," he croaked in a strained voice. "I warned you, Tiana. Come, I have a medicine to wash away the dead past and its unpleasant shades."

His handsome Highness opened a cabinet and snatched forth a decanter. Picking up two wide goblets of excellent workmanship, he poured but enough bright amber liquid into each to cover its bottom. He handed her one, swirling its contents.

"I think you will enjoy this, Tiana. It is made from apricot wine by a secret process called distilling." He swirled his goblet, inhaled deeply with his nose nigh within the bell, and took a tiny sip.

Tiana had observed the seeming ritual with some puzzlement. Though sniffing was a good means for the detection of poison, certainly sipping was not. Ordinarily she'd have checked for poison herself, but the prince was right; the dead past needed drowning, and she had no patience. Besides, there was the matter of quivery calves. She set down the glass with its mere touch of amber fluid, took up the decanter, and took a deep pull.

Liquid fire seared her throat. Choking and sputtering, she

nearly dropped the handsomely decorated decanter. The prince curbed his smile.

"One must sip this, Tiana."

"Oh."

Some sipping later, both of them were considerably more relaxed, and with a lovely warmth upon them. Eltorn asked what he might provide in addition to the severed head of a dead mage of evil.

Smiling, Tiana returned his hands to himself. "A coffin."

"A coffin!"

"Aye. It must be of ordinary appearance, mind, and showing no excellence of workmanship. Inside, though, the lid must be faced with a full length mirror of the highest quality. It must be completely obscured by black cotton, which shall also line the coffin. And it must be possible to whip away the cotton from the mirror swiftly—all at once."

"Most unusual . . . and I think I'll not ask. You are pleased with the mirror in this room?"

Tiana smiled. "I am. It tells no lies."

"Then it is my gift to you, for your strange coffin."

"I shall miss it. Now . . . I'll need clothing for a thin man, six feet in height. The clothing must be shabby in *appearance*—but the lining must be of silver. With silver fastenings, Eltorn, painted over with a dull black."

The prince nodded. "Again, simple. At once. And the silver buckles I shall give you for your boots, Tiana, will *not* be painted black! Tiana . . ."

When he trailed off, she put her head to one side and looked her question. "Tonight is the first formal palace dinner since the siege. Will you attend with me, wearing not what you might choose but what I shall have the royal dressmaker provide?"

Tiana readily agreed, with a smile that had His Highness reeling when he left her. *My appearance seems most important to him*, she mused, and she smiled anew.

The dressmaker was more than expert, and she commanded a small army of seamstresses. In a few hours, Tiana was arrayed in a lovely gown of scintillant green silk. She loved it, not merely because its beauty enhanced hers, but because it was intelligently made. It covered her in a way that seemed modest, but its effect was not. She particularly admired the exhibition the gown afforded her fullformed breasts, though it was annoying to have to be so mindful of sudden movements.

The dress was of Eltorn's choosing; Tiana provided her own

jewels, and not from those the dressmaker proffered. Bedizened in the richest of the gems she had stolen from the Tomb of Kings, the royally bedecked pirate admired herself in the mirror that would soon line a coffin's lid. She was an absolutely breathtaking vision, and she very well knew it.

"This mirror, after all, does not lie."

Dinner was less magnificent, for her. The prince was constantly harried by minor matters; that is to say, his attention was diverted from Tiana. On the new coins, did he want his face three-quarters or full profile? —What thought His Highness of thigh-high boots for the palace guards? (like Tiana's.) Had he considered how long to wait before sending a delegation to Thesia's king, whose brother they'd slain? —at next week's state dinner, who had precedence, the ambassador from Bashan or Ilan? ("Ilan, of course," Tiana said, and the prince smiled and nodded.) Given that the kingdom was nearly bankrupt but that Thesia's monarch might well feel that he must avenge his brother's death, how was a new navy to be outfitted?

With Eltorn thus occupied, a number of silly women chattered at Tiana. She paid them little heed; girls they were, she mused, of all ages. The food—which she was careful to tongue-touch before eating—was good if overly fancy. So were the eating utensils, of which there was a variety only slightly less complex than Turgumbruda's surgical tools. Yet there was no sharp knife, and so Tiana used her dagger—aye, and cut the Countess of Clearspring's meat for her too bidding her eat more of it and less of the excellent pastry and she'd not have to spend so much time bemoaning her lost figure.

After dinner, Tiana was escorted by the prince into a council chamber, along with his closest advisers. It puzzled her that so brave a man as Eltorn Bihal of Collada was suddenly so obviously nervous. The mystery was soon solved; His Highness rose to speak.

"My Lady Tiana, my learned and wise advisers. We are met tonight to discuss a matter which will deeply affect the kingdom. As you know, during the late siege my royal father set an example of courageous austerity by eating rations smaller than the humblest citizen received. His Majesty is now greatly wasted and still unable to discharge the burdens of the crown. I proposed a temporary regency, but the king desires the peace of retirement. Further, he feels that after all the people have suffered, they deserve a joyous holiday, a coronation. In two weeks, I shall officially assume the coral crown and reed scepter of Collada."

His Highness lifted a palm against happy comments, and continued.

"I now propose that the people be given a double occasion for celebration. My Lady Tiana, savior of Lieden and Collada and perhaps other lands as well from the mad dog Lokieto, any man else is free to deal with his personal concerns in private. Not so I. I am and must be public, for my life and decisions affect many. I beg you not to be offended by this necessity. My lady, I love you. Collada loves you; I ask you to marry me and be my queen."

Tiana was hardly offended by the public proposal. A king, no less! Why, she was almost flattered.

In a rather oily manner, Counselor Orld leaned her way and spoke. "My lady Tiana, it is evident from your poise and bearing that you are well born and reared to the gown and jewels you flatter by wearing. Might one ask his future queen from what house and lineage she springs?"

Tiana gazed blandly at the man. "One might well ask, and it is a sensible question, directly put. Surely, my lord, a simple and direct reply is called for. I am a bastard."

Eltorn hastened to assure shocked faces that under Colladan law the marriage between Tiana's mother and her father, Duke Sondaman, would be valid. Only an unjust technicality of Ilani law prevented Tiana from being a Duchess of Ilan.

"One must ask," the Chancellor of the Exchequer said, a man lean as the kingdom's treasury, "about the handsome jewels my lord Orld mentioned. An inheritance from your noble father the duke, my lady?"

Tiana smiled pleasantly on the bald man. "Oh no, these I stole while robbing the royal graveyard in Calancia but a short time ago."

As that lean, bald man fell back in his chair and silence gripped all others, the Chief of Protocol fair leaped with his query. "I noticed the Lady Tiana's gentle table manners, though they are of a style I have not previously seen. May I ask what master of etiquette instructed her ladyship?"

The question was sincere, she was sure. This man knew that customs varied greatly through the world, and he doubtless wanted to know in what nation of the world it was considered good manners to touch each bit of one's food with one's tongue, and then to attack it like a ravenous wolf.

"My foster father, Caranga, instructed me, my noble lord."

"Ah. And whence comes he, this noble Caranga?"

"Originally, he is from the Dark Continent, where he was a

cannibal, but he had to give that up when he took up residence with civilized folk. As a pirate. Now may I say something? I think I can be just the sort of queen this land needs. The treasury is depleted and I have a number of sound moneymaking projects. First, though there is great commerce on Lake Belanda, there are no pirates. As queen, I shall recruit pirates and serve too as admiral of our pirate fleet. This will be a major new source of revenue. Too, as you see from my jewelry, graverobbing can be most profitable. I fear that I accidentally flooded the Tomb of Kings at Calancia, but several of our neighbors have royal cemeteries well worth plundering. I shall lead those expeditions. Ah yes—also, I know several skilled counterfeiters who need a good base of operations. With them minting large quantities of our neighbors' currency, our balance-of-payments problem will be greatly eased. It was after all no fault of Collada's that we were forced to fight off a ravening boar from Thesia!''

Tiana went on, outlining a domestic program that included such social reforms as nationalizing the monasteries, breaking up large baronial estates and giving the land to the farmers. . . .

Soon the advisers were howling in incoherent rage. At last, Orld emerged as spokesman.

''Your Highness,'' he said with asperity, ''we know that this woman was somehow connected with the favorable weather during the battle against Lokieto. If you insist on this absurd marriage to a witch, we cannot prevent you. But it must be made clear that as queen this . . . *woman* will provide only the normal royal duties. Except when she leaves the palace to attend state functions, she will remain at home and bear royal heirs.''

Tiana's sigh nearly bereft her dress of her bosom. ''I see that you won't let a queen have any fun hereabouts. I'm not surprised, as you've never let the prince have any fun. Prince, here is *my* proposal. I am captain of the best pirate ship on the Great Sea. Marry me and you can be second mate—aye, and *commander* of marine forces. Our life will be one glorious adventure after another.''

Prince Eltorn smiled rather sadly. ''Yes, I'm sure such a life with you would be joyful, and at least I'd appreciate your jokes as these men do not. But—I can't abandon my duties here. You very well understand that, as you have been at pains to make us realize you cannot remain.''

Tiana nodded, rising. ''Then there is naught to do but kiss and part friends, Eltorn. Might you first be interested in showing me the sip-wine you . . . told me of?''

* * *

Tiana slept that night in comfortable self-satisfaction. Proposals were ever so awkward to reject. Her straightforward answers and absurd proposals had been effective; she'd not had to refuse a royal proposal, and only Eltorn knew she had done so. Humorless old men! A wicked thought entered her mind, even in her dreams; some day, some day wouldn't it be fun to be queen and do the things the very thought of which had outraged the humorless old aristocrats of Collada!

In the morning she and the prince kissed a last time and, as she was indeed fond of him, she said, "I have something for you to remember me by. This necklace should be easily turned into two or three ships—mind you sell it elsewhere than in Nevinia! And have your gardener plant these."

After handing His pensive Highness some oddly-shaped bulbs, she mounted and rode away.

It came to pass in a later time that the children of Lieden learned and spoke of Saint Tiana, who rode the thunderstorm and hurled lightning bolts to destroy the alien invaders. Though she loved the handsome prince and he her, she was too pure to dwell among mere men. Her parting gift was the flowers of light that still illumine the parks of the City of Light.

14

Pyre of Ice

Success, Goriarch Redbeard of Reme had said two centuries before Tiana's birth, is a treacherous friend, inclined to depart with little or no warning.

Bearing in mind those words of a pirate become duke and slain ignominiously in gamic bed, Tiana eschewed the quickest route back to Reme. She chose instead the safest, though it was a perdurably divagating one. She avoided the excellent Hangtree Road that would have taken her directly westward across Morcar, by way of Scepter and teeming Kla, instead wending south-westward through sunlit sheepherding land that sprawled for the most part in clear, well-grassed plains. With her black cloak drawn about her, her face veiled, and the coffin resting on the cart that rattled along behind her mule, she was treated with respectful avoidance. Alas, poor widow!

On the evening she reached the little border village of Taromplexis, she stopped at its only inn. The Ram's Head was small, comfortable, cozy; its family proprietors were most hospitable and pleasant. The woman, fat and bustling about in constant scutter saw to the few customers. Her husband, also fat and as taciturn as she was bubbly, remained for the most part out of sight; he was the cook, and a good one at that.

A cheery little fire warmed the room Tiana was given rather

than a cot in the common sleeping room, as she was a woman alone and a widow besides, poor thing. She saw to it that the firm oaken door was securely barred, though against what, in this pleasant out-of-the-way place, she had no idea. Outside, the dark of the moon reigned, and thick clouds shrouded the stars. A brumous wind wailed through the trees and around the eaves. The fire with its riant rays was comforting indeed.

The wind came from the north.

Far to the north, a table was crowded with excellent models; the burned ruin of the chapel of the Sisters of Death was there, and the opened cairn atop Mount Erstand, and the flooded Tomb of Kings in Escallas of Nevinia; here sprawled the scarious remains of Turgumbruda's garden and here was Lieden's royal palace and not far away the house of Sulun Tha. Scattered here and there on the table, too, were three blots of char that had been at once hawks and men, and yet neither. And there was a model of a little inn in southwest Morcar, nudging up against the border of Ilan.

In a cruelly straight chair beside the table sat the rigid form of a man. Motionless he was, without breath or heartbeat. The staring eyes were empty, exanimate, the face without expression.

Tiana had stowed away a good supper. Her possessions, including the several pieces of Derramal's body, were safely stacked in a corner of her room. She was content. From here her peregrinating trek appeared easy; an Ilani widow disconsolately towing home her husband's coffin, across the pasturelands of Ilan, where people were happy and minded their own business.

A disturbing factor arose. Despite the fire, her room was growing chilly. She moved closer to the hearth, frowning. There was no window, yet the northerly wind was puffing flagitiously right through her room. It was not her imagination; the candles flickered. The walls were alive with strange, moving shadows.

The candles died. Only the dull glow of the fireplace lit the room, making the shadows the more sinister amid the flickers. Suddenly even the flames were oddly, inexplicably, subdued. The room grew colder still. Tiana reached for the poker and, as though abruptly sucked up the chimney by a giant mouth, the fire gave a spasmodic leap and died utterly.

In the blackness of the tomb—which Tiana knew only too well—she snatched up flint and steel.

She was able to produce not so much as a spark.

The situation had become worse than incongruous. Tiana knew the preternatural when it stalked her; a veil of sorcery had been flung over her room.

She straightened in the dark, listening, straining to see the unseeable. Now came sound: *something* was walking along the hall toward her door. From the sound of its tread, it came not on two or four legs, but on eight. Her rapier was somewhere over there in hellish darkness. The poker was a thick and comforting chunk of smooth iron in her hand. She hung onto it, staring into the darkness and not able even to see her door, where the footsteps stopped. She heard a snuffling that was definitely not human. Then something began scratching at the door.

There came the trill of a songbird, but Tiana was reminded of a hunting hound that had treed its prey. And aye, here came the hunter. Heavy footsteps sounded in the hall with such force that the building seemed to quiver. She heard the sound of heavy breathing. Squaring her shoulders against the horripilation that was an unpleasantness all up and down her arms, Tiana sensed that the cold wind now came in spurts, as if it were the icy breath of one of those creatures the men from the Northland spoke of— a frost giant.

Surely some kind of a giant, this second visitor stopped and instantly pounded at her door with a fist like a sledgehammer.

Tiana gripped the poker, and waited, all still in the dark, and she gave the matter her best excogitation. An attack, and not a natural one. Yet she had defeated the three brothers, the were-hawks; the acolytes. Then . . . this must be the master himself! Pyre! Come to Tiana himself!

The acolytes, though, had attacked in suddenness and without warning, seeking to kill swiftly ere she prepared. Why then did the dread wizard thus *announce* his coming?

For the matter of that . . . even if he left his lair in the north the moment I obtained Derramal's head, how can he have got here so swiftly?

With a sudden flash of insight, the springing forward as if by intuition to a more than logical conclusion that some had seen in her as sorcerous, Tiana knew. Pyre thus proclaimed his presence because he was in fact absent! This was a Sending, an illusion. There was no eight-legged creature at all. The most brilliant and accomplished of thaumaturges had sent werehawks in physical attack, swift and vicious. Their objective was to slay. Now the attack was mental, and the chief weapon was fear. And the objective . . .

The knowledge was small comfort and little help. She was at

once freezing cold and covered with sweat. Her heart was beating like a war drum, and her breath came in short rapid gasps. Her bones felt like molasses on a warm day; her will made threat to crumble.

If I'm to keep my sanity, much less prevail, I must counter-attack. . . but how?

She could launch no physical assault on a man who wasn't there, an ephemeral Sending. The only weakness Pyre could have brought with him was his vanity. And his object—*Ah! Either to frighten me to death, or. . .*

Thought fathered deed; springing forward, Tiana pulled the bolt and threw wide the door.

"Come in, Pyre of Ice. You are late."

"Death," came the reply hollowly from the hall's blackness, "makes no appointments."

The speaker was visible to her only chatoyantly; a pair of burning red eyes surrounded by blackness. They stared with evil intent.

"Oh no, but *men* do, when they want to parley. For two weeks I've had the head of Derramal. Tomorrow I'll be in Ilan, and you are lamentably out of werehawks. Since you can't stop me by force, you must either try to frighten me to death, or parley. You must know that I am without fear," she said, noting that her legs were firming again and that the fine hairs on her arms were lying down, "and you should have come sooner." *Besides . . . all this noise I heard has not roused the inn-keeping family!*

"Pertinacious little fool, do you think you can thus defy *me* and escape my vengeance?"

"Certainly, red eyes. You wish to prevent me from putting Derramal's body into the hands of Lamarred—*returning* it, that is. Once I have done that, I will no longer be important to you—and you'll be far too busy battling real enemies to waste time on empty vengeance. Too, 'twould be as unworthy as this . . . showmanship."

Silence held the dark only for a moment as Pyre took those words—hopefully, Tiana Highrider thought, like slaps across the face. Then he reacted.

Candles and fire leaped into life. In their light stood revealed Pyre.

A tallish man the wizard of wizards was, spear-straight, with the hard polish of a diamond. Ferocious setose brows ambushed dark eyes bright as a hawk's. The tiny beard, pepper sprinkled lightly with salt, covered only his chin and was clipped close, as though it were the growth of less than a fortnight. The planes of his face were sharply defined; this, with his rigid erectness and slenderness, made him appear even taller than he was.

Pyre of Ice, come to Tiana! Aye, and when she spoke, this arresting, pride-radiant man's voice was bitter with defeat, his deep-voiced words like calx.

"For the first time in many years I must tell the truth. This is an unpleasant act for a wizard, but there is no other way now to stop you. Once—what do you now plan to do with that poker, might I ask?"

"Put it down right here," Tiana said, and she did so—and fetched her rapier.

Pyre affected to ignore that fact. "Once you return Derramal's body to Lammared, it is true that I shall take no vengeance. You will be beyond all harm, so-arrogant hoyden, for you shall have been eaten body and soul. Lamarred promised that you might rescue your brother, Bealost. Now I will reveal to you your brother's fate—and the true nature of Lamarred."

"You needn't. I already know. There were several clues. When first I met Lamarred, I recognized his face as that of one I had seen at court when I was but eight. It is the face of Derramal. When he handed me my brother's locket, it had been reversed—as Lamarred is the mirror image of Derramal."

"Mirrors, indeed. Your mind is as extraordinary as your contumely and your . . . daring."

"And Pyre, of course, is above mentioning the extraordinary body," Tiana said with affected comity. "I found an inscription on Mount Erstand. It said that the demon Derramal's soul is free and reigns 'beyond the silver plane. He cannot be slain save by a countless host of swords striking from beyond infinity.' "

"And you understand that?" The great Pyre was impressed.

"Pertinacious I am, Pyre, but I am no little fool. It's become clear to me that when that long-ago conspiracy against King Hower failed, Derramal transferred his *ka*, or soul, to his reflection in a tavern mirror. Since his ka was thus absent, his body did not die even when it was dismembered. Since then he has remained in an inn, the Smiling Skull in Reme, like a spider catching flies in a web. For nourishment he eats the souls of the inn's patrons—like that of my friend Gunda. His promise concerning my brother was that he was not dead and, if Derramal's body were brought him, it could tell us Bealost's hiding place. This he swore on his Power."

"Meaningless! He—"

"I know. From Turgumbruda I learned that such an oath

indicates the most evil possible meaning. My baby brother is hidden in the monster's stomach because he ate him, body *and* soul. Derramal's victims do not thus find the peace of death, true death—and so Bealost is dead and not dead."

Pyre made no effort to conceal his surprise at her having reached such conclusions on her own. "Knowing this, you *help* Derramal/Lamarred?"

"Of course. *Think*, wizard! How else may I avenge Bealost? When the soul and body of Derramal/Lamarred are united, I can make him pay in full. It should be very easy, since he will hardly expect me to attack him. I am to be *his* victim, of course."

Pyre heaved a great sigh that Tiana recognized as partially drama. The man had a fine sense of it! "With all your titles- . . . my lady Captain Tiana Highrider Duke's bastard of Reme . . . you are without doubt the most contumacious and bravest *fool* in creation. Now learn the black mystery you so recklessly challenge."

"With pleasure, and seated," Tiana said, and she sat.

Not so the genius mage who wore black tunic over tights of deep magenta, his heel-length magenta cloak loose and free of his arms. He stood over her, and spoke as if lecturing.

"There are beings, Tiana, who dwell apart from Man, high in the heavens and deep in the bowels of the earth and in the waters beneath it. There are those who were before Man, and they seek to re-enter this world from which they are banished. There are dwellers in the cosmic abyss and the eternal night. Some are as indifferent to our plane as man is to a hill of scuttering ants—and could nigh as easily wreak havoc on our world. Others desire things of this world: to eat the enriching souls of men . . . to drink the blood of virgins . . . and other favors a wizard of this plane might grant." He stared at her with those eagle-sharp eyes.

I am neither man nor virgin, fortunately, she thought, but she said nothing. His words were more full of horror than his earlier showmanship.

"It is the art of a wizard to invoke these beings by spells and by deceit and guile, and bind them to his will. Thus they serve him, not willingly. All, all, Tiana, share with us the common property of existence. But—there are *others*. These others are non-beings, which are not part of this cycle of the cosmos. Their presence is a violation of the order and harmony of the universe. They seek to cause death and destruction and agony, not to achieve their ambitions or to gratify their egoism."

The implication, Tiana mused, *being that those two are worthy motives!*

"These non-beings, these *others*, desire disaster solely for disaster's sake! Because they lack what we understand as existence, they are not subject to limitations we can understand. They are not 'real' then . . . but they are nonetheless most effective at the working of evil."

"In other words, dealing with normal, everyday demons is all right, a wizard's business—but to deal with these is pure evil. You are going to tell me that Derramal is guilty of trafficking with these . . . others, the non-beings?"

"Be patient. *I* have trafficked with them, Tiana. Derramal went far further. Once he was a minor sorcerer whose ambitions considerably exceeded his talent. His failures led to a mad desire, which came to horrible fulfillment. He invoked one of the non-beings. His bargain was that he and it should become one. Each ate the other, and so the demon Derramal was born into the world of men. Fortunately, the unsuccessful conspiracy against King Hower came shortly after. Newly born and unsure of its powers, the man-demon retreated into the mirror. There it remains confined. Over the years its powers have greatly increased. Your foolish plan for individual revenge will free that creature, non-being become flesh as un-man. There is no way to envision the havoc it will then proceed to work."

Tiana shook her head. "On the contrary, I know what it will do, *if* freed. It will attack Pyre of Ice!" Tiana's extended finger pointed. "One of the advantages of my plan is that in the unlikely event I fail, you will have to avenge me."

"Wretched *girl*, this is not merely danger for you and for me, but for all that live!"

"As I told Sulun Tha, Pyre, so I tell you: this is a festering wound. At all risks, it must be lanced and cleaned. Delay only worsens the problem."

"Girl! Why are you so careless of your life? If your foster father knew the danger, he would restrain you."

"Oh, unworthy! Tattletale! When I was a little girl and bested the boys, they used to go crying to Caranga. And now you . . . boy."

This shot at Pyre's vanity was clearly effective. For several seconds his lower body flickered, faded to near transparency. Resolidified, at least in appearance, he spoke in a sour voice.

"So I must choose: let you start a war which I must fight at hopeless odds, or accept a loss of pride more bitter than death."

With both hands, she made a gesture almost pleading. "Pyre, Pyre! Surely it is to your advantage—the advantage of 'all that live'—to start the war *now*! By your own statement, Derramal grows stronger every day, and the war if there is to be one can't be postponed forever. Think of what a disaster would be were Derramal free, not while you are strong, but during one of the periods of weakness that are writ in your stars."

Pyre forgot himself and the ephemeral nature of his Sending as he pounced; his attempt to sieze Tiana was without effect. "Witch! My stars are my secret! How did you learn that?"

Tiana smiled seraphically into the insubstantial face that seemed to be but inches from her own. "To be exalted and humbled is the common law of humankind. Why should I suppose you an exception?"

On hearing this, Pyre shut his eyes and faded away.

The room was instantly back to normal, warm and comfortable.

Tiana snatched up a sack of wine and a drinking mug. When she looked into the mug, her heart nearly stopped; from its bottom Pyre stared back at her! Her haste for wine was an admission of fear, possibly a fatal one—but no! His presence was *his* admission of weakness!

With disdain she said, "What's the matter, frightmaster, does it disturb you when you can't scare someone?" And Tiana poured wine in his face.

The reply came from everywhere and nowhere, in the voice of Pyre.

"Tiana, your beauty is a flame and your wit is as sharp as your rapier. You have been a thorn in the side of many of the great and powerful. Were I not so far down the lonely path of black arts, I myself might desire you. The world will be a poorer place when you leave it. I, Pyre, who knows he is supreme, vow by the fires which shall destroy the earth that I shall avenge your death."

And I, Tiana, who knows she *is supreme,* Pyre, *vow that we'd be a marvelous couple indeed!*

But she said nothing and he was gone, truly gone.

Tiana quaffed wine in quest of the settling of her nerves. She had won this encounter—but to what result? The mightiest wizard had sworn to avenge her, in an act of bravado to assuage a wound to his pride. In a way it was a cheap oath, for he had vowed to do only what he expected he must do.

But—the third oath! The consequences of the vow by the means that shall destroy the world at the end of time were never pleasant.

Well, that is Pyre's problem—or, would be, were I the sort who fails.

Tiana finished her wine and retired.

There was soon no sound or visible movement in the windowless little room at the Ram's Head. But there was movement.

Within the white ivory box the head of Derramal lay, its right ear pressed against the side of the box. Its lips made no sound, for they were not connected to lungs. But their motion was of a giant, laughing.

15

Egg of the Phoenix

"Why kill him? At most, the sot has a few copper coins."

"Idiot—some profit for the night is better than none."

The muttered words were passed between two waterfront footpads; in question was the immediate health of a drunken sailor. Having decided to slay and take what he might have left after his sojourn in the winehouse, they drew daggers and stole up behind the humming, staggering man. He who went first was raising his dagger to stab when a voice came from behind him. It was not that of his fellow thief.

"Are you sure you want to do that, you cringing crawling slime-toad?"

He whirled to see a slip of a flamehaired girl. Swallowed in a great black cloak, she stood athwart the corpse of his comrade. Her bloodstained rapier flashed, and he saw no more.

"Cap'n Tiana!" the drunken sailor exclaimed. "You—you're back in Reme."

"Clever of you to notice, Parsh. Judging from your presence here, *Vixen* must be in port. How fares my ship—and Caranga?"

"The ship remains the best afloat, Cap'n. But Caranga is in a black mood from worry over you and from the great tragedy he's suffered."

"Tra—— *What happened?*"

"Methinks he'd rather tell you of it hisself, Cap'n."

"Very well then; in which whorehouse is my father running riot?"

"He's on the ship, Cap'n, sulking in his cabin."

"He *must* be in a bad mood!"

And so Caranga was, but he was overjoyed to see his foster daughter; his fears for her well-being had gnawed at him more than he liked to admit. Shortly, she was hurling rapid questions at him until he raised his hands.

"Avast your questions, daughter! Sit down, sit down, and I will tell you the story of my calamity, my monstrous misfortune, even though I wrote it all down as we agreed." He glanced about the cluttered cabin wherein she'd found him. "Though my throat is bone dry, and—what's this? My marvelous, beautiful, dutiful daughter has brought her poor but kindly old father some wi—— the famed sip-wine of Collada, no less! Ah, it's been many a thirsty year sith I tasted this ambrosia! Sit back, my dear; the lamp has oil and now that I have . . . oh, have some?"

"Very nice of you to offer, I'm sure," Tiana told him. "Look here, I'm just back from a *long* ride. At least let me fetch a jack—so, and fill it for a careful sip—ahh. And sit down and get—these—boots . . . off—Ahhhhh! Now one puts one's grateful feet up on the chart table between us, so. Tickle my feet and be carved, poor but murderous old father. Now. I'm all attention. Knowing how you do love to spin a tale, I'll not even ask whether you have the legs and feet of Derramal." Tiana smiled, lifting her mug in hail to the huge black man with the almost ludicrously dolorous face. "Besides, I know you'd not be here else!" *And besides* that, *I want you so drunk you'll not interfere in what I must be doing, dear father mine.*

Caranga did not smile. Having nigh emptied his handsome goblet of beaten silver studded with garnets and a rather nice emerald—off a Sinchorese ship, if Tiana recalled properly—he, too, sat back. And, somewhat lengthily and in his own way, Caranga related the tale of the Isle and elixirs of Serancon, and the temptresses who were not.

As he reached the end of that narrative, he squinted into his goblet, then shook the winesack.

"How can this be, daughter? This little sack you brought me all the way from far Collada was a valiant soldier, but now 'tis slain ere my tale be half-told! What? You brought a *second*? Ah, my dear, my dear, you are too good to your old father."

And Caranga told her of the awful experiences in the City of Shadows.

When she had heard out how all had been loaded aboard *Vixen* and anchor was being weighed, Tiana had to interrupt. "Well, then—but what's this talk of tragedy? You gained what you went for, and a fabulous treasure as well." She glanced about with a sudden frown. "Caranga . . . you didn't lose the Egg on the way home, did you?"

"Nay! We returned to Reme without incident or loss."

"Then why are you not off cavorting in a whorehouse? Surely that little incident with the were-spiders or whatever did not sour you on women?"

"Nay. The . . . Old One did that." Caranga took a mighty pull direct from the sack of Colladan liquor, shook his head, showed her a disconsolate face. "Have you not taken note that I wear long pants and high boots?"

"They . . . become you well enough," Tiana said, with caution.

"Hmp! I wear them because that monster's acid saliva *ruined* me! From the waist down, I am as white as you! *Weeks* will pass ere I gain my color ba——"

Tiana's fit of helpless laughter brought him to pause, nor did he do aught but stare until she gained control of herself. Then he was sulky, and it was necessary that she thrice apologize and thrice beg ere he'd tell her of the Egg of the Phoenix.

"Sith it was obviously too valuable to sell to any one sweet buyer, I took it to the diamond cutters. Naturally, they were passing surprised when I removed the cloth to reveal a diamond large as a man. The astonishment rapidly turned to dismay and anger and, ere I knew what was happening, soldiers seized both me and the Egg."

"The cutters couldn't chip it?"

Caranga waved a hushing hand. "I was brought before the magistrate, but he said that only the king could decide such a matter. I feared I would long languish in prison, awaiting His Majesty's pleasure! But this *was* important; within an hour, I and Egg and angry jewelers stood before King Hower himself. The jewelers, y'see, swore that the Egg was *too* big. If 'twere cut up, they said, the market would be flooded and the price of diamonds drop to that of mere copper. It occurred to me then that I was the wealthiest man in the world! But—all diamonds, including our greedy liege's crown jewels, would be nigh worthless. That nonsense persuaded His Moneygrubbing Majesty!

"In desperation, I told him the obvious solution—we would trade! He would have the Egg and be marvel and envy of the world, while I would heroically settle for no more than the considerably less valuable . . . crown jewels of Ilan!"

Tiana chuckled. "Beautiful! Logical, too—where are they?" Swinging her long legs from the chart table with a thump, she looked about his cabin.

Only looking mournful, Caranga decanted more of Prince Eltorn's gift. "Ahhh! King Hower saw how he'd profit from such a transaction, but those damned advisers of his practically frothed at the mouth. Mouths. To keep peace, the foreign minister has made treaties with a half-dozen several lands, promising each to go to war with the others. Playing each against the other, by Susha! Should His Majesty accept the Egg, our sweet neighbors in all directions would burn with envy and launch attack on Ilan forthwith. Hmp—*that* scurvy offspring of Drood is now in prison where he belongs. *But*: after much discussion, the king and his advisers agreed that the Egg should be taken to the deepest part of the ocean and . . . sunk! I was paid nothing, Tiana, *nothing*, and told I'm lucky not to be jailed as a troublemaker."

Tiana was tight of lip. "We must find an opportunity to *help* His Majesty some fine day—and steal him blind and staggery!"

"One hopes. Meanwhile, a ship of the Royal Ilani Navy soon set sail, bearing that great wonder of our modern world. It returned only yesterday, a burned-out hulk that wallowed into port with half a crew. Captain Julnis swore that the Egg had suddenly sprung into flames, whereupon it disgorged a giant bird of incredibly beautiful plumage. The bird flew away, leaving Julnis with a burning ship. Many crewmen died extinguishing the flames, he says. Naturally, some immediately said that Julnis secreted the egg and murdered those of his crew who'd not join such thieving treachery, then fired his own ship to cover. Captain Julnis, curse his name, has of course powerful friends, and it appeared the rumors would be ignored . . . but the powerful friends have powerful enemies, who saw this as a perfect opportunity to embarrass the powerful friends."

Caranga paused to draw breath and wag his head. "His Muddleheaded Majesty has appointed a supposedly impartial board of inquiry: four knaves who stand to grow rich by the captain's conviction, four who will profit by his acquittal, and one senile old hog. Who knows what will come of it?"

"Politics and muddleheaded leaders!" Tiana snapped. "I doubt muchly if the facts and your words about the history of the

Egg of the Phoenix will influence the decision of those . . . fine upstanding men.''

"Aye. So I am shamed, daughter, shamed. Caranga won the most fabulous of treasures and returned it to Reme . . . and in full view of all our fellow pirates I've lost it. I dare not so much as show my face; I am a laughingstock!''

Morosely, Caranga upended the second winesack. He squeezed and pressed, as though milking a reluctant cow. At last, with a long sigh, he dropped the useless bag of leather. "There's the end of my story and my shame, daughter—and of the sip-wine.''

"And of you,'' Tiana said, seeing the mist claiming his eyes.

"Aye,'' Caranga said, whereupon he collapsed on the table and commenced snoring loudly.

Tiana gazed upon him with fondness. At last she firmed her mouth and squared her shoulders. It was time to act. She had braced Pyre, and faced him down, however tenuous that face at the time. She'd be no readier for Lamarred next month than she was right now. Caranga was safely out of the way, too; in this her perhaps insane and certainly ill-advised confrontation with the demon in the mirror, Tiana would not allow her stepfather to share her danger.

And it took two full sacks of Eltorn's super-wine to put him under the table, too, she thought with an admiring and indulgent smile at the snoring Caranga.

16

Paying the Devil

Beloved Father,

We began this quest to save my brother. I found that he needs not saving but avenging. I am going to try to take that vengeance. If you read this letter, I have failed and am dead. Bardon sails under my orders. I write to tell you two things. The first is that you should not waste your life trying to avenge me. If I fail, there is naught that steel and human courage can do. Nor is there need. Two mighty wizards, Pyre and Sulun Tha, will for reasons of their own avenge me. The second is that I love you very much. When I was an orphan wanted by no one, you adopted me. You fed me, sheltered me, loved me. You taught me all my skills and developed all my strengths. You taught me courage, wisdom, and above all, honor. In all these things you are far more my father than he who sired me. What I do now is what honor requires. I hope you will be as proud of me as of a son dying under similar circumstances. I know you would rather have me less honorable, and alive. Hence, I give you no chance to stop me. Please remember me with pride, and spend your days in peace, Father. I leave you all my love.

She signed the brief letter, "Your daughter, Tiana," and half-lifted, half-dragged Caranga to his bunk. He did not so much as interrupt his snoring. After covering him, she kissed him tenderly.

"Farewell, Father," Tiana whispered. "Fair seas and peaceful harbors."

Then Captain Tiana Highrider of Reme—wept.

She loved life; she *enjoyed* life, and thus she feared death. It grieved her to know that her dying would cause Caranga great pain. Yet she saw no choice. Her taking this desperate chance was the only hope for her brother Bealost to find peace. Too, she had excellent motivation in addition to the personal reason.

Isolated on Mount Erstand and in the custody of the mighty and good Sulun Tha, the parts of Derramal's body had lain in harmless repose. Everywhere else they had abode, the pattern had been the same: evil. Nuns discarded their vows for vampirism; ghouls defiled the royal cemetery; shrubs seized control of Turgumbruda's garden and stole the bodies of living men; Serancon became totally inhuman and spiders grew to monstrous size, by illusion seeming to be beautiful women for the entrapment of men; the people of Killiar were slain or driven from their homes when their own shadows rebelled and attacked them.

All amounted to the same horror-haunted abomination: each several portion of the demon's body had inspired rebellion against the natural order, against the very harmony of the universe. The nonbeing Lamarred had brought into her world was a cancer on it, and destiny had appointed Tiana the surgeon to remove it.

This she believed.

Though risk to doctor and patient was great, the alternative was certain disaster.

Steeling herself, the pirate queen dried her tears and cursed her weakness in shedding them. She gathered up the legs and feet of Derramal and carried them to her own cabin.

Here the few crewmen aboard had placed the rest of that noxious demonic corpse, along with the clothing from Collada, a large jug of oil, and Turgumbruda's surgical tools. Surgery had long been her post-combat province aboard *Vixen*, and this task was fascinating. Nor had she reason to take overmuch care; the bones snapped errily together and, once she'd stitched the muscles together, they knit before her dread-sickened eyes. Nor did a single part of the body now exhibit any sign of preternatural life.

She left the head in its ivory box while she dressed the corpse in the silver-lined clothing, and made a few other preparations. Only then did she open that ivory chest to look upon the severed head of Derramal. Yes, she recognized the face. Though the open eyes neither moved nor focused, she felt sure that they *saw*.

In a few minutes she had attached the head to the body and placed the corpse in the coffin with its black lining and black-covered mirror in the lid. Stepping back, she gazed thoughtfully for a time on that silent, sinister corpse. Then she closed the lid and summoned Bardon, Gunda's successor as second mate.

To him she handed the finest jewel she had taken from the Tomb of Kings. "In the House of Delightful Women," she told that scion of a long-impoverished noble family, "there is a girl named Darvra. Caranga greatly favors her, partly because she is black and too because she possesses some character. Go to her. Tell her that if she sails one voyage on *Vixen* and makes Caranga happy, this jewel is hers. Make clear that she will have no easy task. Neither she nor anyone else is to arouse Caranga. I'm for shore, Bardon. Prepare to set sail. If I return by dawn, well and good. With or without me, though, *Vixen* is to sail at sunrise with Bardon commanding."

"Sail . . . for where, Captain?"

"It doesn't matter. Just put all possible sea betwixt you and Reme before Caranga wakes. And then give him this letter."

Tiana knew that puzzled or no, Bardon would obey. Once Caranga awoke, command would be his. Her letter would protect Bardon from his wrath—and Caranga would be far from Reme, distracted by a woman he was considerably taken with. He'd want to avenge Tiana's death, of course, but with no notion whom to attack—or where. His only logical course would be to wait and see whom Sulun Tha and Pyre attacked, and Caranga did frequently take note of logic. Hopefully, she had saved his life.

Tiana had made what preparations she could for defeat.

The time was now for her to test her preparations for victory.

Soon a strange procession wended through the nighted streets of Ilan's captial city and chief port. At its head was a lithe, bemazingly shapely young woman in tight silken shirt and scandalously short pants, also snug. She wore neither black cloak nor rapier, but carried a heavy cutlass. Behind her came six seamen, obviously pirates, carrying a coffin. Footfalls melted into the brooding shadows at sight of them; so did a band of no less than three stalwarts of the City Watch.

The Inn of the Smiling Skull was dark and empty. Tiana easily gained entry. Lighting a candle, she bade her men *stand* the coffin before the curtained wall. They braced a table on either side of it; on one Tiana set her single candle. Nor did those stout pirates make demurrer to her command to return to *Vixen*.

Tiana was alone in the doom-haunted web of Lamarred/Derramal.

With a sudden motion, she snatched the curtain of mauve king's cord from the wall in a great rustle of heavy fabric. Revealed was the mirror that housed the demon's soul. The face that stared at her from the glass seemed mild, harmless, not at all the monster that threatened unbelievable peril to all the world.

"Greetings, Lamarred," Tiana said equably. "I have brought you the body of Derramal."

She opened the standing coffin, revealing the body and arranging the lid so that the inner surface faced the tavern mirror.

"And you've even *clothed* him! Ah thank you, my dear, sweet, *overbosomed fool!* Now shall I keep the promise I swore on my Power."

Lamarred's gaze swerved from Derramal to her, and Tiana was instantly and completely gripped in paralysis. "Ignorant trull! You were placed on this plane to please ruttish men with that arrogantly spectacular body, not to match wits with me!"

And leaving her helplessly immovable, he spoke on, in a language not of humankind but of demons. His words were baneful echoes of the phantasmal night and the desolate void. T. hear him was for a human to grue and stand on the brink of gibbering madness.

The incantation accomplished its dark purpose.

The dead lips of the corpse opened, and Derramal made reply. "The hiding place of Bealost is our belly, for I ate both the babe's body and soul."

And then the body returned to inertness, braced erect in the coffin.

"There," Lamarred smiled, "poor stupid blowze, I have kept the letter of my promise—and so I am free to drink your soul." The sorcerer's gloating eyes were filled with the cold triumph of a cobra that has captured a lovely songbird. "As Derramal's head, I heard you plotting my demise with Pyre! But you shall have no opportunity to carry out your silly little human plan, wench!''

The demon-wizard's eyes swelled, changed from a burning red to maleficent black. Now they were become great empty voids, sucking at her soul, tearing it from her body.

Tiana's despair and dismay were mingled with bitter self-reproach: she'd been so sure the monster's ego would spur him to play the enjoyable game of cat and mouse. Now she must pay a ghastly price for her own ego-wrought error. Neither her strength of body nor of will was of aught avail; this demon-man's terrible Power was dragging forth her very soul. She was completely powerless.

Then the pressure eased, though she remained unable to move.

"Tell me, my sweet supper," Lamarred purred, "have you any last words? For instance . . . art sorry you slew old Sulun Tha, that revolting embodiment of Order and Good?"

Lamarred was indeed playing cat and mouse, did indeed have to gloat, and might still enter her trap. But only Tiana's lips were free to move. She must make the most of that. . . .

"Sulun Tha lives."

"*What*?"

"I did not slay Sulun Tha of Lieden in Collada."

"Then . . . how could you possibly have got the head?"

"He gave it to me, saying that he and others—meaning Pyre, of course—would war against you." On speaking those words, she felt the iron grip of paralysis weaken a whit; news that his great enemies were alive and allied had shaken Lamarred! "Oh . . . but they'd rather have peace—Sulun Tha sent you a present. . . ."

"Slut! I shall release only your right hand—show me."

The hand of his piratical captive came alive—and flashed to the lid of the open coffin. In one swift motion, she tore away the black covering to reveal the excellent Colladan mirror. Lamarred stared into it—and Tiana was free in every limb.

Her voice lilted with clear triumph. "Atop Mount Erstand I found an inscription, monster. It said that Derramal's soul is free and reigns beyond the silver plane, and that only a countless host of swords striking from beyond infinity could slay him. Tell me Demon . . . is this a countless host of swords?"

Tiana accompanied those words by raising her cutlass between the tavern mirror and the one in the coffin lid, so that its reflection was repeated and re-repeated and doubled to infinity. And she saw horror in Lamarred's eyes.

Yet Lamarred did not quail or freeze with fright. As she aimed a blow at the coffin mirror, the demonic wizard unleashed a desperate catalog of black spells. He was like a warrior who had need of striking one true blow but in panic hurled a flurry of inaccurate strokes.

Paralysis gripped every part of her body save her swordarm, for it was amove and could not be stopped. It seemed to enter thick mud, and was terribly slowed. She strove to force arm and cutlass toward the mirror.

Icy winds and searing flames raged at her body.

Hands plucked at her obscenely.

The black eyes sucked at her soul, and her body was racked with pain when diabolical claws slashed across her breasts.

Her sword and the mirror vanished. She saw that she was driving her arm into the mouth of a ravening, drooling wolf whose finger-long teeth were sharp as needles. With desperate effort of will, Tiana told herself that it did not exist, and she continued to force her arm forward. The wolf wavered—an enormous cobra appeared in its place. Its yawning mouth gaped hugely and rushed at her head. Tiana had a fleeting glimpse of shining dagger-teeth and dripping venom and the mouth's scarlet interior.

Then the serpent too vanished, and she was enveloped in slimy, wet blackness that brought on shuddery feelings of the ultimate distaste.

That illusion prevailed, and she shivered—and then her will prevailed and all was normal and real again as the cutlass smashed into the mirror.

For an instant the sword appeared to have penetrated the glass without breaking it. She could see Lamarred's reflection, writhing, pierced by swords without number. Then both mirrors erupted into flying pieces of glass. The light of the single candle was multiplied by the fragments so that the room was alive with an insane kaleidoscope of blazing colors. The sound of the shattering mirrors was like the tolling of a great bell, heard from within the bell.

Mirrors, sound, and Lamarred passed; candle and Tiana and sword remained. She stood alone but for a coffined corpse in an empty tavern. Lamarred, who had called from the abysmal void and united with a baleful nonbeing, was no more. Tiana bore not a mark.

The corpse of Derramal opened its dead eyes. The eyes contained not hatred, but a dreadful avid hunger.

It spoke in the voice of Lamarred, and Tiana's back crawled.

"I see we underestimated you. You have destroyed much of our Power. Why brought you this body here? Had you smashed my mirror while my body was dispersed, my soul would have been destroyed."

"Two reasons, soulless monster! First, I knew that the parts of your foul body inspire evil wherever they lie. Nor could they be destroyed unless reunited with your vomitous soul. And second . . . for what you did to my brother, chaos-spawn, I want you to suffer a painful death!"

"You are most confident in your sword," Derramal said, with a sneering smile.

Sudden jerks of the creature's arms smashed the coffin to splinters. The demon-thing stepped forth and a long arm shot out. Bare fingers closed on Tiana's razor-edged blade—and snapped it, as easily as a hammer smashed glass.

"Now, luscious trull of a human, it is time for you to pay for the inconvenience you have caused me with your pitiful efforts. It is long since I tasted human flesh, and you will be especially delicious."

Tiana still clung to the broken cutlass as though it were a useful weapon. In a tone calm as one discussing the weather, she made reply.

"You say I'd taste good. I'm surprised that the reanimated corpse of a nonbeing would have any sense of taste or smell."

"My lack of sense of taste as humans understand it will make no difference to you," it said, and reached for her.

Tiana backed and sidestepped a pace. Her hip jarred the table beside the coffin. "Aye," she said in the same calm voice, "but the lack of smell will make a great deal of difference to you."

Suspicion grew from vagueness to a yellow-tinged light that approached fear in Derramal's eyes. Its hand paused, with cold fingers at her throat. "Why say you so?"

"Because, if you could smell, you would know that I soaked your handsome new clothing in lamp-oil!" And with the broken cutlass Tiana swept the candle from the table onto Derramal's chest.

In terror the monster leaped back, but flame sprang up brightly. His beating at himself succeeded only in spreading fire over oil saturated clothing. Nor could the fingers that snapped steel rip away the burning clothing; Derramal was from beyond the silver plane, and silver was a barrier that bound him. He was unable to tear the silver lining of his clothes. Flames spread in a rush and he was completely enveloped in dancing oily fire. Dry flesh commenced to burn with an acrid odor.

"Derramal!" It was the triumphing voice of an arrogant pirate. "How tastes the *fire*, chaos-spawned monster who ate my brother?"

The demon charged, flame-enveloped. She easily evaded him, dodging here and there so that he was constantly amove— feeding the flames with the air he himself stirred. He was howling now. Tiana danced close to the monster become torch, letting his flaming arms pass within inches of her while she hurled taunts at him. Vengeance was like the finest of old wines. None of his—its—blindly flailing blows found her, but the tavern's furniture suffered. Soon the floor of the inn where so many had vanished, soul-eaten, was strewed with the flinders of t oken tables and chairs. Some burned.

Many times oiled and long greased-spattered, the inn floor caught.

Flames leaped up all about and the room filled with blinding smoke. Despite the danger, Tiana continued to mock the anguished demon. When a sudden rush carried it charging past her, it slammed into the stone wall. Pain and rage drove it now, and Derramal smashed blindly through that wall of mortared stone. In rushed cool air from the sea, and flames whooshed and waxed in brightness.

A hundred yards away lay the beating surf. Tiana assumed the monster could neither see nor smell that water, the entire reassembled body a torch that lit the Reman night in awful eeriness. Nevertheless, Derramal rushed blazing toward the sea. Tiana raced after that living torch that streamed flame like a bright yellow-and-orange cloak. She strained for speed, for even now she could lose and condemn the world thereby, if the nonbeing could hurl its unnaturally renewable body into the water. It was nearly there—

In a burst of the speed of desperation, Tiana outstripped it, paused and half-turned, and shot out a booted foot.

Tripped, the monster fell headlong with a crashing impact— and seemed to split in twain.

Half that flamebound apparition was the burning skeleton of the wizard; the other was the same shape but was a void, an empty vacuum in the universe.

The bones of half the apparition were white and blazed with a yellow-white flame; the other was black and burned with a weird, green flame that radiated darkness and cold. The fusion of human wizard and demonic nonbeing that was Derramal was split. Each tore furiously at the other. The suit had been reduced to a fine web of silver by the flames that now devoured the battling skeletons.

Heat and cold became intense, and Tiana backed away. The sand, where touched by the fiery bones, was melted and fused to glass or frosted with ice. Strangely, though the silver flashed in the red and green fires, it was not harmed by them. The demon could not break the bondage of silver, neither by the superhuman strength of its arms nor by the dully roaring flames that enwrapped its writhing bones.

There came a sudden blast of total darkness and blinding light, so that Tiana blinked. When she opened her eyes, the fires were gone. Of Derramal nothing remained but a fine sift of the white powder of calcined bones. The breeze from the sea blew it up, dispersing it along the shore. Tiny grains of calx clung to Tiana's boots. Then it was gone. Lamarred was gone. Derramal was gone.

Suddenly alone on the shore, Tiana was not alone.

All about her eddied a half-defined haze, a tenebrous cloud of people. She could see through them and yet she was able to distinguish expressions and recognize faces. There was Gunda, and there was Bealost; there was a host of others. They were thanking her, she realized, for she had slain their horrid slayer and host and rescued them from the foul misery of undeath within it; now they could rest or prepare to return in new forms, whatever became of those who were at last really dead. One by one, while Tiana stared and streamed tears, they closed their eyes and faded away.

And then she was truly alone on the Reman shore of the Great Sea.

For the first time this night, indeed for the first time in months, Tiana breathed freely and relaxed.

She had gambled her life on the quest, jeopardized and nearly lost that life far more than once. Tonight she had gambled it knowingly, deliberately, on three wishful guesses. The first was her interpretation of the inscription on Mount Erstand and her preparations in accord with that interpretation. The second was that even Derramal would be vulnerable to fire. This had been a fairly safe guess, as his left hand had fled, panicky, during the fire in the chapel of the Sisters of Death. The third and vital guess, and hope, was that both Sulun Tha and Pyre had greatly overestimated Derramal.

Doubtless the demon sorcerer's powers had been as great as those two brilliant and strong wizards believed . . . but his powers amounted to little without courage. He or it had fled originally into the mirror; the hand had fled the flame; Tiana had gambled that Derramal/Lamarred was a coward and, that if attacked strongly and with confidence, he would be unable to use his deadly arts effectively.

She had wagered her life. She had been right. She had won her vengeance.

Incidentally, she had saved the world from the liberated mannonbeing-demon.

With a long sigh, she felt a flow of great weariness—and then noted the pearly glow at the meeting of sea and sky . . . and the pink light that was beginning to pale the gray.

Victor or no, weary or no, Tiana ran.

The sun was breaking over the horizon when *Vixen's* captain came running onto the pier and without slowing leaped into space. She alighted aboard her departing ship and ran full into Bardon, who prevented her from falling. Men stared; grins broke out on piratical faces. The captain was back. She snapped out a series of crisp orders and noted that Bardon seemed grateful. She took from him the letter to Caranga, bade him take the helm. The breeze was strong and favorable under a rising topaz sun that was painting the ocean a flickering gold. *Vixen* moved out to sea.

Tiana tore the letter to shreds as she went below, to Caranga's cabin. How embarrassing if her foster father had read her soupy note!

He snored still, and would for hours, with the liquorish load he'd taken into his hold. The jet-black, almost purple Darvra was there, waiting. Tiana smiled and gave the patient temptress a finger-to-lips sign. She rolled her eyes at Darvara's bare, painted breasts; the girl grinned. The captain of *Vixen* went back up on deck and, though she should have been weary unto dropping, it was with the springy step of victory and elation and relief that she went to take the helm.

"Come, *Vixen*," she murmured, with the breeze tugging her hair as it bellied the sails. "The sea is full of rich ships owned by men evil and unworthy. Let us redistribute their wealth!"

Thus Tiana Highrider sailed away from Reme. Naught has
been said concerning the second half of the bargain between
Lamarred and the mage Ekron, or of the consequences of Pyre's
swearing the dread third oath; and these things remain to be told.
But they are another tale.